THE LIFT DOORS OPENED . . .

. . . and Picard got inside. But he didn't get inside alone. The X-Man known as Archangel came with him.

As the doors closed, Archangel turned to him. "You're going after that cluster missile, aren't you?"

The captain didn't return the winged man's scrutiny. "As it happens," he said, "I am. Computer—Shuttlebay One."

The lift began to move.

"Take me with you," said Archangel.

Finally, Picard looked at him—his expression a skeptical one. "Why would I do that?"

"Because I can help," the mutant told him. "I may not be a hundred percent, but I can probably fly at peak efficiency for a short period of time. With a little luck, I can make it to the missile and disarm it."

The captain shook his head. "We don't know anything about the technology that went into it."

"But we *will*," Archangel insisted. "When we're up close and personal with it, you'll scan it with those high-powered, sophisticated instruments of yours and figure out what makes it tick."

"Even so," said Picard, "the friction created by its passage through the atmosphere will render it too hot to handle."

"Can you slow it down?" the mutant asked.

Picard glared at him. "Yes, with a tractor beam. But if you make a mistake? And the device explodes in your face?"

Archangel smiled a taut smile. "Then you'll have one less annoying X-Man flying around your ship."

PLANET X

MICHAEL JAN FRIEDMAN

Based on
Star Trek: The Next Generation
created by Gene Roddenberry

X-Men Based on the Marvel Comic Book

POCKET BOOKS
New York   London   Toronto   Sydney

This book is a work of fiction. Names, characters, places, and incidents are products of the author's imagination or are used fictitiously. Any resemblance to actual events or locales or persons, living or dead, is entirely coincidental.

An *Original* Publication of Pocket Books

POCKET BOOKS, a division of Simon & Schuster, Inc.
1230 Avenue of the Americas, New York, NY 10020

ISBN-13: 978-1-4516-9151-1

First Pocket Books printing May 1998

10   9   8   7

POCKET and colophon are registered trademarks of Simon & Schuster, Inc.

Manufactured in the United States of America

For information regarding special discounts for bulk purchases, please contact Simon & Schuster Special Sales at 1-800-456-6798 or business@simonandschuster.com.

For Matt Dittman, Tommy Zebroski, Frankie Coughlin, Henry Klion, Chris Sciacca, Pascal Spagna, Brandon Mays, Johnny Marx, Danny Kavanagh, Matt Lazar, Jake Paisner, Andrew Preston, Matt Ciancimino, and, of course, Brett Friedman . . . all of 'em heroes in my book

Acknowledgments

As always, a number of people who don't get to put their names on the cover put a lot into this book. John Ordover, my editor, and Scott Shannon, my publisher, are tops on the list for smoothing what could have been a very bumpy road. Mike Thomas and Steve Behling of Marvel Creative Services, as well as Chip Carter at Viacom, helped shape the book in the beginning and also at the end. Viacom's Paula Block put in a welcome two cents at a critical time, and Tim Tuohy, Marvel's Star Trek editor, was eminently cooperative in coordinating this book with his related comic project. Keith R.A. DeCandido, mutant editor par excellence, read the manuscript for me, and Bob Greenberger remains the source.

I'd also be remiss if I didn't tip my hat to Gene Roddenberry and Rick Berman, on one hand, and Stan Lee, Jack Kirby, Chris Claremont, and Dave Cockrum on the other. They are, after all, the ones who came up with most of the characters you're about to meet.

PLANET X

Prologue

"I WILL BE a new person," Erid Sovar told his friends, savoring the warmth of the afternoon sun on his face. "I will be a person this world has never seen before."

His companions laughed good-naturedly and reminded him that *everyone* is like that—a person the world has never seen before. And they said that was true even before a person went on his adulthood quest.

But Erid wouldn't have his enthusiasm dampened. "I will be *truly* different," he said. "I will be so different from anyone else, you won't know me when you see me again."

They laughed again. And this time, he laughed with them.

Over the next several hours, Erid and his friends completed their hike into the barren highlands of Ra'ad Cuhloor. At the doorstep of the gigantic Vuuren Pass, they paused to eat something. While Erid prepared himself for the task ahead, his friends traded scandalous stories about him and laughed even harder than before.

1

Then, as the sun began to set, he hugged each of his companions and said goodbye to them. After all, he was certain they would never see him again—at least, not as the Erid Sovar they had known.

Continuing his journey on his own, he mused that one other should have been there to say goodbye to him. Unfortunately, that one was gone from his life forever. It was best to forget about him, the youth told himself, and to move on.

Without benefit of food or water, Erid made the long climb up to Otros Paar, the legendary Field of Heaven. When he got there, he saw the dozen tall, lonely stacks of rocks that awaited him.

Erid chose the pile farthest from the ruddy light of the setting sun and, therefore, nearest the light of the sun that would rise the next morning. Then he climbed the rocks, laid one on top of the other in ancient times, until he reached the highest and most precarious of them.

Sitting, he crossed his legs. Then he took a breath and composed himself, his light clothing barely any help against the cutting lash of the wind. Putting aside all thoughts of the life he had led to that point, thoughts both good and bad, he began to sing.

It was the way it had been done by his ancestors for the last seven hundred and fifty years. It was what tradition demanded of him. And Erid was only too eager to comply.

So he sat there, alone under the terrible and unexpected brightness of the stars, and sang psalms to the inclinations of his spirit. Nor was it like any other spirit in all the universe—his elders had assured Erid of that again and again.

All he had to do was sing the song, they had said, and he would find the elements that made him unique . . . the elements that finally and irrevocably made him Erid Sovar.

For a brief time, the stars were obscured by a herd of gray clouds. Erid felt a cold, eventually numbing sizzle of rain, but he sang his way through it. Then the rain stopped, and the clouds dissipated, leaving only a few breeze-rippled puddles as evidence of their passing.

As he sat there shivering, he was again haunted by thoughts of the one who should have been with him at Vuuren Pass. Anger and resentment rose in him. And pain as well.

No, he told himself. *You must clear your mind, driving away such thoughts as the clouds have been driven from the sky.*

Closing his eyes, Erid dropped deeper into his song, seeking solace. He wrapped it about him like a cloak against the chill, and in time his thoughts became pure again.

He pursued mystery after mystery, seeking who he was and who he might yet be. He came up with questions, a great many of them, but nothing at all in the way of answers.

Not at first, anyway.

Then, with the first pale hint of dawn, a change began to take place in Erid. As the wind lost its edge and the land grew still, the answers he craved started to come to him, one after the other—slowly at first, and then in a dizzying, breathtaking rush.

The youth felt a rush of confidence, a heady unfolding of grand potentials and possibilities. With great satisfaction, he realized that he was doing what he had set out to do—shedding one existence and donning another. Finally, the song having served its purpose, he stopped singing—but the feelings of joy and transformation continued.

Now the sun was rising over the uneven line of the horizon, its warmth moving down Erid's body like a lover's caress. It immersed his hands and his feet, then took the chill from the stone surface beneath him. He breathed deeply again and at last opened his eyes.

The world was . . . *beautiful.* Even this place, with its dark, graceless flats and slopes and rock piles, with its stubborn refusal to support life—it was as beautiful as anything he had seen.

His teachers were right, Erid thought. There had been a new way of seeing things locked inside him, a way that belonged to him alone. And all he had needed to do to find it was to follow their path.

Wishing to share his feelings with his friends, knowing how glad they would be to see him, Erid uncrossed his legs and tried to dismount from the rock pile. However, his limbs wouldn't cooperate. They were stiff and awkward from his long night's vigil.

He had to go slow, to allow his feet time to find the niches between the stones. As the light moved down the ancient pile, so did he—little by little, rock by rock, his legs tingling painfully as the circulation began to return to them.

Then one of his feet slipped and missed its niche, and the rest of Erid followed it with amazing quickness. The next thing he knew, he was lying on the ground, the side of his head feeling raw and bludgeoned.

He touched his fingertips to his temple. They came away with a purplish smudge on them. *Blood,* he thought vaguely. *I'm bleeding?*

But even that couldn't dim Erid's jubilation. Rolling over onto his belly, he raised himself on his hands and knees. Then, laughing at his helplessness, he hauled himself to his feet.

Turning, he saw the place where Otros Paar descended into the Vuuren Pass. With his back to the rising sun, he set out in that direction.

At first, it got easier and easier, as the blood rushed back into his legs. He made his way past one stack of rocks and then another. But after a while, Erid's legs began to feel heavy again.

Sensing that something was wrong, he looked down at them. Was it his imagination, or were the veins in his legs swelling?

As he pondered the question, feeling a tiny trickle of

fear running down his spine, he realized it wasn't just his legs that felt heavy. His arms felt that way too.

Weighted down. And thick. Swollen, somehow. And their veins were popping out as if they wanted to burst through his smooth bronze skin.

Erid shook his head helplessly. It didn't make sense. There were no poisonous animals lurking this high up, no toxic plants he might have brushed against. And if he had eaten something bad for him the day before, he would have known it long before this.

It didn't make sense at *all*. And yet, his veins and arteries were swelling before his eyes, standing out under his flesh like metal cables.

But, strangely, Erid felt no pain. Even the numbness had gone away. The only discomfort he felt was the sensation of weightiness.

He swallowed, his throat dry with fear. He could feel the vessels in his neck and his temples were swelling, too, now—and that wasn't all. His flesh was beginning to darken around them, turning a hideous shade of purple—except in his fingers, which remained their natural bronze somehow.

What's going on? Erid wondered, his heart pounding savagely against his ribs. *What's happening to me?*

At that moment, he chanced to look into one of the puddles left by the night's rainshowers. In it, he saw his reflection, almost as clearly as he might have seen it in a mirror.

He was hideous, his blood vessels enlarged and darkening all over his face, his long, narrow brush of blue-black hair starting to thin and fall out. As he staggered away from the sight of himself, repulsed beyond words, he heard someone screaming.

It took Erid some time to realize it was *him.*

He fell to his knees, too weak and scared to support himself any longer. Only his fingers remained normal, resisting whatever had befallen him. Staring at them, he tried to hang on to the remnants of his sanity. Then something happened to his fingertips as well.

They began to glow with a pale, hazy light. Erid studied them, wondering what would happen next. He wasn't left wondering for long.

A brilliant white beam shot out suddenly from one of his fingertips and struck a nearby stack of rocks—shattering it with explosive force. He stared at the stunted pile that remained.

Did I really do that? he asked himself.

Then, before the fragments created by the first beam could stop rolling, a beam projected from another finger and hit the ground. It pulverized the rocky surface and sent a blinding spray of pebbles into his face.

Erid got up and staggered backward, eyes watering, trying to hold his hands as far away as possible—but a third beam shot over his shoulder, missing his ear by only a few inches. Then another shot out, and another and another after that, all of them losing themselves in the blue-green heavens.

But what if one of them hits me? he wondered. *If these beams can shatter rocks, what will they do to flesh and blood?*

Unfortunately, there was nowhere Erid could run where the beams wouldn't follow. They were coming from parts of his body, after all—or, anyway, the wretched thing his body had become.

The beams began to manifest themselves faster and faster, like a pair of fireworks wheels on Tala Day. One after another, the surrounding rock piles burst apart and littered the landscape with their gravel. But as terrified as Erid was, as shaken to his bones, he couldn't help but be fascinated by the sight as well.

Where is all this power coming from? he asked helplessly. *How could it have gotten inside* me?

He had barely completed the thought when there was a burst of white-hot splendor, beams jumping from all ten of his fingers with a fury that dwarfed anything that had gone before. He stumbled backwards, hit a rock with his heel, and sprawled on the ground.

But when Erid looked at his hands again, the beams were gone. His fingers had stopped glowing. They were normal again.

It was as if the nightmare had passed—as if it had never happened in the first place. Then he looked at his arms, with their huge, purple blood vessels, and knew in his heart that the nightmare was just beginning.

Chapter One

SECURITY OFFICER MARCO PALMIERI shone his palm light down the long, dimly lit corridor, one of a multitude of corridors he had patrolled since his arrival at Starbase 88.

Palmieri didn't see anyone attempting to break into one of the cargo bays. He didn't see anyone sabotaging any of the internal sensor nodes. He didn't see anyone, period.

No surprise, he thought. There was never anyone there to see.

Palmieri had shipped out from Earth several months earlier, propelled by an academy graduate's dreams of excitement and adventure. After all, these were dangerous times, with the Dominion an ever-present threat and the Cardassians again at odds with the Federation.

But somehow, none of those dangers seemed to materialize on Starbase 88. Instead of finding excitement and adventure, Palmieri had managed to draw the most routine assignment he could imagine, in one of the least inspiring places in the galaxy.

Naturally, he had mentioned his problem to Security Chief Clark, his superior. But she had been less than sympathetic.

After all, Clark had reminded him, Starbase 88 received just as many potential troublemakers as any other Federation space station. If it didn't experience the turmoil other stations did, that was a *good* thing—a sign that Palmieri and his colleagues were doing their jobs.

At the time, Palmieri had found it difficult to argue with the woman's logic—and it was no easier now. But that didn't make his inactivity any easier to take.

Coming to the end of the corridor, he turned right and illuminated another walkway with his palm light. Like all the others, the passage was orderly and unpopulated, devoid of anything that might make a security officer's heart beat faster.

Palmieri sighed. Maybe it was time to ask for a transfer. He knew that berths on starships were hard to come by, but there had to be some starbase somewhere in need of an eager if untested security officer.

Suddenly, his tricorder began to beep. Taking it out of its loop on his tunic, he checked its tiny screen to see why. What he saw made him wonder if the tricorder was on the fritz.

It was indicating a temporal flux artifact in Cargo Bay Six. But that didn't make sense. The base's security station routinely scanned for such phenomena. If they had . . .

"Clark to Palmieri," came a voice, shattering his thought.

Dutifully, he tapped the communications badge he wore on his chest. "Palmieri here, Chief."

"Are you getting a temporal-flux reading down there?"

"As a matter of fact," said Palmieri, "it just registered on my tricorder. You don't know anything about it?"

"No more than you do," Clark told him. "Go check it out, but be careful. If there's anything at all to be concerned about, let me know immediately."

"Will do," he said. "Palmieri out."

Obviously, he thought, the chief wasn't seriously worried about the temporal-flux reading, or she would have insisted on checking it out herself. Frowning, he put his tricorder away and headed for Cargo Bay Six.

It wasn't far. Palmieri took a left at the end of the corridor and found the entrance a few meters down on the left.

Laying his hand against the security pad on the bulkhead, he watched the door slide aside. It was dark in the bay, but he had his palm light. Palmieri took a few steps inside and played the light over the uneven terrain of stacked cargo containers.

Nothing to see. But when was there *ever?*

Taking out his tricorder, the security officer scanned the bay from one side to the other. There was evidence of flux, all right—not a lot, but enough to make him wary. He looked around again with the help of his light, seeking the exact location of the phenomenon.

Abruptly, without warning, the cargo bay blazed with a brilliant blue-white light. Instinctively, Palmieri threw a hand up to protect his eyes. Losing his balance, he staggered backward a step.

By the time he righted himself, the source of the illumination was gone. The bay was dark again—the neon afterimage on his retina the only evidence the flare-up had happened at all.

Then he glanced at his tricorder, and he realized the afterimage wasn't the *only* evidence. For a moment, apparently, the temporal-flux reading had gone off the scale. Now it was back to a trace level again.

Strange, Palmieri thought. *I'd better let the chief know about it.*

But before he could tap his communicator, he heard a sound. Something muttered. *A curse,* he thought.

Whirling, he saw he was no longer alone in the cargo bay. There were shadowy figures at the far end among the largest containers, where before there had been nothing and no one. From what he could tell, they hadn't noticed him yet.

"Where are we?" one of them asked the others.

"Weren't we just standing in the woods outside the mansion?" someone else asked.

"I've got a better question," said a third voice. "Where are our wee timehook devices?"

A fourth one spoke up gruffly. "Gone, it looks like. And don't *that* take the flamin' cake."

Putting away his tricorder and drawing his phaser, the security officer took a breath. Then he played his palm light on the figures.

"Hey!" one of them rasped at him. "Whaddaya tryin' ta do, *blind* us with that thing?"

Counting quickly, Palmieri saw there were seven of the intruders. Five males and two females, one of the latter rather young-looking. All humanoid, he decided quickly, though at least two of them looked like no species he'd ever seen before.

One had light-blue skin, but no Bolian, Andorian, Benzite, or Pandrilite ever had such yellow hair to go with it. And the great, white wings he wore looked like they had sprouted right out of his back.

Another one sported golden eyes and a dark-blue complexion—or was it some kind of fur? Also, the being had only three toes on each foot and three fingers on each hand—in itself, not so unusual, maybe. But he had a tail as well, which seemed fully maneuverable and ended in a sort of arrowhead shape, and that part *was* unusual.

There was also a short, stocky specimen, in yellow and blue garb and an elaborate, yellow and black mask. Though Palmieri knew of races whose people went hooded for cultural or religious reasons, he had a feeling this was something else—some kind of disguise.

A strange group indeed. But it wasn't just the strangers' appearances that made him wary. It was where and how they had shown up—in an obscure part of the starbase, without any kind of warning or prior notice.

Clearly, their appearance was linked with the blinding flash that had taken place a moment earlier—and the flux build-up that had accompanied it. It was too much of a coincidence for Palmieri to believe otherwise.

But what was the connection? Who *were* these people?

"Stay right where you are," he barked.

He trained his phaser on the intruders. They didn't seem to have any weapons in hand, but that didn't mean they weren't armed—or dangerous in some other way.

"Careful," said the one with the wings on his back. "That looks like a weapon he's holding."

"I believe Archangel's right," the one with the tail chimed in.

With the hand that held the palm light, the security officer tapped his communicator. "Palmieri to Chief Clark. Trouble on level ten, section four—request back-up."

Help would be on its way in a matter of seconds. All he had to do was hold these people until then.

The man in the mask took a couple of steps toward Palmieri. "How about ya put that toy away, Sparky, and tell the ol' Canucklehead what kinda fryin' pan we landed in?"

Frying pan? thought the security officer.

He remained calm and aimed his weapon directly at the stocky stranger. "I told you to stay where you are!"

"Or what?" asked the masked man. "You'll slap my wrist? Lemme tell ya, bub, I been slapped by bigger and better."

I warned him, thought Palmieri. Pressing a stud on his phaser, he hit the stranger square in the chest with a ruby-red beam, sending him flying backward into the arms of his companions.

What happened next turned the security officer's knees to jelly. The biggest of the strangers, who had looked perfectly normal to that point, suddenly grew even larger, produced a skin of shiny armor plating, and interposed himself between Palmieri and the others.

The security officer could think only one thought: *shapeshifter!*

That would mean the strangers were Dominion

agents—all of them. And they'd had the gall to materialize right in the middle of the station, as if they somehow
owned the place.

Palmieri grated his teeth as he tried to remember what
he'd learned about changelings. Did phaser beams even
have an effect on them? And if they did, at what setting?

"Stop," said the shapeshifter. "We have done nothing
wrong."

Suddenly, the security officer heard a pop, and realized one of the strangers had disappeared. As the scent of
sulfur reached him, he realized it was the one with the
dark-blue skin.

But where had he gone? Back to whatever vessel they
had come from—even without the benefit of a temporal-
flux incident? And why hadn't the others gone with him?

Before Palmieri could come up with an answer, he felt
something grab him from behind and spin him around.
Before he knew it, that same something had ripped his
phaser from his grasp.

Only when it was over did he realize it was the
stranger with the tail who had disarmed him. Instinctively, Palmieri took a swing at him, but the stranger did
a backflip and avoided it.

"Drop it!" came a shout from Palmieri's right.

Turning, he saw that it was Chief Clark who had
voiced the warning. Phaser in hand, she was entering the
cargo bay with a half-dozen armed security officers right
behind her.

Reinforcements, Palmieri thought. And none too soon.

"Lights," said Clark.

Instantly, the cargo bay was illuminated. Palmieri
could see the intruders better than ever—but it didn't
prepare him for what came next.

One of the strangers—the younger of the two females—began to sink right through the floor. One of the
other security officers fired at her, but the phaser beam
stabbed right through her and left a char mark on the
bulkhead beyond. A moment later, she was gone.

"That does it," growled the masked man, who seemed

to have recovered already from the blast he'd taken earlier. "Ya want a fight that bad, I'll be glad ta oblige!"

"No!" cried the remaining female, a tall, dark beauty with hair that looked like spun platinum.

Her comrades stopped dead in their tracks—even the man in the mask, though he grumbled about it. Obviously, they were accustomed to taking orders from the woman.

She turned to Chief Clark. "This is unnecessary," she said.

"I'll go along with *that,*" the chief agreed. She glanced at the stranger with the tail, her dark eyes blazing. "Of course, you'll have to return that phaser if you want to keep this cordial. And I want your friend—the girl—back where I can see her."

The woman with the silvery hair nodded to the one with the tail. "Give it back, Nightcrawler."

"Your wish is my command," he replied. And with a casual air, he tossed Palmieri's phaser to him.

The man with the wings then turned to the floor. "It's all right, Shadowcat. You can come out now."

Before Palmieri's wondering eyes, the younger woman's head floated up out of the deck surface. Then, when she was satisfied there wasn't any danger, she ascended the rest of the way.

Palmieri shook his head. *Who are these people?*

"Wait a minute," said another of the strangers—a fellow with closely cropped red hair, decked out in yellow and green. He took a couple of steps toward Clark.

"That's far enough," she told him.

Suddenly, the red-haired man grinned. Then he turned back to the woman with the silver hair and indicated Clark with a gesture.

"D'ye not see it?" he asked, in what Palmieri was beginning to recognize as an Irish brogue.

The woman's eyes narrowed, then widened again. "Yes," she answered at last. "It's the same uniform, isn't it? And the same insignia."

"Exactly th' same," the redhead confirmed. He turned to Clark again and spread his hands in a gesture of peace. "Tell me, Lass . . . would ye happen t' know a lad by th' name of Picard?"

The name sounded familiar to Palmieri. Then he realized where he had heard it before.

Jean-Luc Picard was the captain of the *Enterprise,* the flagship of the fleet. If the stories about the man were true, he had saved the Federation from destruction more than once.

"What do you want with him?" Clark asked the man with the brogue.

The redhead smiled. "Believe it or not, he's a friend o' ours."

Chapter Two

PRADDIS AMON, ESTEEMED Chancellor of the planet Xhaldia, paced his high-ceilinged summer office with a heart full of trepidation. He no longer had to study the rounded monitor on his desk to know what kind of reports were coming in—and at what seemed like an ever-accelerating rate.

In Brellos Province, a woman named Nikti Eilo had nearly killed her newborn twins when her body began drawing heat and light out of everything and everyone around her. Two hundred miles away, in the city of Cardriil, a mental patient named Tessa Mollic had thrown his ward into chaos when he began incinerating beds with the power of his mind.

Off the Nornian Coast, a recreational fisherman was lucky to escape with his life after accidentally punching a hole in the bottom of his boat. A Mercasite gymnast had come close to suffocating when she somehow encased herself in an impermeable, metallic skin. And at Otros Paar, in the midst of an adulthood quest, someone named Erid Sovar had inadvertently blasted several prayer perches to dust with energy beams.

Such bizarre incidents were taking place all over the globe, if the reports could be believed—and as much as Amon didn't want to believe them, it appeared he had little choice in the matter. After all, they had been filed by sane, reliable regional administrators.

People turning invisible, indeed undetectable except by the most sophisticated instruments . . . moving more quickly than the eye could follow . . . and one who could create illusions so real, so powerful, she had already caused a fatal hovercar accident.

The fact patterns were always different, but one thing remained constant. In each case, the individual at the heart of the incident had recently reached the age of twenty-two.

Why that span of years? Amon had no idea. But it was the only common thread that seemed to exist, tantalizing him with the hope that he might understand what was going on if he just tried hard enough.

A voice filled the room, startling him out of his meditation. "Chancellor? It's the security minister."

Amon nodded. "Send him in."

A moment later, Minister Tollit entered Amon's office, his white garb marked by the black ribbon of the security corps. Taller and broader than Amon, he inclined his silver-tufted head and spoke in a deep voice.

"Good to see you, Chancellor—though I wish more pleasant circumstances had brought us together."

"So do I, Tollit," said the chancellor. He tilted his head in the direction of his desk. "You've seen the lastest reports?"

The minister nodded soberly. "I have indeed. They're . . . disturbing, to say the least."

"Yes," Amon agreed. "But the repercussions may be even more so."

Tollit looked at him. "What do you mean?"

"The public feels endangered," said the chancellor.

"Our people are frightened. And perhaps they are right to feel that way."

The security minister shrugged. "I have yet to hear of these strange twenty-two year-olds using their abilities to hurt anyone."

"But it will happen eventually," Amon insisted. He eyed his colleague. "Mind you, the youth in question may only be acting in self-defense, or perhaps what he *perceives* to be self-defense. But he will lash out at someone and there will be a tragedy. And when that happens, the news will spread like wind-driven fire."

Tollit considered the possibility. "Then we must prevent the spark . . . and thereby the fire."

"Agreed," the chancellor replied.

He turned to the oval window behind his desk, where the cloudless sky was mellowing to a dusky orange. He could still make out the dark smudge of the Obrig Mountains on the distant horizon, with the lights of the area's only city clustered at their base.

"Verdeen," he said.

The security minister regarded him. "I beg your pardon?"

"Verdeen," Amon repeated. "There's a fortress there left over from the Seven Years War."

"An *ancient* fortress," Tollit reminded him.

"But still, our best option. I want you and your people to round up those who've been . . . transformed . . . and bring them to Verdeen. For their own safety, as well as everyone else's."

The minister frowned. "We can't keep them there forever, Chancellor. We haven't the right."

Amon sighed deeply. "I'm afraid this goes far beyond the issue of anyone's rights, Tollit. Though, as you must know, I don't like that idea any better than you do."

The minister nodded. "Yes, Chancellor. I know."

"That will be all," Amon told him. "At least for now."

Tollit inclined his head again and left the room. In his wake, there was a silence the chancellor could only describe as oppressive.

Xhaldian society had been built on the privileges and responsibilities of the individual. It pained Amon to take a barbaric step backward in that regard, to imprison people when they hadn't done anything wrong. But the transformed represented a new kind of danger, unlike anything any Xhaldian had encountered before.

And, as someone had once said, desperate times called for desperate measures.

As Commander Worf got up from the center chair of the *Defiant,* he glanced at each of the men and women operating the ship's key bridge stations. Finally, he settled his gaze on Chief O'Brien.

The engineer smiled at him. "Say hi to all our old friends for me, won't you?"

The Klingon no longer believed in showing a lot of emotion in public—especially when he was in command of the *Defiant.* Many emotions were undignified, after all.

Naturally, Jadzia believed otherwise. But then, Worf and his new mate differed on a great many subjects. It was hardly a shock that they would differ on that one as well.

"I look forward to it," the Klingon said simply.

Of course, O'Brien had known Worf a long time—longer than anyone else on the Defiant or, for that matter, on Deep Space Nine. The engineer's smile turned into a grin.

"Whatever you say, Commander," he replied.

Tapping his communicator badge, the Klingon raised his bearded chin, imagining it gave him an air of self-possession. "Worf to Enterprise. One to beam over."

"Ready, sir," came the response.

The voice was unfamiliar to Worf. But then, he hadn't set foot on the *Enterprise* in almost a year. In that period of time, considerable changes would have taken place in ship's personnel.

"Take care, sir," O'Brien told him. "And don't let

them kid you too much about your wedding, all right?"

The Klingon didn't respond to O'Brien's reference about his recent nuptials. However, he fully expected that the chief was right. No doubt, some of his former comrades would find something humorous in his marriage to Jadzia Dax.

Others would simply congratulate Worf on the event. Captain Picard would be one of the latter, he expected. After all, the captain was a man who showed others the proper respect.

"Energize," said the Klingon.

There was no sensation to signal the fact that his atoms were being scanned, reorganized, and shot across the void. There was only the always-strange recognition that he was suddenly somewhere else—in this case, one of the *Enterprise*'s several transporter rooms.

The operator was a slender woman with short red hair. As Worf had gathered from hearing her voice, he didn't know her.

That came as no surprise to him. What the Klingon *did* find unusual was the absence of his friends and colleagues. Except for the transporter operator, he was all alone in the room.

"Welcome aboard, sir," the woman said cordially.

"Thank you," said Worf. He couldn't help frowning. "I had . . . expected there would be someone here to meet me. Other than yourself, I mean."

The transporter operator just looked at him. Obviously, she didn't know what to say to that.

"Never mind," the Klingon told her. "It is not important."

Clearly, he thought, the captain and his command staff were engaged in some urgent and unexpected business—though Worf had difficulty imagining what that business might be. Stepping down from the platform, he crossed the room and headed for the exit.

He was almost there when the doors slid aside and

revealed Captain Picard. The man looked distracted—so much so, he almost walked into Worf before he realized his former tactical officer was there.

"Mr. Worf!" the captain exclaimed.

The Klingon suppressed a smile. "I am pleased to see you, sir."

"You look well," said Picard.

"As do you, sir." He eyed the captain more closely. "Has something pressing come up? Something of which I should be aware?"

Picard looked at him. "I . . . don't believe so," he responded finally. "Why do you ask?"

Worf sighed. "No reason."

True, he had expected a bit more of a reception. However, he had hardly seen the captain over the course of the last few years. The same was true of the Klingon's other former comrades—Deanna, Data, Geordi, Dr. Crusher, and Commander Riker.

Times change, he told himself. People change. They make other friendships and move on.

"Well," said Picard, "why don't we repair to the observation lounge? We can discuss the diplomatic conference. No doubt, you already have some ideas as to how you would like to approach it."

Worf nodded, reminded of the reason for his visit. With the efforts of the Klingon Empire so vital to Federation security these days, Starfleet Command had decided to hold a strategy meeting with a number of high-ranking Klingon military leaders.

As the Starfleet officer most familiar with Klingon customs, Worf was asked to attend a planning session at Starbase 42. After all, the last thing Command wanted to do was offend or alienate its guests—and who knew the potential pitfalls better than a warrior of the House of Martok?

On the other hand, with the Jem'Hadar a constant threat, Captain Sisko hadn't wanted the Defiant gone too long from Deep Space Nine. Hence, the rendezvous with another starship.

The *Enterprise* was selected for the job because her captain had served as the Klingons' Arbiter of Succession years earlier. As that had given Picard some standing in the Empire, his input was valued as well.

"Indeed," said Worf, "I *do* have some ideas."

"Excellent," the captain replied.

Then he led the way out of the transporter room. The Klingon followed, feeling as if he had just conversed with a stranger. It was not a particularly good feeling.

Catching up with Picard, he cleared his throat. "You know," he said, "I have taken a wife."

The captain glanced at him. "Yes, I've heard. That lovely young woman Captain Sisko depends on so much. She's a Trill, as I recall."

Worf nodded. "That is correct."

"What was her name?"

"Jadzia. Jadzia Dax."

"Of course. Congratulations," Picard said.

The Klingon did his best to conceal his disappointment. He had expected a bit more from the man he had designated his cha'DIch—his ceremonial defender—when he was accused of treason on his people's homeworld several years earlier.

"Thank you," Worf answered hollowly.

Suddenly, something occurred to him. Perhaps it was the captain who was disappointed in *him*. Hadn't the Klingon held his wedding without inviting anyone from the *Enterprise*? And, if he were in Picard's place, wouldn't he have taken offense at that?

"I would have invited you to the wedding," Worf began to explain, "but Alexander was shipping out in a matter of days. There was no—"

The captain smiled at him. "There is no need to make excuses, Commander. I understand completely."

His tone said he was telling the truth. He really *did* understand. And as far as the Klingon could tell, it didn't matter much to Picard that he had missed the wedding.

They entered a nearby turbolift and instructed it to

take them to the bridge. During their passage through the ship, the captain didn't say anything and neither did the Klingon. They simply faced forward and waited to reach their destination.

When the lift doors opened, Picard emerged first. Crossing the bridge, he headed for the observation lounge.

Worf was right behind him. However, he took a moment to scan the bridge and its personnel. His heart sank a little further as he realized there was no one there that he recognized. No one at all.

The doors to the observation lounge slid open and the captain made his way inside. The Klingon shook his head. True, this *Enterprise* was not the one on which he had served for so many years. But he had hoped to feel at least a little bit at home here.

He had hoped to find some sense of *family.*

With that thought echoing in his head, Worf entered the lounge, head down—and was jolted by a loud and raucous sound. He had already assumed a Mok'bara stance and bared his teeth before he realized what it was. . . .

A cacophony of voices shouting a single word: "Surprise!"

Looking around, the Klingon saw all the friends he had looked forward to seeing again—Riker and Crusher, Geordi and Data, Deanna and Guinan. And they were all grinning at him—even Data, who had acquired an emotion chip shortly before the destruction of the previous Enterprise.

But it was Captain Picard who was grinning the widest.

"Sorry to startle you," said Deanna.

"A Klingon does not startle," Worf insisted.

Taking a glass of amber-colored liquid from the eight drinks assembled on the table, the captain raised it and offered a toast. "To Commander Worf, our friend and comrade now and forever."

"And to Commander Dax," Riker amended slyly, raising a glass of his own.

Deanna added her glass to the others. "May they bring honor and gladness to the House of Martok."

"May their hearts always beat together," said the doctor.

"And may their love for one another never lose its edge," Guinan remarked.

She gestured to the one glass remaining on the table. It contained a darker, thicker liquid than the others.

"Have a drink," the bartender told Worf. "It's on the house."

The Klingon smiled, his heart swelling with gratitude and affection. "Perhaps I will," he said. He picked up the glass and raised it as the others had done. "On behalf of Jadzia and the House of Martok, I offer my thanks."

"Well said," Riker noted.

Data addressed the captain. "Your performance must have been quite convincing, sir. Commander Worf seemed genuinely surprised."

"I didn't think I'd be able to pull it off," Picard admitted. "As you know, Mr. Data, I love acting, but I'm afraid it's not my forte."

"On the contrary," said Deanna, "you were flawless, sir."

"A regular one-man show," Geordi added.

The Klingon grunted. "I wish Chief O'Brien could see this. He warned me that you would all taunt me."

"Taunt you?" Data echoed. "About what?"

"My marriage," said Worf.

The android looked confused. "I fail to see what purpose that would serve. As I understand it, marriage is a happy event. One in which two people agree to share the experience of their lives—"

"For better or worse," Geordi chimed in.

"Richer or poorer," Crusher said matter-of-factly.

"In sickness or in health," the engineer added.

"Wrong culture," Riker pointed out.

Geordi and the doctor looked at each other.

"He's right," said Crusher.

Geordi shrugged.

The first officer put his hand on Worf's shoulder. "Just one bit of advice," he said. "Don't forget your anniversary, Commander. I understand the little woman swings a mean bat'leth."

"Though, from what I've heard, not half as mean as your mother-in-law's," Geordi added.

The Klingon looked at Riker, then at the engineer, and scowled. "Perhaps Chief O'Brien had a point after all."

Worf had to maintain the pretense that their gibes annoyed him. A warrior could act no other way. But, truth be told, he found himself basking in the warmth of their company—ridicule or no ridicule.

Suddenly, a voice cut into their conversation. "Lieutenant Sovar to Captain Picard. I have a subspace message for you, sir. It's from Admiral Kashiwada on Starbase 88."

The Klingon turned to the captain. In fact, they all did. Picard frowned back at them.

"Stay here," he said. "I will attend to the admiral's communication. If I need any of you, I will let you know."

"Are you certain, sir?" asked Worf.

The captain nodded congenially. "Quite certain, Commander."

And with that, he left them.

Chapter Three

As Picard emerged from the observation lounge, he pulled down the front of his uniform top and advanced to his captain's chair. Unfortunately, a commanding officer's duties took priority over family reunions.

"Put the admiral on screen," he told Ensign Suttles.

A moment later, the image of a flowing starfield was replaced with a familiar visage—that of Admiral Yoshi Kashiwada. Thirty-odd years earlier, the admiral had served as the captain's tactics instructor back at the Academy.

Kashiwada smiled, deepening the wrinkles around his eyes. "Good to see you, Jean-Luc. I trust you're well?" The admiral was of the old school, where nothing was so urgent it superceded the need for good manners.

"Quite well, thank you," Picard replied. "How are you, sir?"

Kashiwada shrugged. "As you can see, I survive."

"And will for another hundred years, no doubt. But I suspect you called about a more immediate concern."

The admiral nodded. "In fact, I have. I find myself

playing host to a most unusual group of guests, whose method of arrival is no less strange to me than they are. What's more, they claim to know you."

Picard leaned back in his seat. "Their names?"

Kashiwada frowned ever so slightly. "They insisted you would know them more readily by their aliases." He peered at a monitor alongside him. "Storm. Wolverine. Banshee. Arch ""

The captain felt a thrill of surprise shoot through him. "Arch*angel?"* he blurted, completing the name.

The other man cocked an eyebrow. "Then you *do* know them?"

Picard leaned forward again. "I met them some time ago. Though . . ."

The admiral looked at him. "Yes?"

"Frankly, I am at a loss to explain what they're doing here. They reside in another frame of reference—another universe, as it were."

"I have a grandson who is said to do the same," Kashiwada commented. "But I have a feeling you mean it in a more literal sense."

The captain confirmed it. "Did the X- . . . that is, did your guests say how they got here? Or what purpose they had in mind?"

The admiral held his hands out—a gesture of helplessness. "From what they tell me, their arrival was not a matter of design, but an accident. Their only intention, they insist, is to return home."

"I see," said Picard.

"I can send you the information they gave us concerning their arrival. You may find it helpful."

"I would appreciate it," the captain told him.

"In any case," Kashiwada went on, "since these people seem to know you, and since Starbase 88 is more or less en route to your destination . . ."

"You thought I might come by and pick them up."

The admiral smiled. "It might be a good idea for everyone concerned. At least one of our guests seems ill-suited to a Starfleet environment. And, given his rather . . . let us say *surly* disposition, I would be surprised if trouble did not ensue."

Picard nodded. "That would be Wolverine," he guessed.

"It would," Kashiwada agreed.

The captain sighed.

Even if Wolverine weren't threatening to become a problem, he would have felt compelled to help the X-Men. After all, they had proven themselves dependable and courageous allies in their own universe. The least he could do was stand by them in his own.

He turned to Lt. Rager, who was manning the helm. "Make the necessary adjustments," he told her. "Warp six."

Rager nodded. "Aye, sir. Setting course for Starbase 88."

Picard regarded the admiral again. "The *Enterprise* should be there in a day or so, sir. In the meantime, I trust you'll find a way to keep your guests properly entertained."

"Oh, yes," the older man assured him. "One way or the other. See you then, Jean-Luc. Kashiwada out."

A moment later, the admiral's image was supplanted by that of the starfield. The captain stroked his chin thoughtfully.

The last thing he had expected was to run into the X-Men again. However, he had to admit that the prospect intrigued him . . . especially when it came to one X-Man in particular.

As Erid Sovar entered the room, he took note of three things.

The first was the presence of a thickset, blue-uniformed administrator behind a large, blackwood desk. His name was Osan, or so Erid had heard. The man didn't look the least bit surprised by Erid's appearance. But then, by that time, he had probably seen even stranger transformations.

The second thing Erid noticed was the light streaming

in through a large, oval window. It slashed across the only other chair in the room, which was positioned opposite Osan's.

Erid's third observation was that there were no guards in the room. The two who had escorted him from his room had remained outside. It was a sign of trust—one that seemed strange to the youth, as it stood in direct opposition to everything Erid had experienced over the last two days.

Ever since he had been discovered and taken into custody near the Vuuren Pass, he had been handled like a criminal. He had been transported by silent guardsmen and locked up in this old, stone fortress, where he was surprised to see others who had changed in bizarre ways.

In Erid's case, maybe there was some justification for such treatment. After all, he had destroyed some of the ancient prayer perches at Otros Paar, even if it wasn't his intention to do so.

But the others to whom he had spoken, or—more often—whose conversations he had overheard in the yard . . . they hadn't destroyed anything. They had been incarcerated simply because of their transformations.

Because the government was afraid of them, some said—afraid of what they might do if they remained free. The fortress guards had told the transformed that wasn't true. The guards said that they had been gathered here for their own protection.

To Erid's mind, only one thing was certain: the transformed were inside the walls of the fortress and every other Xhaldian was outside them. Nothing else really mattered.

"Please," the administrator said in an almost paternal way, "sit down." He indicated the empty chair with a beefy hand.

Erid considered the chair. It gleamed in the shaft of light.

"What is it?" asked Osan, noticing the youth's hesitation.

"I cannot sit there," said Erid.

The administrator's eyes narrowed. "Why not?"

The youth indicated the window with a tilt of his head. "The light. It activates the energy in me."

Understanding dawned on Osan's face. Understanding . . . and something else as well. Something like concern, only stronger.

Erid was almost tempted to call it fear.

"I see," Osan said. "In that case, you may move the chair away from the light. Or stand, if you prefer."

Erid chose to stand, though it made his legs feel even heavier. "I want to speak with my family," he declared. "When can I do that?"

The administrator looked sympathetic. "That's difficult to say. Right now, all our resources are concentrated on the rescue operation. New transformations are taking place every day, you understand."

The youth shook his head. "I *don't* understand. What have your resources got to do with my speaking with my parents?"

Osan leaned back in his chair and frowned. "We have to regulate the flow of information. If people find out what we're doing here, they may misinterpret our actions. The situation could instantly spiral out of control, to the detriment of all concerned."

"In other words," Erid said, "you have no intention of letting me speak with my family."

The administrator's frown deepened. "As I said, we're regulating the flow of information. But that's just a temporary condition."

"How temporary?"

Something stiffened in Osan. "I believe I answered that."

But he hadn't. Not really.

"Do my parents know what's become of me?" Erid asked. "Do they know where I am? How I've changed?"

The administrator sighed. "That, too, would constitute potentially incendiary information. It's in everyone's best interests that they *don't* know. At least, not yet."

31

Erid glanced at the window. Somewhere beyond its glare was the yard, where the transformed were allowed to congregate twice a day.

He recalled how it had been for him there a couple of days earlier. Frightened by his transformation and his subsequent imprisonment, still uncertain of how his powers worked, Erid had made the mistake of wandering into the center of the yard.

In moments, beams of brilliant laserlight had sprung from his fingers, just as they had that first time at Otros Paar. And the guards who lined the battlements had fired their weapons at him, making him shiver and convulse and finally lose consciousness.

Perhaps Osan was right. Perhaps it was better his parents didn't know. It would be easier for them to think their son had perished than to picture him as a monster in a stone cage.

But that wasn't the point, was it? It wasn't a matter of who would suffer if word of his transformation got out. It was a matter of his right to make that decision for himself.

"You had no right to take me," Erid told the administrator. "And you have no right to keep me here."

Osan regarded him. "You may be right about that. We may have no right at all. But we have a responsibility to the people of Xhaldia, and we must carry it out as best we can."

Erid saw he would get nowhere with this man. Still, it irked him that it should be so.

A part of him even considered stepping into the light and becoming what Osan feared—a dynamo of deadly and unpredictable energy. But that would only earn Erid a barrage of stun fire from the guards outside, and he dearly wished to avoid another experience like the one in the yard.

"Some day," he told his captor, "you'll regret what you've done here." It was less than a threat, but more than a prediction.

Osan smiled a grim smile. "This may surprise you," he said, "but I regret it already."

Erid was still pondering the meaning of the man's words as he left the room and returned to his barracks.

Captain Picard got up from his center seat and eyed the bridge's forward viewscreen, where he could make out a speck of gray against the sea of stars. "Maximum magnification," he said.

"Aye, Captain," replied Data, who was sitting at Ops.

A moment later, the speck became a full-blown Federation starbase—in this case, Starbase 88. Picard considered it for a moment, then cast a glance over his shoulder.

Lt. Sovar, a security officer with bronze skin and a brush of blue-black hair, was manning the tactical console. He looked up from his monitors, seeming to sense the captain's scrutiny.

"Lieutenant," said Picard, "hail the station. Tell them I would like to speak with Admiral Kashiwada."

"Aye, sir," Sovar replied.

Before long, Kashiwada's countenance replaced the image of the starbase. By the frown lines around the man's mouth, the captain could tell the X-Men's stay was proving stressful for the admiral.

"Jean-Luc," said Kashiwada. "I see you made good time."

It was a joke, of course. Starship travel was precise. Seldom did a vessel vary from its schedule by more than a few minutes.

"I was eager to see you in person again," Picard replied.

"More likely," said the admiral, "you were eager to see my guests. As you may have guessed, they are eager to see *you* as well."

The captain smiled. "I imagine they are. I trust their visit with you has been mutually profitable?"

Kashiwada grunted. "That would be one way to put it.

I'll meet you in our transporter room, Jean-Luc. Say, in . . . half an hour?"

"Half an hour will be fine," Picard assured him.

"Excellent," said the admiral.

His face disappeared, the image of the starbase taking its place. But Kashiwada's expression remained with the captain.

Quite clearly, it hadn't been a happy one.

Chapter Four

Erid Sovar walked out of the fortress's low, stone mess hall last and alone. But then, that wasn't unusual. More than most of the transformed, he mainly kept to himself.

As he emerged from the coolness into the hot, crowded yard, Erid hugged the high, curving wall on his right. That way, he could protect himself from the rays of the sun and the indignity of another energy fit.

Others among the transformed had the same problem. Erid had learned that over the previous couple of days, as the prisoner population had grown from twenty to just under thirty. In fact, fully five or six of them possessed powers triggered by sunlight.

Like him, those individuals kept to the shadows as best they could. And in the rare instances where they forgot to do so or defied fate, and their powers ran rampant, the guards on the ancient battlements buried them in a storm of stun fire.

Of course, some fits seemed to take place without any provocation at all. Suddenly, one of the transformed would emit a web of electrical energy or grow twelve feet tall. And while they were trying to come to grips with what had happened, the guards would turn them into convulsing wretches.

Erid shivered at the thought. It had become almost as hard for him to watch such an event as to experience it.

Of course, not everyone was quite so sensitive to the feelings of others. Some seemed hardly to care at all. But then, the transformed at Verdeen were as diverse as any cross-section of the population.

The youth was reminded of that fact as he skirted the yard, watching his fellow prisoners meditate, or exercise, or talk in small groups. No two of the transformed were exactly alike.

There were shy, quiet types, and those who were loud and angry about what had happened to them. There were friendly, compassionate people, and those who hated everyone they looked at. There were young men and women who were frightened and wanted only to go home, and those who seemed to barely mind their imprisonment.

What's more, they had all changed in different ways. Even with his enlarged, purple blood vessels and the loss of his blue-black skull brush, Erid was hardly the most grotesque of them.

Some of the transformed had grown an extra set of arms. Some had sprouted horns or some similarly peculiar appendages. Still others had seen an alteration in skin texture or eye color. Only a fortunate handful seemed to have undergone no outward change at all.

Their powers were unique as well. Where one had become immensely strong, another had become lightning-quick. Where one could draw energy from everything around her, another could turn solids into liquids or create illusions in the minds of others.

All of them different. And yet, all bound by a common destiny—to become something their world had never seen before, near the occasion of their twenty-second birthday.

No one knew why they had changed. No one knew

how. They knew only that they had been altered, and for the time being—at the very least—there was nothing any of them could do about it.

As Erid's eyes adjusted to the bright light in the yard, he picked out the transformed who had arrived only that morning. There were three of them, the smallest group of newcomers he had seen yet.

One was a small, slender woman named Denara, who spoke with a Mercasite accent. To look at her, one would never know she could grow a metallic exo-skin capable of withstanding the most punishing force. Yet Denara could do exactly that—or so she claimed.

The second of the new arrivals was a handsome young man named Paldul, the skin of whose forehead had become pocked with tiny, green craters. Paldul's power, apparently, was a mental one—he could tell what others were thinking, in the manner of a Betazoid.

But it was the third of the newcomers who seemed to command everyone's interest. His name was Rahatan, and like Denara, he looked much like any other Xhaldian. A little taller than normal, with perhaps a little more swagger in his step, but nothing terribly out of the ordinary.

The nature of Rahatan's power? He had neither demonstrated nor described it, so Erid didn't have any idea. However, he had a feeling the man's talent was something formidable.

Perhaps it had something to do with influencing others. That would explain the small crowd that had gathered around Rahatan, hanging on to what he was saying. Curious, Erid came as close as he could without exposing himself to direct sunlight.

"You haven't been *allowed?*" said Rahatan.

"That'sright," replied a woman named Corba, who had been seen to move in amazing bursts of speed. "Notevenacalltoourfamilies,toletthemknowwhereweare. Theydon'twantanyoneontheoutsidetoknowaboutus."

"Slow down," said a man with luminous, red eyes,

37

whose name Erid had forgotten. "We can barely understand what you're saying."

"*I* understood her," remarked a transformed called Leyden.

Most of his skin had turned into something hard and translucent, like the armored shell of an insect, and he was reputed to have the strength of ten normal Xhaldians.

Leyden smiled bitterly. "Corba said we can't make contact with the outside because the government doesn't want anyone to know about us. It's the truth, too. Osan hasn't made an effort to deceive us on that point."

Rahatan grunted. "It doesn't seem right."

"It's not," responded an attractive woman named Seevyn, who could create powerful illusions. In fact, it was said that her transformation had made her something hideous, and that her appearance was an illusion as well. "But there's not a great deal we can do about it."

Rahatan eyed her. "And why's that?"

Seevyn jerked a thumb over her shoulder, indicating the guards perched on the parapets above them. "In case you haven't noticed, *they're* the ones with the stun weapons."

"And they're not afraid to use them," added the man with the luminous eyes.

Rahatan shrugged. "So what? We've got weapons, too, haven't we?"

He looked up at the guards, his expression a defiant one. What's more, they seemed to notice.

"Look at them," Rahatan said softly. "It's *they* who are afraid of *us.* That's why they're clutching those weapons so tightly. They're scared we'll climb up there and show them how powerful we've become."

Erid found himself nodding. The guards *were* scared of them. He had seen it in their eyes, even as they raked him with stun fire. He had seen it in Osan's face, as he stood before the administrator's desk.

"Are you suggesting something?" asked Seevyn.

Rahatan looked at her. "All I'm saying—for now—is that they need to treat us better. And if I have anything to say about it, they *will.*"

Erid was impressed with the newcomer's bravado . . . even if he didn't think anything would come of it. Still, he resolved to keep an eye on the transformed called Rahatan.

Picard materialized in the large, well-lit transporter room of Starbase 88, flanked by Counselor Troi and Commander Data. He found Admiral Kashiwada standing beside the base's transporter operator—waiting for Picard and his officers, as promised.

"Admiral," said the captain.

"Welcome," Kashiwada replied.

Picard indicated his officers. "This is Deanna Troi, our ship's counselor. And Commander Data, our second officer."

The admiral inclined his head slightly. "My pleasure."

"The pleasure is ours, sir," Troi responded.

"No," said Kashiwada. "The pleasure is *mine,* believe me. For when you leave, you will take our guests with you." He gestured to the door. "Follow me, please."

Picard allowed the admiral to lead the way out of the transporter room. Once they had emerged into the corridor outside, however, he accelerated to catch up with Kashiwada.

"You must understand, sir," said the captain, "it is not easy for the X-Men to be here. Their world is very different from ours."

"I'm sure it is," the admiral told him. "And believe me, Jean-Luc, I harbor no ill will toward them. In fact, I find them intriguing in many respects. It's just that—"

Suddenly, Picard saw something red-and-white flash into view at the end of the corridor and come hurtling in their direction. Before he knew it, it was almost on top of them.

"Watch out!" he snapped.

The captain barely had time to duck before the thing flashed over his head in a loud, almost tangible rush of air. Whirling, he saw it disappear around a bend in the passageway.

He cursed. "What *was* that?"

"That was Archangel," Data answered matter-of-factly. "I imagine he was in a hurry, or he would have stopped to speak with us."

Picard straightened and made an effort to regain his composure. "No doubt," he muttered.

Kashiwada sighed. "It's been my experience that Archangel travels that way as often as possible. I think he enjoys startling my base personnel with his comings and goings."

For all the captain knew, the admiral's observation was an accurate one. But he kept his speculation to himself.

"Then again," said Data, "as you yourself have pointed out, sir, a starbase is hardly the ideal environment for the X-Men—particularly one who is used to the freedom of an open sky. Perhaps this is simply Archangel's instinctive response to being—"

"Cooped up?" the admiral suggested.

The android nodded. "Precisely, sir."

Kashiwada shrugged. "No doubt, you're right, Commander."

He resumed walking. Picard and the others followed suit.

"Nonetheless," the admiral went on, "understanding the stresses on Archangel's psyche doesn't make his mode of travel any less startling. Why, just a little while ago—"

Before he could finish his sentence, a sinister, dark figure popped into existence in the corridor ahead of them. The captain tensed, his nerves already taut from their encounter with Archangel.

Then he saw who it was—just another of the X-Men. Taking a breath, he forced himself to relax.

"Nightcrawler," said Troi.

"In the flesh," the mutant responded playfully, with a German accent. "Or the fur, if you prefer. You may take your pick, Counselor."

"How did you know where to find us?" asked Data.

Nightcrawler grinned. "A little bird told me—the one that went rushing by you a moment ago. Fortunately, I've come to know some of these corridors pretty well by now."

"Me, too," said a youthful, feminine voice.

Tracing it to its source, Picard turned and saw the head of a young woman emerging from the deck behind him. It would have been a bizarre sight indeed had it not been preceded by the equally bizarre appearances of Nightcrawler and Archangel.

"Shadowcat," the captain noted. "Remind me to instruct you in the use of a turbolift sometime."

Floating the rest of the way up through the metal deck surface, revealing her blue and yellow garb, the girl appeared to ignore Picard's comment. "It's about time you got here. Storm and the others are waiting for you in the admiral's office, and they are *not* happy with what's going on."

The captain turned to Kashiwada. "What's . . . *going on?*" he repeated.

The admiral nodded. "You see, we had some trouble with your friend Wolverine last night. I was forced to incarcerate him."

"You put him in the brig?" Picard asked.

"That's correct," Kashiwada replied. "Reluctantly, of course. However, it was necessary if we were to maintain order on the base."

"I see," said the captain.

"Can we go see Storm now?" asked Shadowcat.

"We are doing our best to make progress," the admiral told her. "If people stop flying by and floating out of the floor, perhaps we will actually arrive at our destination someday."

Shadowcat started to say something, but Nightcrawler held a hand up. "Admiral Kashiwada is right," he said. "The sooner we leave him alone, the sooner he and our friends here—"

Out of the corner of his eye, Picard saw a blur of red and white. He knew what it was this time, but it was still disconcerting to see it bear down on him and then zip just over his head.

"—will get where they're going," Nightcrawler finished, as Archangel negotiated a bend in the corridor and sped out of sight.

"Okay," said Shadowcat. Without another word, she walked into the bulkhead and vanished.

A moment later, Nightcrawler disappeared as well. In his place, he left a small implosion of air and a scent not unlike brimstone.

Kashiwada let the captain see his suffering for a fleeting moment. "A most stimulating group indeed," the admiral said.

Picard didn't answer. He just followed Kashiwada to his ready room. Without any further interruptions, it was a journey of but a few minutes.

As they entered the admiral's sanctum, the captain saw that Nightcrawler, Shadowcat, and Archangel were there already. So were Storm, Banshee, and Colossus, as well as a dark-haired woman in a gold and black Starfleet security officer's uniform.

The pips on the woman's collar told Picard she wasn't just *any* security officer. She was in charge of that function here on the starbase.

"Captain Picard," said Storm, rising from her chair. "I am glad to see you." She acknowledged the captain's colleagues. "And you as well."

Colossus and Banshee got up, too. The former was in his human state, so he didn't tower over the others in the room by quite so much.

"There has been a problem with Wolverine," Colossus noted, not one to beat around the bush.

"Aye," said Banshee. "Or rather, there *was* a problem.

42

But it's over now, so there's nae reason for him t' be sittin' in that silly wee brig."

Picard knew the X-Men could have prevented their comrade from being incarcerated if they had wished to—or freed him any time they wanted. Yet they had allowed Wolverine to be taken to the brig and to languish there.

In a way, they were doing what the captain would have done in the midst of an alien culture. They were showing respect for their hosts by trying to obey the laws set out for them.

Picard turned to Kashiwada. "Admiral? Do you have any objection to Wolverine's being set free at this time?"

"None," Kashiwada said reasonably. "As long as the fellow doesn't linger here on the base." He glanced at his security chief. "Lt. Clark, would you be so kind as to see to Wolverine's emancipation?"

The woman nodded. "Aye, sir."

Archangel's wings beat once, quickly.

Storm glanced at him with her blue eyes, seeming to know what the gesture meant. "What is it, Archangel?"

"Wolverine isn't too fond of Lt. Clark. After all, she *was* the one who phaser-blasted him." He turned his cold, almost haughty gaze on the security officer. "No offense."

"None taken," said Lt. Clark, though her expression said otherwise.

Storm turned to Picard. Her look was an appeal for help—a request that he not put her in the position of intervening.

"If it's all right with you," the captain told Kashiwada, "perhaps Counselor Troi could accompany the lieutenant. She has, after all, established something of a rapport with Wolverine."

Not *that* much of a rapport, Picard knew. However, the counselor had been trained to defuse explosive situations, and this had the possibility of becoming one of them.

The admiral thought about it for a moment. "Lt.

Clark," he said at last, "Counselor Troi will go with you, as the captain has suggested. If a confrontation seems to be developing, you'll defer to her."

"Aye, sir," the security officer responded dutifully.

Then she and Troi left Kashiwada's ready room.

Picard turned to Storm again. "Don't worry. The counselor will make sure everything goes smoothly."

"I'm sure she will," said Storm.

But, judging by the glances the X-Men were exchanging, not all of them were quite so confident.

Chapter Five

As TROI ACCOMPANIED Security Chief Clark along one of the starbase's curving corridors, she used her Betazoid senses to locate Wolverine and probe the mutant's state of mind. What she found in him was anger and frustration, in equal parts.

The anger was primitive, instinctual—what an animal might have felt at being caged. The frustration came from the restraint he had to exercise, lest he compound his offense by attempting to tear up his cell.

"I don't mind telling you," said Clark, "he did quite a bit of damage."

Troi let her empathic contact with Wolverine lapse. "Oh?" she replied.

"Two tables, several chairs, and a replicator," the security officer enumerated. "And, of course, one of the bulkheads."

The counselor looked at her. "One of the *bulkheads?*"
Clark nodded.

The counselor nodded. "I see."

"He's just up ahead," said Clark. She turned to her guest. "You're sure you can handle this?"

Troi nodded. "If the prisoner acts up, I'll just use a few Mok'bara moves on him."

The chief looked at her. "You're joking, right?"

The counselor didn't sense any real amusement on Clark's part. "Trying to," she said.

A moment later, they came in sight of the brig. Its forcefield was transparent except for an occasional white spark. As Troi got closer, she could see a pair of booted feet inside, one crossed over the other.

"Lt. Clark," Wolverine said without turning around.

Troi took up a position in front of the brig, where she could get a good look at Wolverine. He was masked, as always.

"Counselor." he acknowledged.

His anger was gone now. The frustration, too. A new complex of emotions was taking hold in the mutant—a mixture of happiness and relief, along with a hint of . . .

Troi blushed.

Wolverine grinned. "Ya don't know how glad I am ta see ya, Darlin'. Whatever they say I did, don't believe it."

"They say you were acting disorderly," the counselor told him.

The prisoner shrugged. "All I wanted was a glass o' milk before bedtime. Izzat so much ta ask?"

Troi didn't answer his question. Instead, she said, "Captain Picard's arranged for your release."

"Huh," Wolverine grated. "I knew he'd come through for us sooner or later."

Clark glanced at the Betazoid. "Last chance to reconsider," she said. "If I try real hard, I could convince the admiral to keep him here."

Troi couldn't help chuckling a little. "Orders are orders," she said. "I think you had better release him."

Reluctantly, Clark placed her hand against a plate set into the bulkhead. Then she tapped out a command on the pad below it.

A moment later, the forcefield was gone. Wolverine put out his hand and confirmed the fact for himself. Satisfied, he grunted.

"Now that," the mutant said, "is more like it." He looked at the counselor. "Where's Picard?"

Troi gestured for Wolverine to come along.

Then, with the mutant at her side, she followed Lt. Clark back to the admiral's ready room.

As Commander Riker entered Transporter Room One, he saw Lt. Robinson manning the controls. Nodding in a friendly way to the willowy brunette, the first officer took his place beside her.

After all, the captain and their newfound guests would be beaming aboard in less than a minute. Picard had called from the starbase to say so only a little while ago.

"Sir?" said Robinson, as she checked her monitors.

Riker turned to her. "Yes, Lieutenant?"

She looked up at him. "Are these people—these X-Men—really as super-powerful as people say they are?"

The first officer began to say that Robinson would know as well as anyone. Then he remembered.

The lieutenant, a veteran of the *Enterprise-D,* hadn't remained with the crew when it launched the *Enterprise-E.* She had spent some time on Earth first—and had thereby missed the ship's crosstime battle with the Borg, not to mention its encounter with the X-Men.

"They have some unusual talents," said Riker. "One of them can teleport himself around. Another one can dent duranium with a single punch, and the youngest can travel through solid matter."

"I heard one of them can fly," Robinson told him.

The first officer chuckled. "Like a bird."

"Hard to believe a man can do that," she said.

Riker shrugged. "Not when you put them in context."

Robinson looked at him. "Context, sir?"

"Think about some of the other beings we've run into in our travels. Take Q, for instance."

Their frequent visitor from the Q Continuum had demonstrated his amazing powers for them time and again. Once, he had even granted the first officer a taste of them.

"Or the Traveler," he continued, "who can manipulate the very fabric of space and time. And don't forget the Douwd, who was able to wipe out an entire race with a single thought."

Riker wasn't done. In fact, he was just warming up.

"Then we've got the Founders of the Gamma Quadrant, who can reshape themselves into anything they can imagine. And our own Mr. Data—who's as fast or powerful as any of the X-Men."

The transporter operator smiled. "Actually, I was thinking more in terms of other humans."

He looked at her. "What makes you think the X-Men are *human?*"

"Well," said Robinson, "they're from Earth, aren't they? Maybe not *our* Earth, but something a lot like it?"

"They're from Earth, all right," Riker confirmed. "But apparently that doesn't make them *homo sapiens.* As I understand it, some people consider them a different species entirely."

The lieutenant absorbed the information. "Interesting."

Suddenly, she looked down at her control console. "They're on their way," she reported.

Just then, the doors to the room slid open and Worf walked in. He nodded to the first officer and took up a position beside him.

"Come to renew old acquaintances?" asked Riker.

The Klingon grunted. "I seem to be doing that a lot lately."

Before he had finished his comment, the transporter platform came alive with a half-dozen pillars of sparkling light. In a matter of moments, they solidified into Data, Troi, and four of the X-Men—Nightcrawler, Banshee, Colossus, and Wolverine.

The first officer smiled at them. "Welcome aboard."

Nightcrawler stepped down from the platform. He walked with that strange, bowlegged gait Riker remembered.

"Vielen dank," said the mutant. "It's nice to *be* aboard."

"Worf," grunted Wolverine.

Coming forward, he held his hand out to the Klingon. Worf grasped it enthusiastically—and no wonder. In their last meeting, he had developed quite a respect for Wolverine's prowess as a warrior.

"You are well?" asked the Klingon.

"Well enough," the mutant told him. "Ya don't have a brig on this bucket, do ya?"

Worf's brow creased. "In fact, we do. Why do you ask?"

Wolverine waved away the question. "Never mind. Now that I'm here, howzabout you show me that game you were tellin' me about—the one we didn't have time to play last time?"

"Game?" said the Klingon.

"Yeah, what'd ya call it . . . some kind o' holo-whoozis?"

Worf suppressed a grin. "Ah, yes. My calisthenics program on the holodeck."

The mutant pointed to him. "Yeah. That's the one."

He hooked Troi by the arm.

"Hey, Counselor—wanna join us fer some calisthenics?"

Troi sighed. "Maybe another time."

As she moved away, Wolverine leaned closer to the Klingon. "Is it me, or has the counselor gotten a little stuffy all of a sudden? She needs to lighten up—be more like you, Worf."

"Please clear the platform," said Robinson. "Captain Picard and the others are ready to beam over."

Banshee sighed and motioned to Colossus. "Come on, Piotr. I think we're standin' in th' way o' th' fast lane."

As Riker watched, they stepped down and stood alongside their teammates. A moment later, three more columns of light appeared. In short order, they gave way to Picard, Storm, and Shadowcat.

"The gang's all here," said Wolverine.

The captain approached Riker. "Number One, would you see to quarters for our guests?"

"It'd be my pleasure, sir," said the first officer.

"In the meantime," Picard told him, "I'd like to have a word with Storm." He turned to the silver-haired leader of the mutants. "If that's all right with you."

Storm nodded. "It is not as if I have urgent business elsewhere."

The captain smiled. "I suppose that's true."

Riker looked at his commanding officer. He hadn't seen that kind of expression on Picard's face in years. He was pleased and more than a little intrigued to see it now.

Pondering the possibilities, the first officer led all the X-Men except Storm out of the transporter room.

Chapter Six

PICARD ESCORTED STORM into his ready room. Offering her a seat, he went over to the replicator unit built into the bulkhead.

"Something to drink?" he asked.

She shrugged. "Some tea? Herbal, if you have it."

"On the *Enterprise,*" he replied, "we have everything."

Selecting a blend of rosehips, orange peel, and blackberry leaves, the captain programmed the replicator to manufacture it. Then he added an Earl Grey for himself.

A moment later, there were two steaming cups of tea on the grid in front of him. He removed them and set them down on his desk. Then he came around and sat down opposite Storm.

"There's a problem," she said, "isn't there?"

Picard knew exactly what she meant. "Getting you home," he replied. "Yes, if the information I received from Admiral Kashiwada is accurate, it appears there is."

The mutant smiled bravely. "I had a feeling."

"As I understand it," said the captain, going over what he had learned just to be certain, "your timehooks malfunctioned—and then disappeared."

"That is correct," Storm replied. "Obviously, the timehook *you* used produced more satisfactory results."

"Eminently more satisfactory," said Picard. "It worked perfectly, returning us to our own time and place. Nor did it disappear, as yours did."

"Then why is there a problem?" asked the mutant. "Can you not use that timehook to help *us?*"

"Actually," he said, "we shipped it off to Starfleet Command on Earth, for testing. As it happened, it was then sent back to the Enterprise. But war with our enemies broke out and . . . well, a few things were misplaced. The timehook was one of them."

"But . . . can it be still be retrieved?" she asked.

"I do not believe that will be a stumbling block," the captain told her. "It is simply a matter of tracking it down." He paused. "On the other hand, there may be a problem with your using it. You see, if the other timehooks failed to work for you, there is every possibility this one will fail as well."

Storm nodded soberly. "I see."

"When the admiral first notified us of your presence in our universe," Picard said, "we speculated that *our* timehook had somehow dragged *yours* along with us. However, you would then have appeared at the same point in time and space that we did."

She sighed. "And you probably appeared light years away from Starbase 88."

"Light years in space," he confirmed. Then he imparted the bit the woman would undoubtedly find more jarring. "And nearly twelve months ago, Federation standard time."

Storm looked at him, surprised. "Twelve months? You mean . . ."

"It has been nearly a year since we returned to our timeline," the captain explained, as gently as he could.

The mutant shook her head, appearing to wrestle with the concept. "So you haven't seen us for quite some time . . . though it seems to me as if I saw you the day before yesterday."

"Indeed," said Picard.

Storm grunted softly. "No doubt, you were surprised to hear from us."

"I was," the captain agreed. "Though to be honest, I often found myself thinking about you."

He realized how that must have sounded and felt his cheeks flush. It was not a pleasant sensation.

"That is," he added quickly, "about your group. To be honest, I had never encountered anyone quite like you."

The mutant took a sip of her tea, her blue eyes gleaming with reflected light. "As much as a man like you must have encountered, I imagine that is saying a lot."

It *was*—but that didn't make it any less true. In all his years of space exploration, Picard had never come across anything exactly like Storm—or, for that matter, her fellow X-Men.

Then, on his way back from a confrontation with the Borg in Earth's 21st century, the captain had found himself embroiled in a scheme by someone named Kang the Conqueror to disrupt established timelines—not only the one to which Picard himself belonged, but also the one where the X-Men fought oppression and injustice.

With the mutants' help, the captain and his crew had crossed timelines to thwart Kang's scheme. Then, using the villain's own timehook device, they had returned to their proper time and place. The X-Men had employed Kang's timehooks as well—with very different results, it seemed.

Picard leaned forward in his seat. "Rest assured, Storm, we will do everything in our power to find a way to get you home—and to do so as expeditiously as possible. Even without the timehook devices, there are other methods . . . other options at our disposal. However, finding the right one will require your cooperation."

"Ororo," she said.

He looked at her, puzzled by her response. "I beg your pardon?"

"My name is Ororo," she told him. "Storm is just my *nom de guerre.*"

The captain smiled. "Ororo, then." He resisted inviting her to call him Jean-Luc. "As I was saying, we will require your cooperation if we are to help you. We need to determine why the *Enterprise* returned to its programmed time and place and your X-Men did not."

"What sort of cooperation did you have in mind?" she asked.

"Dr. Crusher and Commander La Forge would like to conduct some tests," Picard explained. "They will be painless, of course. But with any luck, they will tell us why you were deposited in our timeline."

The mutant thought for a moment. "I cannot say I love the idea," she said, "but I do not think these tests will pose a problem."

The captain nodded. "Good."

Storm glanced at one of the observation ports, where she could see stars streaking by. "Do you deal with things like this all the time?" she wondered. "Cross-temporal anomalies and such?"

"More often than I would like," Picard admitted.

She turned to him again, able to joke despite her team's plight. "Then whatever they pay you, it is not enough."

"Since we aren't paid, as such, certainly not," he said.

The mutant glanced at the observation port again. "We are moving at a considerable rate of speed. I take it you have been assigned a mission."

"Only in the broadest sense. I have been asked to attend a planning meeting on another starbase. It pertains to an ally of our Federation known as the Klingon Empire."

"Commander Worf's people?"

"The same," the captain told her, pleased that she had made the connection. "Fortunately, neither Dr. Crusher nor Commander La Forge will be involved in the planning meeting, so your problem will not be neglected. In any case, I hope you and your comrades will make yourselves comfortable while you are here."

"Thank you," Storm replied. "You are very kind."

For a second or so, neither of them spoke. But it wasn't an uncomfortable silence by any means. Strange as it seemed, Picard felt as if he had known the woman all his life.

"May I ask you a question?" she said at last.

"By all means," he responded.

The mutant leaned forward. "Do you never get lonely here, so far from the planet of your birth?"

The captain shook his head. "Not at all. I chose this life. In fact, I aspired to it." He smiled. "Nothing gives me more pleasure than traveling from star to star, seeing what no one has seen before."

She smiled, too. "I cannot say the same."

"And why is that?" he asked.

"I have a bond with Earth's biosphere," Storm explained. "It is an essential component of my mutant powers. I find it . . . difficult to be away from Earth for too long."

Picard regarded her. "You would have gotten along with my brother, Robert," he said.

She tilted her head to one side. *"Would* have?"

"He perished in a fire," the captain told her. "Along with my nephew. It took me a long time to accept their loss."

Silence again. And again, it was Storm who ended it.

"I know what it is like to lose people close to you. I lost my parents when I was very young."

Picard saw the pain in the woman's eyes. "It must have been hard for you to go on."

"It was," she answered frankly. *"Very* hard. Even as an adult, I have nightmares about it."

The captain was surprised to see how vulnerable Storm could allow herself to be. To this point, he had seen her only as a warrior and a leader. Now he saw the lonely child in her as well, and he felt privileged to have the opportunity to do so.

Her eyes seemed to lose their focus. "How lovely," she said.

Picard didn't understand. "To what are you referring?"

Storm pointed to the Ressikan flute he kept on his desk. A small, simple instrument made of a tinlike material, it was one of the few personal items he had been able to salvage from his quarters on the *Enterprise-D.*

She turned to him again. "Do you play it?"

The captain nodded. "On occasion. I love the music that comes out of it—but it represents another tragedy, I'm afraid. The death of a civilization on a planet called Kataan."

"You mourn the death of an entire civilization?" Storm asked.

"In a way," he said. "You see, when the people of Kataan were dying, they wanted desperately to be remembered—so they sent out a space probe containing the memories of an ironweaver named Kamin. As it happened, I was the one who received Kamin's memories, as well as the flute and the knowledge of how to play it."

She looked at him. "There is more."

"More?" Picard asked, surprised.

"Yes. Something about the flute you have not mentioned."

Suddenly, he realized what she was talking about. "I had . . . a friendship with someone a few years ago. She played an instrument as well. We enjoyed participating in duets."

Funny, the captain thought, how dry he managed to make it sound. How lifeless. But then, he was unaccustomed to opening up to someone as he was opening up to the mutant.

"You no longer have these . . . duets?" Storm asked. It wasn't so much a question as an observation.

"No longer," he said. "Our careers got in the way of our . . ."

"Friendship?" the mutant suggested, using Picard's word for it.

"Yes. I found I could not act effectively as her commanding officer and care for her at the same time."

Storm digested the remark. "Leaders seldom enjoy stable relationships. It is one of the burdens one must bear when one assumes responsibility for the lives of others."

"So I learned," the captain responded.

"Except . . ." she said.

He looked at her. "Except?"

Storm returned his scrutiny for what seemed like a long time. At last, she shook her head.

"Nothing," she told him at last. "Sorry. I did not mean to pry so into your personal life."

Rising, she picked up her cup and saucer and returned them to the replicator slot. Then she turned to Picard and smiled.

"Thank you again," Storm said. "For everything."

The captain stood, too. "It is nothing," he assured her.

With a last glance at him, she crossed the room and left through the sliding doors. A breeze seemed to attend her, making her hair and her garments undulate in response.

Picard sat back in his chair and sighed. He would have given much to know what thought Storm had declined to finish.

Chapter Seven

His ARMS FOLDED across his chest against the late-afternoon chill, Erid watched the shadows lengthen in the fortress's yard. They had already reached the opposite wall and climbed halfway up its stone surface.

Soon, the guards would call down to the transformed and send them back to their rooms. It was difficult enough to keep an eye on the growing prisoner population during the day; at night, it would be nearly impossible. At least, that was how the transformed interpreted the situation.

Suddenly, Erid experienced an unexpected sensation. He felt as if someone were whispering in his ear, though he couldn't see anyone within several meters of him.

And it wasn't exactly a whisper. True, there were words in his head, but they seemed to manifest themselves without sound.

"Don't be afraid. My name is Paldul."

Erid looked around. He saw the youth with the green pockmarks in his forehead sitting among some of the other transformed. The others were talking, but Paldul didn't seem to be listening to them. His eyes were closed, his head tilted back slightly.

"Yes," Erid thought. "I know your name. I heard someone say it the day you arrived here."

"And yours?" asked the telepath.

"Erid. Erid Sovar."

"Pleased to meet you, Erid." There was an undercurrent of something like humor. "I'll bet you've never spoken with your mind before."

"That's true," Erid replied.

"Neither did I," said Paldul, "before my transformation. Now, I do it quite a bit. Every chance I get, in fact."

"How many others have you spoken with?" Erid inquired. "Here in the fortress, I mean?"

"Almost everyone," Paldul told him. "Except for Mollic, of course."

"Mollic?" Erid had never heard the name before.

"He's insane," the telepath thought matter-of-factly. "And dangerous, too. He can set things aflame just by looking at them, so they don't dare let him out into the yard."

Erid wondered what it was like to visit the mind of a crazy person.

"Not pleasant," Paldul thought, surprising him. "At least, in Mollic's case, it's not. I've never visited the mind of any *other* mental patient, so I can't say that's true as a rule."

Erid frowned. "It must be nice to have a power like yours. You don't have to worry about it getting out of control. And you can exercise it without the guards trying to stun you."

There was another undercurrent of humor. "That's true. But it wasn't nice at all when the power first came to me. I kept hearing the thoughts of everyone around me, all the time and all at once. It took me a couple of days to learn to shut them out—to focus on hearing only what I wanted to hear."

"Two days," thought Erid.

He had had his power a lot longer than that, and he

still hadn't learned to control it. But then, he didn't have the luxury of using his talent in public. He was forced to practice it in his cell at night, projecting tiny rays of energy over and over again until he was too tired to keep his eyes open.

"I envy you," he thought at Paldul.

The youth smiled. "The one I envy is Rahatan. He's the only one with the courage to stand up to our guards. In fact . . ."

"What?" thought Erid.

"You'll see," Paldul told him, with just a hint of amusement.

Erid asked him for an explanation again, but there was no answer in his head. Paldul had gone away. With that realization came a great emptiness—a loneliness Erid had never felt before.

But then, he had never shared his thoughts with another Xhaldian.

Suddenly, he was jolted by a loud sound—a voice from directly above him. "Day's over," the prime guard bellowed. He was a tall, rangy man with a long, lined face. "Time for last meal."

Erid studied the wall on the opposite side of the yard. Sure enough, the shadow had climbed almost to the top of it. In half an hour or so, the sun would go down.

He started in the direction of the mess hall, telling himself it wasn't so bad they had to leave the yard. As much as he had eaten at second meal, his hunger was already beginning to gnaw at him.

"This is ridiculous!" someone cried out in a strident voice.

As the cry echoed from wall to wall, all eyes turned to its source. Erid was no exception.

What he saw was Rahatan. The transformed's gaze was fixed on the prime guard, his hands held out in a plea for reason.

"It's still light out," said Rahatan.

Erid was reminded of the thought Paldul had sent him

moments earlier. *The one I envy is Rahatan. He's the only one with the courage to stand up to our guards.*

"That may be true," the prime guard allowed, "but it doesn't change anything. Rules are rules."

"There's no reason to rush us," Rahatan insisted. He took in some of the other transformed with a glance. "Am I right?"

His challenge was met by a rumble of assent. After all, none of the prisoners ever liked to leave the yard.

Denara looked up at the prime guard as well. "Would another few minutes really hurt?" she asked.

"It's little enough to ask," agreed Leyden.

The head guard raised his weapon and pointed it at Rahatan. "Don't make me use this," he said.

The youth smiled. "I'm not making you do anything."

Seevyn came over to him. "This is unnecessary," she told Rahatan.

"I'll decide what's necessary," he returned, glancing at her.

"You'll just get yourself stunned," Seevyn insisted.

Rahatan chuckled. "Will I?" Then he looked to the head guard again. "Just leave us alone and there won't be any trouble."

The guard's eyes narrowed. "Trouble? Is that a threat?"

Rahatan shook his head. "A force of nature doesn't threaten. It acts *without* warning."

Suddenly, the high stone wall began to shudder under the guards' feet, loosening tiny pieces of mortar. Wide-eyed, uncertain of his footing, the prime guard thrust a hand out to support himself—almost dropping his stun weapon in the process.

"What's going on?" one of the other guards barked.

Erid knew the answer. He could see it in Rahatan's smile, in the way he held his hands out. So that was the newcomer's power, he thought.

Rahatan could *move* things—perhaps a great many things. But what he was moving at that moment was the earth beneath the fortress wall, causing the barrier to tremble and scare the life out of the guards.

"It's *that* one," the prime guard concluded at last. He pointed to Rahatan with his weapon. *"He's* doing it."

"And what if I am?" asked Rahatan, seemingly unconcerned.

The prime guard didn't answer. He just braced himself as best he could, took aim, and fired a stun blast. Nor was he the only one.

Rahatan didn't make a move to elude his fate. He stood there and accepted it—and before the eyes of everyone assembled, endured the indignity of the guards' barrage.

It made him shiver and twitch uncontrollably, then fall to his knees. His eyes rolled back in his head and his jaws worked furiously. Spittle ran from the corner of his mouth.

The ordeal lasted only a second or two. By the time the guards stopped firing, Rahatan had pitched forward and lost consciousness. He lay stretched out on the ground, paler than any living being had a right to be.

"Monsters!" bellowed Leyden, shaking his fists at the guards.

"What have you done to him?" Denara demanded.

Meanwhile, the shuddering of the walls had stopped. But despite that, the guards didn't look as if they felt very secure.

"Disperse!" cried their prime, aiming his rifle at Leyden and then at Denara. "Walk away!"

"Or what?" asked the youth with the luminous eyes. "Will you do to us what you did to *him?"*

Clearly, the guards didn't want to fire at anyone else. Their expressions were proof of that. But the cries of the transformed had begun to sound too much like a rebellion.

Then a handful of them began to move in the direction of the prime guard—or more accurately, the wall beneath his feet. Leyden and Denara and the man with the luminous eyes were among them. Corba might have advanced with them too, but she had paused to kneel at Rahatan's side.

"Stay back!" the prime guard yelled sharply, glaring at Leyden and Denara and the others.

His admonition had no effect. The transformed kept coming.

When Leyden reached the wall, he hit it with the heel of his hand. Amazingly, the stone and mortar cracked under the blow, giving him a handhold. With the heel of his other hand, Leyden smashed another hole in the wall.

To Erid, at least, the transformed's intention was clear. Making hand- and footholds as he went, he was going to climb the barrier. Leyden could never do it quickly enough to actually reach the prime guard, but that didn't seem to discourage him in the least.

"Stop him!" cried the prime guard.

With that, he and his men unleashed another barrage. No doubt, it would have wracked Leyden as it had Rahatan, except Denara advanced to the strong man's side.

Erid had never seen her activate her shielding until that moment. He hadn't known she could extend it to protect someone else. But as he looked on, that was just what she appeared to do.

The stun barrage should have subdued Leyden. It should have sent him crashing to the ground.

But thanks to Denara, it didn't. Together, the two of them withstood volley after volley from the guards. Leyden even got a chance to take a couple more pieces out of the wall.

In time, however, Denara's shielding seemed to weaken. The stun blasts began to get through. Leyden cried out as if in agony and went lurching away from her. And once he was no longer under Denara's protection, he was as vulnerable as any of them.

In a moment or two, he was writhing and convulsing like a fish out of water. In another, he was on the ground, spent and senseless.

But the guards weren't finished. After all, Denara had defied them as well. They kept up their barrage until she, too, began to stagger. She cursed them through clenched teeth, dropping to one knee.

Then her shielding gave way and the stun fire got to her. For a moment, the woman convulsed so badly it was agony for Erid to watch. Then, mercifully, she too lost consciousness.

The guards looked around, wary of the other prisoners. But the yard was quiet—ominously so. No one moved. No one even breathed, it seemed.

In the wake of the battle—for that was what it had been, without question—the prime guard wiped his brow with the back of his hand. Then he indicated Rahatan, Leyden, and Denara with a gesture.

"Pick them up and put them in cells," he told his men. "And lock them so they can't get out."

Some of the guards descended from the battlements and entered the yard, their weapons at the ready. None of the transformed moved to stop them as they carried out the prime guard's orders.

It was only after they had disappeared with Rahatan, Leyden, and Denara that the remaining prisoners began to exchange glances. Erid found himself studying Corba's face.

He saw pain in her eyes. And hatred.

He couldn't help wondering what she saw in his.

Chapter Eight

As GEORDI ENTERED sickbay, tricorder in hand, Night-crawler was already standing there waiting for him.

Not far away, Colossus—whose real name was Piotr—was lying full-length on a biobed while Dr. Crusher ran some routine scans on him. But the doctor's responsibility began and ended with medical anomalies.

It was the chief engineer's job to put the X-Men's *abilities* under a microscope. Figuratively speaking, of course.

As he caught sight of Geordi, Nightcrawler held his hands out. "So what can I do for you?" he asked congenially.

Clearly, he was the blithe spirit of the group. The engineer had always appreciated people like that.

"What I want to see," Geordi explained, "is how your teleportation ability works. For instance, if it's anything like our transporters."

"And how do *they* work?" asked Nightcrawler.

"Basically," said the engineer, "they convert matter to energy, then send it from one place to another along a sort of guide beam. When the energy reaches the second location, it's converted back into matter."

The mutant dismissed the idea with a wave of his three-fingered hand. "My teleportation ability works nothing like that."

"How do you know?" Geordi asked.

"Professor Xavier has explained it to me."

The engineer looked at him. "And he would be . . . ?"

"The mutant who saved my life from an angry mob," said Nightcrawler, "and recruited me into the X-Men. A brilliant geneticist and perhaps the most powerful telepath on Earth."

Geordi nodded. "Okay. And what did Professor Xavier tell you about your teleportation talent?"

"What happens," the mutant replied, "is I enter an entirely separate dimension. Somehow, though I have no awareness of it, I travel through that other dimension. Then I come out again in my own dimension, an equivalent distance from where I started."

The engineer smiled. "An intriguing theory. Still, I'd like to check it out for myself . . . if you have no objections."

"None," the mutant told him.

Geordi finished calibrating his tricorder. "This'll just take a second . . ."

"Just say the word," Nightcrawler advised him.

Finally, he looked up. "All set."

A moment later, there was a soft pop, and the teleporter was gone. In his place, there was a puff of smoke and a burning smell.

Almost instantly, Nightcrawler was back again—but this time, he was on the other side of the room, his lips pulled back in a grin. "Miss me?" he asked the engineer.

Geordi chuckled, then consulted his tricorder. "How about that?"

"How about what?"

"You were gone, all right. For a fraction of a second, it was as if you didn't exist."

"At least, not in this dimension," Nightcrawler noted.

The engineer continued to study his readout. "Now, *that's* interesting."

"*What* is?" asked the mutant.

Geordi showed him the tricorder. "When you left, there was nothing remarkable about you. But when you came back, you were literally dusted with verteron particles."

Nightcrawler looked at him. "Verteron . . . ?"

"Sorry," said the engineer. He'd forgotten that in the mutants' universe, which was roughly equivalent to his own in the twentieth century, verterons probably hadn't been discovered yet. "They're subatomic particles associated with subspace phenomena."

Nightcrawler still didn't look enlightened. "Subspace . . . ?"

"A spatial continuum," said Geordi, "with different properties from our own. It's by ducking into subspace that the *Enterprise* is able to travel at faster-than-light speeds. In fact, one might call subspace another dimension—which leads us to an interesting question."

The mutant tilted his head. "That being?"

"Whether this other dimension you're traveling through isn't related to subspace. I mean, we don't come out of warp smelling like brimstone—at least, I don't think we do. But the presence of those verterons suggests you're doing with mind and body what we need an entire warp drive to accomplish." Geordi looked at his guest with newfound respect. "Let me tell you . . . if that's true, it's pretty amazing."

Nightcrawler stroked his blue-furred chin, his golden eyes fixed on the possibilities—of which there were many. "Does that mean," he said, "there's a way for me to travel from world to world . . . maybe even star to star . . . without benefit of a ship?"

Geordi thought about it. "Maybe," he conceded at last. "But then again, maybe not."

Nightcrawler looked at him quizzically.

"You see," the engineer said, "even after we enter

subspace, we still have to apply a lot of power to move the ship from place to place. It's true, your mass wouldn't be anywhere near that of the *Enterprise*—but then, in subspace, mass isn't really the main issue."

"In other words," said the mutant, trying to boil down Geordi's comment, "it wouldn't be enough just to access this continuum, or whatever it is. I would also have to have a way to propel myself across it."

The engineer took a breath, then let it out. "I think so—but honestly, I'm just taking a stab at it. I'd have to study you a lot more closely to come up with an accurate answer."

Nightcrawler shrugged. "I'm game if you are."

"Maybe later," said Geordi. "Right now, I want to run some computer models with regard to those verteron particles you're wearing."

The mutant's brow creased. "Why? You think they had something to do with our timehooks malfunctioning?"

"I think it's a possibility," the engineer told him.

"And if that's the case," said Nightcrawler, "it'd be silly not to check it out."

Geordi smiled. "You said it, not me."

When Erid emerged from the mess hall, hugging the high wall on his right as always, he saw new faces among the guards on the parapets. Apparently, Rahatan's act of rebellion had gotten the government's attention. Reinforcements had arrived overnight.

A few new transformed were in evidence also. But there was no sign of Rahatan, Denara, or Leyden. Osan had restricted them to their cells, as the prime guard had recommended the day before.

Still, Erid thought, Rahatan had a powerful talent at his fingertips. So did Leyden, for that matter. If either of them had wanted to escape their containment, they might have done it.

In fact, if he were Osan, he would have seen to it that Rahatan and Leyden were guarded around the clock—

and maybe Denara as well. Anything less would have been foolish.

Then Erid had a terrible thought. What if Rahatan and the others had been deemed too dangerous to confine? What if the administrator of the fortress had decided to kill them instead?

It was hard to believe someone could be destroyed for an insignificant offense. However, worse offenses might follow—probably *would* follow, if Erid was any judge of character. And the government had never faced anything like the transformed before.

"Erid?" came a voice from behind him.

He turned and saw it was Corba who had spoken to him.

She tilted her head slightly. "That'syourname, isn't it?"

Erid nodded, intrigued by her strange, quick way of talking. "Yes."

"Youdon'ttalkmuch," Corba observed.

He shrugged. "I think a lot."

"Aboutwhatyou'vebecome," she said.

"That," he replied, "and other things."

Corba glanced at the opposite wall, where the guards were looking down on the yard. Erid glanced that way, too. Their conversation hadn't drawn any special attention. But then, they were hardly the only ones conversing.

"Otherthings?" she echoed. "Likewhat?"

"Like how much I hate it here," he told her.

He hadn't intended to say that. But it had been days since he exchanged more than a couple of superficial words with anyone, and the sentiment had simply come pouring out.

"We*all*hateit," Corba answered. "That'swhyRahatan didwhathedidyesterday. Becausewe'repeople, notanimals. We'renotsupposedtobecagedup."

"No," Erid agreed. "We're not."

Her gaze seemed to harden, become more resolute. "Andwithanyluck, wewon'tbecagedmuchlonger."

He didn't understand. He told her so.

Again, Corba cast a glance at the battlements. "Rahatanwantstobreakoutofthisplace."

Erid looked at her. "Break . . ." He shook his head. "But how do you know?"

"Paldulcontactedhiminhiscell," she said. "Hecando that. Rahatantoldhimwedon'tneedtostayhereanylonger —not withthepowerswe'vegot "

He swallowed. "But the guards . . ."

Corba frowned. "Allweneedtodoisworktogether. That's whatRahatansays. Ifwedothat,theguardscan'tstopus."

Erid felt his cheeks flush. "And the others . . . ?"

"I'vespokenwithhalfadozentransformedmyself," she said. "Noone'sturnedmedownyet. They'reallsickof being here."

Suddenly, Erid was more frightened than ever. It was bad enough he had become some kind of freak, and worse still that he had been imprisoned because of it. But now he was contemplating an act of violence—one that would forever alienate him from Xhaldian society.

And yet, he thought, if he *didn't* do it, he would be alienated from a different kind of society—maybe the only kind realistically left to him. He took a breath, then let it out.

"Has Rahatan got a plan?" Erid inquired.

Corba nodded. Then she told him what it was, and what role had been chosen for Erid in it.

"Soyou'rewithus?" she asked. She quirked a smile. "Ordoyou*like*thewayitfeelswhentheystunyouintheyard?"

He thought about it. If Rahatan was right and they were able to break out of the fortress, he might never have to feel a stun blast again.

Erid swallowed even harder. "I'm with you."

Chapter Nine

THE HOLODECK DOORS opened with a soft hiss. Worf found himself bathed in sun and shadow as he studied the scene in front of him. Wolverine, who was standing beside him, just grunted.

They were in a clearing in the middle of a steamy, tropical jungle. A blood-blackened, white-stone altar was the only man-made structure in sight.

Birds screamed from high up in the lush, golden foliage and darted across a patch of crimson sky. Half-seen creatures peered out from their sun-dappled hiding places with wide, frightened-looking eyes.

"Nice place ya got here," Wolverine rasped. He wiped sweat from his eyes with the back of his hand. "I prefer somethin' a little frostier myself, but to each his own."

As it happened, Worf had no particular liking for this place either; the flora gave off a most unpleasant scent. Still, the program had been a gift from his son, Alexander, who had been living with Worf's foster parents back on Earth at the time. And if one could ignore the smell, the opportunities for battle were most exhilarating.

71

Hefting his batt'leth, the Klingon turned to his guest. "You're certain you do not require a weapon?" It wasn't the first time he had asked.

The mutant held up his fist, showing Worf the deadly-sharp spars of bone that protruded well past his knuckles. "I've got all the weapon I need right here," he said.

The Klingon had seen Wolverine use his claws to considerable advantage. "Very well," he said.

Taking a couple of steps in the direction of the altar, he felt the program respond to his presence. The shrieks of the birds grew louder, the wind in the trees fiercer, the sense of danger more immediate.

Worf could feel his pulse quickening, his blood growing hotter. His lips pulled back in anticipation of the battle to come.

And Wolverine was right behind him, his eyes sliding warily from side to side, his nostrils flaring beneath his mask. It seemed he could sense the danger as well.

But then, as Worf understood it, the mutant's faculties of smell and hearing—not to mention his most basic, primitive instincts—were far superior to those of normal humans. In that regard, Wolverine was more like the Terran predator he had been named for.

Or—Worf thought—more like a Klingon.

The only thing about Wolverine he didn't understand was the mutant's disguise. If a warrior concealed his identity from others, how could he bring honor to his house?"

"They're out there," Wolverine whispered.

"Indeed," Worf responded.

The mutant's lip curled. "So what are they waitin' for?"

As if that were a cue, adversaries charged them from four different directions. Worf flung his bat'leth up in time to ward off the mace-stroke of a hulking, blue-skinned Pandrilite, then whirled and parried the sword thrust of a lightning-quick Orion.

A glance told him Wolverine wasn't bored either. A Chardeni whipmaster was trying to snare the mutant's ankles while a Drilikan assassin looped a garrot around his neck.

With the claws of one hand, Wolverine sliced off the business end of the whip and drove his fist into the Chardeni's face. Unfortunately, he wasn't quick enough to prevent the garrot from taking hold around his neck—but even then, he was far from vanquished.

Driving his elbow into the Drilikan's ribs, the mutant cracked a couple, forcing his adversary to loosen his grip. Then, with some room in which to work, he slashed the assassin's belly.

Worf, meanwhile, was getting a workout. No sooner had he opened the Pandrilite's throat with his bat'leth than the Orion was on the attack again. Ducking the green man's flashing steel, the Klingon parried a second assault and a third.

Then, just when the Orion thought he was gaining the advantage, Worf struck low and swept his legs out from under him. With a single, quick thrust, the Klingon finished off his adversary.

Some of Worf's colleagues might have been shocked at his love of violence. But not Wolverine, he knew. Turning to the mutant, the Klingon grinned.

Wolverine was grinning too. "Not bad for a start," he gibed. "But when're we gonna see some *real* action?"

In answer to his question, a shaggy Bandelaar dropped on him from the trees above. Pinning the mutant to the ground, he raised a large and deadly looking axe over his head.

Taking two quick steps, Worf hurled himself at the Bandelaar. He managed to knock the alien off-balance before he could bring his weapon down on Wolverine's head. Then, before the Bandelaar could recover, the Klingon sliced his axe-handle in two.

Weaponless, the alien reached out and grasped Worf's naked throat. The Klingon felt his windpipe closing in the Bandelaar's vicelike grip. Reluctant to let his enemy finish the job, he plunged the point of his bat'leth into his opponent's ribs.

That made the Bandelaar let go in a hurry. With his throat open for business again, Worf raised his weapon and savagely terminated his adversary's brief existence.

That's when he saw someone big and dark hurtling out of the jungle at him. A Shriiton trident-warrior, he thought. Whirling, he tried to brace himself for the newcomer's attack.

It turned out not to be necessary. Before the Shriiton could get anywhere near the Klingon, Wolverine tackled him.

For a moment, the trident-warrior and the mutant rolled across the clearing, driven by their momentum. Then they scrambled to their feet, separated by less than a meter. The Shriiton thrust his weapon at Wolverine, who caught it and broke its shaft over his knee.

As the alien tried to regain his balance, the mutant drove his heel into the Shritton's belly. When the trident-warrior groaned and doubled over, Wolverine laced his fingers together and delivered a two-handed blow to the back of the neck.

The Shriiton collapsed and fell on his face. After a moment or two, it was clear he wasn't getting up again. The mutant made a show of brushing off his hands, then turned to Worf.

"Don't tell me that's it," he said.

"Actually," the Klingon told him, "we are just warming up." He looked up. "Computer—Level *Four*."

Wolverine's eyes narrowed. "Geez, Worf—ya mean we've been loungin' on Level *Three* the whole time?"

The Klingon shook his head. "No. On Level *One*."

Then there was no time to talk. He was too busy defending himself against one enemy after the other.

As Erid sat with his back against the fortress wall, he felt a voice in his head. He had heard it before, of course, but never charged with such a sense of excitement.

"You'll take out the man to the right of the prime guard."

Erid looked at Paldul, who was sitting in the sun at the other side of the yard. Thanks to his telepathic abilities, he had become the link between Rahatan and the other transformed.

"I hear you," Erid thought. He glanced at the guard in question, gauging the distance between them. "And I'll be ready."

"Good," thought Paldul. "Wait for my signal."

Erid waited. While he did this, he thought about his parents. The first thing he would do when he was free was get in touch with them and let them know he was alive.

And after that? He had no idea, really. As far as he knew, none of the others did either. The need to escape loomed so large in their minds, there didn't seem to be room for anything else.

Maybe there was nothing they *could* do. Maybe this escape of theirs wouldn't accomplish anything in the long run—and they would end up back inside these walls, or in another fortress somewhere else. But if their efforts only alerted the world to their plight, it would be worth the effort.

Abruptly, he felt the voice in his head again. "Ready," it said. "On the count of three. One . . . two . . . *three.*"

Pointing his right hand at the guard assigned to him, Erid unleashed a beam of brilliant, white energy. It struck the man before he had any inkling he was threatened, causing him to drop his weapon and collapse on the battlement.

Erid was pleased with his accuracy. His nightly practices had improved his skill with his energy releases, but he had never consciously sent out a bolt so powerful—or over such a great distance.

Meanwhile, his assault hadn't been the only one. Far from it. All over the yard, every one of the transformed with a projectable energy power had put it to use simultaneously, creating a bizarre, multicolored barrage.

Half a dozen guards were jolted off their feet—and

those who weren't had no better time of it. One was struck by an invisible assailant, who then grabbed his weapon and cracked him across the face with it. Another found himself firing at an adversary who was only an illusion—and hitting one of his comrades instead. A third tried to track a blur of speed and couldn't, firing instead at the places where Corba had been.

It was chaos. But as Erid shot another stream of energy, spinning a guard around, he began to imagine their plan might work.

Then he felt the ground tremble, and by that sign he knew Rahatan would soon be joining the fray. Also, Leyden and Denara, who had been imprisoned in cells alongside him.

"Watch out!" he heard someone cry.

A fraction of a second later, Erid was smashed hard in the ribs and taken off his feet. At the same time, a stun blast splattered against the wall where he had been standing.

He looked up into the face of his savior—and saw the man with the luminous eyes. "Thank you," Erid said.

"Don't mention it," the other transformed replied. Eyeing the guards warily, he got to his feet and began to move off. "Just keep doing what you were doing, all right?"

Erid nodded. "I will."

Whatever the other man's power was, it didn't seem to be very useful in a fight. But to his credit, he was looking for other ways to help.

Turning to the battlements, Erid picked out another guard and extended his hand. Once again, a crackling stream of energy traversed the yard and found its target, slamming the man into the wall behind him.

Additional guards raced out onto the parapets, replacing those who had fallen. They fired down into the yard, stunning a transformed with four arms and another who had generated a net of electricity.

But they couldn't stun everyone. Not when Corba was running around disrupting their aim. Not when one of the transformed had grown twelve feet tall and was throwing them off the battlements like dolls.

And the longer the guards were kept busy, the easier it was for Erid and the other energy-wielders to strike. One after another, they blasted their adversaries into unconsciousness. The guards' ranks thinned moment by moment, until only a handful were left on either side of the yard.

Then a steely voice rang out: "This must stop!"

It was Osan. As Erid watched, the administrator came out onto the battlements, his hands notably empty of weapons. No doubt, he had seen how ineffective such things were against the transformed, and opted to take a different tack with them.

"We need to speak, not fight!" Osan cried out.

He signaled the guards to stop firing and held his hands out. It looked to Erid as if he were praying.

The transformed looked at each other—and desisted, as the administrator had asked. The yard grew quiet, though it was a decidedly uneasy quiet.

But Erid was skeptical. What did Osan think he was going to do? Marshal the forces of sweet reason against the misguided youths wreaking havoc in the prison yard?

As it turned out, that was *exactly* what the man thought. "This is insane," he told the transformed. "We're not your enemy. We're here to help you—to protect you from the outside world."

"We've heard that speech," someone called out.

"If you want to help us, open the gates and let us out!"

"Or is it the outside world you want to protect from *us?*"

The administrator shook his head. "You've got to trust us. Whatever the problem is, we can work it out together."

Suddenly, Erid heard his own voice raised as well. "You wouldn't let me contact my parents!" he shouted.

Osan found him and looked at him. "Perhaps we can change that policy. Perhaps it wasn't necessary in the first place."

"Perhaps you're lying through your teeth!" someone shouted, his voice echoing dramatically in the yard.

Erid turned and saw Rahatan standing there, Denara and Leyden directly behind him. The earth-mover pointed a finger at the administrator.

"You've kept us down and deceived us long enough!" he shouted. "Now it's time for you to reap what you've oown!"

Rahatan gestured and the walls of the fortress began to tremble, as if caught in the throes of an earthquake. Osan tried to protest, but his words were drowned by the sound of stone grating against stone.

Some of the guards were shaken off their perches. Those who managed to stay on their feet tried futilely to take aim at the transformed.

But the transformed had no trouble taking aim at *them*.

Erid sent a burst of energy at a guard. Someone else blasted another one. Then the rest of Osan's men leaped from the battlements, reluctant to get caught in the collapse of the wall.

The transformed in the yard were waiting for them. Leyden disarmed two of the guards and battered them with their own weapons. Denara enveloped one in her shield and cut his air off. And Seevyn sent more of them flying from imaginary pursuers, until they collided and knocked each other out.

Soon, there were no longer any guards on their feet. Of all the uniformed personnel in the fortress, only Osan was still conscious, still able to bear witness to the escape.

But the parapet beneath him was twisting and cracking. Large stones were coming loose and striking the ground with lethal force. Finally, with a sound of thunder, the wall wavered and caved in on itself—not in one place, but in several at the same time.

Osan fell, too. He dropped out of sight into the clouds of dust that billowed in the yard. For several long seconds, Erid choked and gasped for air. Then, as the clouds settled, he spied the administrator lying on a chunk of the ruined wall.

But was he alive? Erid hoped so. He hadn't wanted to kill anyone, just win his freedom.

Rahatan himself approached Osan, inspected the administrator's face. Then he turned to the other transformed, all of whom seemed to have the same question in their eyes.

"He's hurt, but alive," he announced. "Not that he deserves to be, after what he did to us."

Erid breathed a sigh of relief.

"But we're not done yet," Rahatan announced, his voice full of urgency. "Before the guards regain consciousness, we've got to bind them and place them in what's left of the cells. And those of us who were stunned must be revived. Quickly, now . . ."

Erid didn't hesitate. Though covered with dust and sweat, he started to help with the binding of one of the guards.

Then Denara came over to him. "Rahatan wants us to check on Mollic."

Erid recalled the name. Paldul had mentioned it the other day. *He's insane,* the telepath had noted. *And dangerous, too. He can set things aflame just by looking at them, so they don't dare let him out into the yard.*

That was why Rahatan wanted Erid to accompany Denara—because Mollic was too dangerous for one of them. Getting up, he followed Denara in the direction of the cells.

When they got there, he saw that one of the outer walls had crumbled half away—the result of Rahatan's efforts, no doubt. Stepping over the rubble, Erid and Denara went inside and waded through the dust-ridden air.

There were barred cells on either side of a long corridor. Three of the ones on the left displayed ruined masonry and twisted bars. No doubt, they had held Rahatan, Denara, and Leyden.

The cells on the right, however, seemed perfectly intact, despite the tremors to which Rahatan had subjected the entire fortress. If Mollic was inside one of those those cells, as Denara had indicated, he might well have gone unscathed.

Before Erid could find out one way or the other, he heard a bizarre croaking sound. It repeated itself over and over. Turning to Denara, he noticed her lack of surprise.

"What is that?" he asked.

She grunted. "That's the man we're looking for." Then she pointed to the last cell on the right.

Erid followed her gesture. There was something about the croaking that made his skin crawl. Nonetheless, Rahatan had given him a job, and he meant to see it through.

As he walked the length of the corridor, the croaking grew louder and louder, echoing from wall to wall. Erid took the opportunity to glance to his right and left. All the other barred compartments were empty, he noticed. Only Mollic's was occupied.

Finally, he came to the cell he was looking for. All at once, the croaking seem to diminish in intensity, signifying Mollic's awareness of him. Clenching his jaw, Erid peered inside the compartment.

Mollic was in there, all right. But the fellow was naked, his garments shoved into a corner of his cell as if he no longer had any need of them. His skin was covered with razor-thin black stripes, and there were sacs on either side of his neck that inflated and deflated as he breathed.

"Are you all right?" Erid asked him.

For a moment, Mollic just stared at him. Then he smiled slyly and created a flash of fire in the space between them.

Instinctively, Erid flinched. That made the transformed in the cell smile even more. He made another flash, and another.

"Mollic," he said in a reedy voice. "Mollic Mollic."

It was the sound Erid had heard before—but now, he knew it wasn't just a croak. It was the poor man's name.

"Mollic Mollic," said the prisoner.

Erid wanted to free him—but in this case, at least, he had to agree with Osan's approach. It would be better if they left Mollic where he was.

He turned back to Denara. "He seems all right. But if we take him with us, he's likely to hurt someone. Himself, maybe."

She nodded. "We'll have to get him some food, though. He may be here for a while before the government finds him."

Erid agreed.

As he and Denara went to find sustenance for the only transformed who would be left behind, he vowed never to curse his fate again. Ugly and afflicted as he was, he was still a lot better off than some people.

Chapter Ten

IT HAD BEEN a long day.

Weary and begrimed like all the other transformed alongside him, Erid stood silently, almost reverently, amid the rubble of the fortress's eastern wall and considered the not-so-distant city of Verdeen.

It sprawled in the foothills, a scattering of bright lights that housed more than a hundred thousand people. The place looked calm, peaceful . . . unaware of the momentous event that had occurred in the ancient structure above it.

Erid had a hard time grasping it himself. Minutes earlier, he had been a prisoner of the worldwide government. Now he and all the other transformed—with the exception of Mollic, of course—were prisoners no longer.

They were *free.*

"We did it!" Leyden thundered all of a sudden.

As if a dam had broken, a cheer went up from the throats of the transformed—all thirty-seven of them. Fists were pumped into the air. There was a sense of triumph, of invincibility, as if they had proven conclusively that there was nothing that could stand against them.

Nor could it have happened without Rahatan. Erid knew that and he was sure the others did, too.

Without Rahatan's spirit, none of the transformed would have found the courage to defy Osan. Without Rahatan's leadership, they would have been ensconced in their respective quarters at that very moment, staring into the darkness without hope or the prospect of any.

"Rahatan!" cried Denara.

"Rahatan!" sang the youth with the luminous eyes, which seemed even more radiant in the dying, orange light of dusk.

"Rahatan!" Leyden roared.

The earth-mover didn't say anything. He just basked in the glow of their admiration, looking almost humble.

"What now?" asked Corba.

"Where should we go?" another of the transformed asked Rahatan.

He pointed to Verdeen, in all its splendor. *"That's* where we'll go," he told them.

"Into the city?" asked Denara.

He nodded. "We'll take the place over. It'll become *our* city."

Seevyn cursed. "Are you insane?"

Rahatan's eyes slid slowly in her direction. "You have a problem with that plan?" he asked.

"I certainly do," said the illusion-maker. "If we stay in one place, it'll be too easy for the government to find us. They'll have us dug out of Verdeen before the sun comes up."

What she said made sense to Erid.

Corba seemed interested as well. "Whatwould*you*do?" she asked Seevyn.

"We need to split up," the illusion-maker told her. "Put as much distance between ourselves and this fortress as we can. Then we'll have a chance to blend into society again."

"We can't *all* blend in," Leyden objected. *"I* can't."

"Yes, you can," Seevyn insisted. "At first, you can stay with me if you want. My illusions will keep people from seeing you as you are. Then, in time, you can find a way to disguise yourself."

"And live like a hermit," Rahatan noted, "alone and apart." He turned to the other transformed. "I'm offering you a chance to live with your own kind. A chance to stay together and remain strong."

"A chance to be imprisoned again," Seevyn argued.

Rahatan rounded on her, eyes blazing. "Hold your tongue," he rasped.

Erid had never heard the earth-mover take that tone of voice—not even with Osan and his guards. To hear him use it with one of his fellow transformed . . .

Seevyn laughed derisively. "Who are you to order me around?"

He pointed to the broken wall of the fortress. "I'm the one who freed you from your prison," he reminded her.

The illusion-maker's eyes narrowed. "Why? So I could exchange Osan's tyranny for *yours?"* She scanned the faces of the others. "If you value your freedom, now's the time to do something about it. Get as far away from here as you can."

Then she turned her back on them and started down the barren slope—headed in the opposite direction from Verdeen. The wind plastered her garments to her, as if giving her a helping hand.

At first, no one responded to Seevyn's speech. All they did was cast uncertain glances at one another. Then two of the transformed—the four-armed man and a woman who could draw energy from things around her—separated themselves from the group. As the sunset painted a wash of fire across the sky, they followed the illusion-maker down the mountain.

It seemed to Erid that others might leave as well. In fact, he was beginning to wonder if it might not be a bad idea himself . . . when he saw Rahatan point a finger at Seevyn and the others.

"Where do you think you're going?" he demanded.

Seevyn and her companions stopped and looked back at him. "Wherever we want," she called back, the wind snatching at her words. "We're free, aren't we? Isn't that what our escape was all about?"

"You're fools, all three of you!" Rahatan bellowed, his voice echoing savagely down the mountainside.

The illusion-maker didn't answer him. Neither did the other two. She just turned again and kept going, and her companions went with her.

"Fools!" the earth-mover roared at the top of his lungs.

Then, without warning, his hands clenched into fists—and the ground seemed to open like a hungry maw under Seevyn's feet. She screamed and looked back over her shoulder, and Erid saw something big and dark and fearful come flying at Rahatan.

But the thing shivered into nothingness before it could reach him, as if it had never existed in the first place—as if it were only an illusion. And when Erid looked back to see what had happened to Seevyn, he couldn't find her. All he could see was the ground coming together again.

The sight made Erid want to retch. The illusion-maker had been swallowed whole by the mountainside. For the love of the ancients, Rahatan had buried her *alive*.

The two transformed who had followed Seevyn scrambled away frantically from her burial place. Their eyes were wide with horror at what they had seen—and with fear that Rahatan might not be done yet.

But their fears were unfounded. Slowly, Rahatan let his fists fall to his sides. Then he turned to Erid and the other transformed, a guilty expression on his face.

"Seevyn was a cancer among us," he explained in a strangely reasonable voice. "She had to be removed, before it was too late."

No one replied. With Paldul one of Rahatan's staunchest supporters, no one even dared to think.

"You all understand that, don't you?" asked the earth-mover.

85

"Ofcourse," said Corba, though she sounded less than certain.

"You had no choice," added the youth with the luminous eyes.

Rahatan smiled a haunting smile. "I'm glad you see it the way I do," he said. "Now let's go. Verdeen is waiting for us."

As if nothing had happened, as if Seevyn's death had never taken place, he made his way down the slope. And with what seemed like little choice in the matter, the others followed—Erid among them.

Numbly, he wondered if the story about Seevyn concealing her ugliness was true, or if she was really as beautiful as she appeared to be. At that point, it shouldn't have mattered anymore.

But somehow, it mattered a lot.

Lt. Sovar stopped outside his friend's door and pressed the pad set into the bulkhead beside it. A moment later, the duranium panel slid aside, revealing Robinson's neatly furnished quarters.

Unfortunately, Robinson herself wasn't anywhere in sight. "I'll be just a minute," she called from the next room.

Sovar nodded. "Take your time," he said, depositing himself on the transporter operator's couch.

He looked around at the artwork displayed on the walls. One piece in particular caught his eye.

"This is new," he observed out loud.

His friend poked her head in from the next room. "What is?"

Sovar pointed to a striking montage of welded metals hanging above Robinson's workstation. "It's a Richard Serra, isn't it?"

"Very good. But then, as I've always said, that Relda Sovar knows his twentieth-century artists."

The montage was merely a copy, of course. An authentic Serra would have cost more than any Starfleet officer could afford. Sovar sat back and admired the piece nonetheless.

Robinson withdrew her head again and finished dressing. "So . . . is everything all right?" she asked after a moment.

Sovar turned and considered the wall his friend was standing behind. "What do you mean?" he asked.

"Come on, Relda, it's *me.* I can tell when something's got you down. Besides, you don't often visit the lounge in the middle of the day."

He marveled at how well Robinson knew him. "Well," the Xhaldian said, "maybe I *am* a little out of sorts. A little . . ." He was reluctant to finish the statement. "Homesick, I guess."

His friend emerged from the next room with her dark hair freshly combed. "Homesick?" she echoed. "A big, bad security officer like you?"

Sovar frowned at her. "You're making fun of me."

"Just a little," Robinson assured him. "Now, tell me, why would you be homesick? Didn't you get anything from Xhaldia in the last subspace packet?"

He nodded. "I got something, all right. But it didn't exactly give me reason to smile. My parents told me my brother Erid had left on his adulthood quest."

His friend looked at him. "And that's bad?"

"Not normally, no. But he didn't leave a farewell message for me." Sovar shook his head. "By the ancients . . . me, his older *brother!"*

Robinson considered the information. "I'm sure he didn't mean to insult you," she said optimistically.

"No," he told her. "That's *exactly* what he meant to do."

The transporter operator sat down on a chair opposite him. "Was there some kind of trouble between you and your brother?"

Sovar frowned. "I never told you about it, but . . . yes, there was trouble. It's been there for some time. You see, Erid didn't like the idea of my leaving Xhaldia and becoming the first of our people to join Starfleet. He wanted me to stay and pursue a more traditional existence."

"Maybe he just liked having you around," Robinson suggested.

"Maybe," he echoed. "In any case, he took my leaving hard. He refused to see me off as my parents did. But I thought when he got older, he would see my side of it." He made a sound of bitterness deep in his throat. "Erid is twenty-two now. And by not leaving me a message, he's showing me he still hasn't forgiven me for leaving."

Robinson's eyes narrowed. "But the packet came almost a week ago. You haven't been in a funk all that time. At least, not as far as I've been able to tell."

The security officer sighed. "It was Commander Worf who rubbed . . . what is the expression you humans have? Salt in my wound?"

His friend looked at him. "Worf? How?"

Sovar shook his head. "I know it sounds foolish, but . . . I envy him. He seems so at home here on the *Enterprise,* as if the captain and the other officers were his family."

Robinson considered what he was saying. "He really does seem at home here," she commented at last. "But then, he spent seven or eight years as an officer on the *Enterprise-D.* When you work alongside someone for that long, they *do* become as close as family."

He became wistful at the thought of it. "My brother hates me. And my parents are far away. What family do *I* have?"

"Hey," his friend told him, *"I* think of you as family."

"Do you?" Sovar asked.

She nodded.

He smiled. "Thank you."

"Don't thank me so quickly," Robinson replied. "I don't particularly like my family."

Sovar's mouth fell open.

His friend giggled. "Just kidding."

The Xhaldian scowled. "Now you're *really* making fun of me."

"Guilty as charged," she said, taking his arm and leading him to the door. Clearly, she was trying to take his mind off his troubles. "Now let's get over to the lounge before all the drinks are gone."

"That's hard to imagine," said Sovar. "But then, in the last several months, I've seen a *lot* of things I once found hard to imagine."

The door to Robinson's quarters slid open as they approached it. Suddenly, they heard the sound of laughter. Coarse, *harsh* laughter.

Robinson looked at the security officer. He shrugged. Together, they went out into the corridor and looked to see where the sound was coming from.

What Sovar saw was a pair of battered-looking figures—Worf and the X-man called Wolverine—negotiating the hallway with a tired air about them. The black exercise clothes they wore were ripped and stained, and Worf had big, purple bruises on his face.

Wolverine elbowed the Klingon in the ribs. "That was a good workout."

Worf winced and shot the mutant a look of mock admonishment. "Just be careful you do not puncture my lungs as you did our opponents.

Wolverine pointed a finger at his companion. "Never can tell who you're gonna have to fight next."

The Klingon broke into a savage grin.

As the two of them walked by Sovar and Robinson, they appeared to realize what a sight they must have been. The mutant stopped to look at Worf. Worf looked at the mutant. Then they shrugged and started down the corridor again.

"Carry on," the Klingon told Sovar and Robinson. Then he followed his companion around a bend in the passageway.

The security officer turned to his friend. "That Worf . . . he finds family everywhere, I think."

Robinson didn't say anything. She just rolled her eyes, took Sovar's arm, and led him in the direction of the ship's lounge.

Chapter Eleven

IT WAS AFTER midnight when Erid and the others reached the outskirts of the city. Despite Rahatan's boasts about making Verdeen *their* place, the earth-mover opted for a more conservative course of action.

He asked a transformed named Cudarris, who had lived in Verdeen until he was almost fifteen, where they might find an area with some condemned buildings. Cudarris described a district called the Old Quarter, where a whole block's worth of residential structures was gradually being razed and replaced with new housing.

Rahatan said that sounded good to him. He asked Cudarris to lead the way, but to take the least-traveled route possible.

The transformed didn't travel all together, either. They would have been too easy to spot that way. They walked in groups of three and four, keeping the group ahead of them in sight and avoiding illuminated windows wherever they could. Luckily, they didn't run into any inquisitive hovercar drivers, and they never saw even a sign of the city guards.

At last, they came to a series of half a dozen likely tenements. None of them were big enough to hold all the transformed, but together they would do the trick.

As they gathered in an alley near the buildings, Rahatan called for a transformed named Inarh, who turned out to be the man with the luminous eyes. Inarh came to the front of the group.

"What can you see?" asked the earth-mover.

Inarh regarded the buildings for a moment. "They're not entirely unoccupied," he said. "There are drifters in every one of them. Not too many—two or three in each."

Erid knew then what the man's power was. He could *see* things . . . at a distance, in the dark and maybe right through solid objects. It was a handy talent to have under the circumstances.

"Unfortunately," Inarh continued, "the power's gone. No light, no heat." He chuckled. "Strangely enough, the water's still on. Nothing like the efficiency of city government, is there?"

"I don't mind it a bit," Rahatan told him, "as long as it works to our advantage." He rubbed his chin for a moment. "Take Leyden, Denara, and Erid and clear out the first building. When you're done, let me know and you can start on the next one."

"Understood," said Inarh.

As it happened, it didn't take long to evict the building's tenants. When they saw Leyden and Erid, their eyes opened wide and they ran away.

In the long run, Erid thought, the drifters would prove their undoing. They would say something about a man with skin like an insect's shell, and another man with huge, purple veins, and someone would use that information to trace the transformed to the Old Quarter.

But in the meantime, they would all have a place to sleep. That wasn't a bad thing at all.

As Erid and the others had promised, they signaled Rahatan when the building was empty. Then they moved on to the next one, and the one after that, with much the same results.

They kept going until they had cleared out all six of the condemned buildings on the block. And each time they emptied one out, a bunch of transformed moved in. Finally, in accordance with Rahatan's orders—which he sent through Paldul—Erid's group settled in the last building themselves, with the understanding that a cou ple of their comrades were to join them.

Erid picked out a set of rooms near the north wall of the structure, where he was less likely to have to contend with light streaming in through the windows. He was pleased to find some furniture in the rooms, even if it was only a bed, a table, and a chair, none of which was in particularly good condition. And as Inarh had said, the water was still in service, though he had to let the faucet run for a while until the water lost its dirty, brown color.

He was just about to taste it when he heard a tapping at the door. Cautiously, he moved away from the wash basin and peered out into the anteroom. Someone was there, all right.

It was Corba.

She smiled. "Iwaswonderingifyoumightwantsome company."

Erid didn't know exactly what to say to that. After all, she had taken him by surprise.

"ItwasjustthatIfeltsolonelyinasetofroomsallbymyself, and . . . well,Ithoughtyoumightbefeelingthesameway."

He nodded. "I was," he said, though he really hadn't had time to think about it. "Come on in."

Corba did as he suggested. Then she shut the door behind her and looked around, her arms folded across her chest.

"There are two bedrooms," Erid told her, trying to be helpful. "You can have whichever one you want."

That's when he noticed Corba was shivering.

He didn't understand. It was warm down here in the city, even at night. Then it occurred to him it might have something to do with her power and the demands it made on her body.

"Idon'twanttobeabother," she said apologetically, "butifyoucouldjustholdmeforawhile . . ."

Erid held her. In fact, he held her for a long time.

"Hmm," said Dr. Crusher, studying the results of her latest scan on the overhead readout.

She didn't like the look of them. Not at *all*.

Her patient, the X-Man known as Archangel, looked up at her from the biobed he was lying on. "Sounds ominous," he told her.

To tell you the truth, she thought, *it* looks *ominous.* But, of course, she didn't say that.

"It's just something in your blood," she replied.

"In my blood?" he echoed. "You mean, besides my bad, old mutant genes?"

The doctor smiled—or tried to. Picking up her tricorder from a nearby counter, she established a link with the biobed and downloaded the information that was bothering her. Then she showed it to her patient.

"See those green dots?" she asked.

Archangel examined the tricorder. "Uh huh."

"Those represent traces of techno-organic material." Crusher frowned. "They remind me of something I've seen before—in a cybernetically enhanced species called the Borg."

The mutant shrugged. "Never heard of them."

"They're immensely powerful," she explained. "They conquer other races and assimilate them into a shared-consciousness collective. If I were prone to nightmares, the Borg would be in all of them."

"And now you're wondering if the techno-organics in my bloodstream make me some kind of threat."

She was impressed with his leap of logic. "It's my job," the doctor said, "to wonder about things like that."

He dismissed the idea with a movement of his hand. "Don't give it another thought. Some time ago, I was captured by a creep named Apocalypse. He severed my natural wings—if you can call having wings 'natural'—and replaced them with razor-edged, techno-organic equivalents."

As Archangel described the experience, his tone remained matter-of-fact—but Crusher noticed a flicker of pain in the mutant's eyes. She imagined she knew why, too.

After all, his wings appeared to be an integral part of his anatomy—in the same way arms and legs were a part of anyone else's. He must have suffered terrible trauma when he realized his wings had been removed in favor of something cold, dark, and metallic.

"Recently," the mutant continued, "it turned out the techno-organics were some kind of shell—a way to protect my real wings until they could grow back. But if you ask me what Apocalypse gained by amputating my wings and then helping them grow again . . . I'd have a tough time giving you an answer."

"But as far as you know," the doctor said, "the techno-organics in your system are dormant . . . harmless."

"As far as I know," he confirmed.

Crusher would have felt better if she had more to go on—more about this Apocalypse character, especially. However, her patient seemed to be telling the truth, if his biosigns were any indication. As far as he could tell, the techno-organics in his blood posed no threat to anyone.

"All right," she said. "I think we've learned all we're going to learn about you."

Archangel looked at her. "Then I'm free to go?"

He made being there sound like a stint in a penal colony. "Not yet," the doctor told him. "All you're free to do right now is join Commander La Forge on the other side of the room."

He frowned. "Whatever you say."

Crusher could feel the tension inside him—the hatred of being pinned down. But the mutant seemed able to cope with it.

Sitting up, he swung his legs over the side of the

biobed. Then, with a flurry of his wings, he propelled himself across sickbay and alighted in front of a very surprised Geordi La Forge.

The doctor grunted. *Show-off,* she thought.

Then she saw Wolverine enter the room, and she prepared the biobed for her next patient.

Geordi closed the door to his office in engineering. Then he sat down in his chair, leaned back, and pondered what he had learned from his studies of the X-Men.

To his regret, very little of it seemed useful.

Not that every one of the examinations hadn't been interesting in its own way. Colossus, for instance, actually seemed to increase his mass when he converted his body tissues into an amazingly tough, metallic substance. Unfortunately, the engineer hadn't been able to determine where that extra mass came from.

Shadowcat, on the other hand, appeared to have control over the very atoms in her body—to the extent that she could move them through the atoms in an object or even another person, faciliating a phasing effect. Years earlier, Geordi and one of his colleagues had experienced a similar effect related to chroniton build-ups— but, as his instruments showed, the X-Man's abilities had nothing to do with chronitons.

And then there were the techno-organics both he and Doctor Crusher had discovered in Archangel. Again, an intriguing discovery, but it shed no light on the X-Men's appearance in the *Enterprise*'s twenty-fourth century.

Only one of the exams had turned up anything potentially valuable in that regard—and that was the one to which he had subjected Nightcrawler. The verterons he had found on the mutant still stuck in his engineer's mind, suggesting a solution he couldn't quite latch on to.

Without question, the proximity of verteron particles could have caused a malfunction in the X-Men's timehooks. Heck, it might have kept them from working at all, though that obviously hadn't happened.

But why had the mutants been whipped into Geordi's milieu, of all places? If their appearance there was just a coincidence, it was a staggeringly unlikely one.

After all, there were an infinite number of points in time-space—an infinite number of destinations. The X-Men could have wound up at the dawn of time or in the fifty-fourth century . . . on Risa or Rura Penthe . . . in a reality with bipedal humanoids or without them.

However, they hadn't done any of those things. They had materialized in a frame of reference not far removed from their own—in which, as luck would have it, they actually had some friends they could call on.

The engineer grunted. Staggering, all right.

But if they were drawn to the *Enterprise*'s twenty-fourth century, why not to the *Enterprise* itself? What was it about Starbase 88 that had pulled the mutants to it like a magnet?

And why several months from the time they had seen the X-Men last? What was it about this time that made it more attractive than any other?

Tons of questions, Geordi mused. And as usual, not nearly enough answers to suit him.

That meant more digging. And the place to do it was on Starbase 88—either personally, or with the help of someone on the station.

Of course, he already had information on the manner of the mutants' appearance there. What he lacked was data on the station itself, background on its day-to-day operations.

If he sifted through enough of it, he might turn up a clue—and sometimes a clue was all the engineer needed.

Chapter Twelve

WHEN ERID AWOKE, he found that he wasn't alone in his bed. Corba was there as well, snuggled comfortably alongside him under the blanket he had found lying around.

He smiled and tried to go back to sleep. After all, it wasn't quite light yet. However, there was a voice in his head.

Paldul's, of course.

"Rahatan's seen to it that we've got some food," the telepath thought to him. "You can pick it up at the third building. From now on, though, you'll have to help with night foraging if you want to eat."

"I will," Erid thought back.

"Be careful about going outside, especially during the day," Paldul went on. "I picked up some thoughts from the normals in the vicinity. They've been warned about our escape from the fortress and the city guards are watching for us—although they have no idea how many of us are in Verdeen."

"I'll be careful," Erid promised.

Then he put his head down and enjoyed Corba's nearness again. But he didn't have a chance to enjoy it for long. A few minutes later, she too woke up with Paldul in her head.

When the telepath was finished with her, the two of them lay there in the darkness for a while. After all, the morning light was coming in on the opposite side of the building.

"Ilikedstayinghere," Corba told him. "Doyouthinkwe mightmakeitapermanentarrangement?"

Erid smiled. "I'd like that," he said.

But deep inside, he couldn't forget that they were transformed. For them, permanence was relative.

As Data entered the *Enterprise*'s lounge, he heard singing. The place being only sparsely populated, it took him only a moment to trace the sound to its source— and to realize it was the mutant known as Banshee.

The X-Man wasn't alone, either. He was surrounded by four crewmen, two men and two women, who appeared to be admiring his voice.

"I wish I were a butterfly," he sang, "I'd fly to my love's nest. I wish I were a linnet, I'd sing my love to rest. I wish I were a nightingale, I'd sing to the morning clear. I'd hold you in my arms, my love, the girl I hold so dear."

As the last of his lyrics faded, Banshee shrugged. "An' that's it," he told his companions, almost meekly.

"Bravo," said Lt. Robinson, clapping with delight.

"That was excellent," Lt. Sovar agreed enthusiastically. "I have never heard anything like it."

"Ah," said **Banshee**, "ye're much too kind. Back home, they tell me t' have mercy and keep me mouth shut."

"Not here," Ensign Saffron assured him.

"That's for sure," Guinan added from behind her bar. "At least, not while *I'm* in charge."

"Sing another one," Lt. Rager requested.

"Yes, please do," called Troi. The counselor had been listening from her table in a distant corner of the room.

The mutant looked at her wistfully. "Unfortunately, Lass, I've exhausted me repertoire. If there's another song of old Eire in me head, I'm afraid it's decided t' stay there."

As Data came closer, Banshee caught sight of him and acknowledged him with a grin. The others turned to look at him as well.

"Welcome, Mr. Data," said the mutant. "I do nae suppose ye've got a ballad or two in that computerized brain o' yers."

"Actually," the android replied, "I have several."

And he began to sing one, in a voice quite different from his own. It was higher-pitched, better suited to the music in question.

"I dreamt," he sang, "that I dwelt in marble halls, with vassals and serfs by my side. And of all who assembled within those walls, that I was the hope and the pride . . ."

Banshee's eyes opened wide. "I had riches too great to count, could boast . . . of a high, ancestral name . . ." He turned to Lt. Robinson. "But I also dreamt, which pleased me most, that you loved me still the same."

Again, there was a round of accolades and applause— Robinson's the loudest of all. But this time, the cheers were directed at the android as well as at the mutant.

Getting up from his seat, Banshee clapped Data on the shoulder. "Well done, lad. Well done indeed."

Data nodded. "Your performance was impressive as well."

"But tell me," said the mutant, "where did ye come across an ol' ballad like that one?"

"It was a favorite of Brian McGonaghy," the android replied.

Banshee shook his head. "The name does nae ring a bell."

"Brian McGonaghy," said Data, "was one of the colonists on Omicron Theta, where I was created."

"He was a friend?" the mutant ventured.

"I am afraid not," the android told him. "Shortly after I gained awareness, I was programmed with the logs and journals of all the colonists, in the hope that they would provide a reference for social behavior."

He paused, experiencing a pang of regret. Emotions were still a new experience for him.

"Unfortunately, Brian McGonaghy died with the other colonists when Omicron Theta was destroyed by a space-going entity."

"I'm sorry t' hear that," Banshee said.

Data nodded. "So am I. However, we should not linger here."

"And why's that, lad?"

"Dr. Crusher asked me to bring you to sickbay. She is waiting to examine you as she has examined your teammates."

The mutant hit himself in the forehead with the heel of his hand. "Of course she is. I completely forgot, Mr. Data, and that's th' honest truth." He turned to his listeners and shrugged. "Perhaps another time, my friends."

"Another time," Lt. Robinson agreed.

"See you then," said Lt. Rager.

As the android escorted Banshee out of the lounge, he turned to him. "May I ask you a question?"

"Anything," the redhead said, obviously in a good mood.

"Why do they call you Banshee?" Data asked. "Does that not describe someone who makes a wailing sound? And warns of approaching death?"

The mutant's smile tightened a bit. "Ye've not had th' pleasure o' hearin' me sing in battle," he replied. "Believe me, lad—if ye had, ye would nae have asked that question."

The android thought about requesting a more specific answer, but decided against it. Commander Riker had fought alongside Banshee. No doubt, *he* could shed some light on the matter.

When one wanted information, Data had learned, it

was sometimes easier *not* to go to the horse's mouth. Or, in this case, the Banshee's.

Troi was sorry to see Banshee leave the lounge. She had enjoyed his songs, not to mention the sincerity with which he sang them.

Still, Data must have had a good reason for dragging the mutant off like that—more than likely, for another of Beverly's exams. Unfortunately, the Betazoid mused, ballads weren't a priority on the *Enterprise* as often as some of the crew would have liked.

Suddenly, she heard a *whoosh* and saw a red-and-white blur in the vicinity of the entrance—one which startled a couple of crewmen into ducking for cover. Troi needed a moment to realize the blur was Archangel.

The mutant circled the lounge in the blink of an eye, causing nearly everyone in the place to flinch. Only when he got to the far wall did he spread his elegant, white wings and stop himself. Finally, with fluid grace, he lowered his legs into a vertical position and floated gently to the floor.

The counselor shook her head. *He'll be fine,* she thought sarcastically, *once he gets over his terrible shyness.*

Seeming to notice Troi's disapproval, Archangel eyed her for a moment. Then, his wings folding up behind him, he made his way toward her through the maze of tables.

"Counselor," said the mutant.

She smiled, because it was part of her job to make guests feel welcome. "That *is* what they call me. Is there something I can do for you?"

He shrugged. "How about offering me a seat?"

"All right," Troi said. "Would you like a seat?"

Archangel smiled, though it was a distant, almost condescending smile. "I thought you'd never ask."

Pulling a chair out from under the counselor's table, he turned it around and straddled it as he sat down. Troi imagined it was more comfortable for him that way.

"I take it you've already made your visit to sickbay," she said.

The mutant nodded.

He was extremely good-looking, the counselor noted. What's more, he seemed to know it.

"I've visited Dr. Crusher's chamber of horrors," Archangel told her. "Commander La Forge gave me a once-over, too. Of course, they didn't find anything that would explain our being here in your universe. Just the same mutant genes the others have—and a little something extra."

He declined to say what that was. And as far as Troi was concerned, it was the mutant's absolute right to keep the information to himself—whatever it was. Still, if he didn't want to go into detail, she wondered why he had mentioned it at all.

Archangel's eyes seemed to lose their focus for a moment—to look right through her. He smiled.

"You're a rich girl," he said.

Troi returned his gaze. "Rich?"

He nodded. "You know. Wealthy. Prosperous."

She felt compelled to explain. "On Betazed, where I was born, no one lacked for material possessions. That's the case throughout most of the Federation. So the term 'rich' isn't really—"

Archangel held up a hand in surrender. "Okay. I'll rephrase my observation. You come from a . . . privileged background. True or false?"

The counselor frowned. "I belong to the Fifth House of Betazed. Some people would call that a privileged background, I suppose. But it's really more of a responsibility than a prerogative."

The mutant chuckled softly. "That's how the privileged classes have always described themselves—as the protectors of society. Noblesse oblige and all that. But you'll notice that when there are wars to be fought, we're always the ones in the strongest armor, on the fastest horses. And the devil take everyone else."

Troi shook her head. "Is that how it is where you come from?"

"That's how it is where *everyone* comes from. It's a fact of life. If you don't see it, it's because you're kidding yourself."

Stung, she lifted her chin. "And you're part of this so-called privileged class as well?"

"Absolutely," he told her. "Born with a silver spoon in my mouth. Went to the Riviera in the summer and Chamonix in the winter. Wore the best clothes, attended the best schools, drove the fanciest cars. Nothing was too good for Warren Worthington III."

The counselor didn't recognize any of the references, but she understood perfectly what Archangel was talking about. She was reminded of the song Banshee and Data had sung.

"I dreamt that I dwelt in marble halls, with vassals and serfs by my side . . . and of all who assembled within those walls, that I was the hope and the pride . . ."

Troi found herself speaking the next verse out loud. "I had riches too great to count, could boast . . . of a high, ancestral name . . ."

He nodded. "Something like that."

"Then," she asked, "if you were so well off, why are you here? What made you decide to put your armor and your spoon aside and place your life on the line to help people?"

He laughed carelessly. "I grew wings. It's tough to lounge on the beach at St. Bart's when you've got these . . . things sprouting from your back."

"No," the counselor said. "That's not what I mean." And you know it, she added silently.

The mutant gazed out the observation port. His strange, blue skin, unlike that of the Bolians or the Andorians, was absolutely flawless. And the contrast with his golden blond hair was . . . striking, to say the least.

"Why did I decide to fight on the side of the angels?"

he asked himself. He shrugged. "Hard to say. It was a long time ago."

Troi sensed bitterness in the man. Bitterness and pain and a hatred of himself she couldn't understand.

And he obviously liked to keep others at arm's length. It was, no doubt, his way of protecting himself from further pain.

But despite all that, Archangel was an honorable man. And a compassionate one as well. And he was as dedicated as any of the X-Men to the principle of helping those who needed it.

The counselor smiled to herself. *Perhaps,* she thought, *we have something in common after all.*

Chapter Thirteen

GUINAN PULLED OUT a piece of cloth from under the bar and took a swipe at its polished surface. It reflected her image back at her.

She wasn't smiling, she noticed. But then, this place didn't feel like home to her—at least, not yet.

Ten-Forward, the lounge she had managed for Captain Picard on the *Enterprise-D*, had been her pride and joy. Through hard work and attention to detail, she had made it a place where anyone could feel comfortable, regardless of their rank or station.

When Ten-Forward was ripped to shreds along with the rest of the *Enterprise-D*, Guinan hadn't dismissed it as a loss of materials. She felt as if her heart had been torn out of her.

After all, a lounge like Ten-Forward wasn't just another venue on the ship. It was a place where friendships and love affairs began, where births and marriages and promotions were celebrated. As far as she was concerned, it was a living thing, with a spirit and a sensibility and a soul.

Sometime after the death of the *Enterprise-D*, Picard had been given command of the *Enterprise-E*—and he had assumed the job of outfitting another lounge. The captain had done his best to pattern it after Ten-Forward, bringing in the same kinds of furnishings and even many of the same waiters and waitresses.

Everyone seemed pleased with the results. It was only in Guinan's estimate that the place didn't feel quite right.

Of course, she was just a visitor these days—someone who had hitched a ride with the *Enterprise* en route to Earth, where she had business with the Federation Historical Society. And it was only over Picard's objections that she had taken a shift at the bar—for old times' sake.

Guinan sighed and took another swipe at the bar with her cloth. Maybe with a little time, the place would grow on her.

Just then, Ben came over with an empty tray. He was one of the waiters Picard had brought with him from the *Enterprise-D*.

"How's it going?" Guinan asked him, stowing her cloth back under the bar.

"To tell you the truth," he said, "I like it better when the place is hopping."

"It'll be hopping soon enough," she told him. "We've got a shift change coming in fifteen minutes."

Ben smiled. "In that case, let me get my order in. Lt. Sovar will have a synthale. Lt. Rager asked for a Gamzain wine, no spices. Lt. Robinson is in the market for—"

"Now, why didn't anyone tell me about this place?" someone growled all of a sudden. "I mighta come here insteada wastin' my time in sickbay."

Turning, Guinan saw a powerful-looking figure in blue and yellow enter the place. Plunking himself down on a stool right in front of her, he gazed directly into her eyes.

"Howzabout some service, Darlin'?"

Guinan recognized the fellow as Wolverine, one of the

visitors the *Enterprise* had taken on recently . . . friends of the captain, she reminded herself, so it wouldn't do to disembowel one of them with a mixing spoon.

"Service?" she echoed calmly. "Oh . . . you mean a *drink.*"

The mutant looked at her askance. "This is a bar, ain't it?"

"It certainly is," she told him.

"Well, I'm lookin' fer somethin' good an' strong."

She nodded. "One good-and-strong, coming up."

It only took a moment to make the mutant's drink. Pushing it across the bar to him, Guinan watched him slug it down. Wolverine frowned.

"Is there a problem?" she asked.

"Geez louise," he said. "You call this a drink?"

"Actually," she replied, "It's the strongest stuff we serve around here."

Of course, that wasn't quite true. But Guinan didn't want to start a riot in the place.

Wolverine seemed to wrestle inwardly with his next remark. "That's a cryin' shame, then," he said. He jerked a thumb over his shoulder, indicating the officers seated at the table behind him. "This may be fine for yer Starfleet types, but I'm in the market for something with a kick."

"A kick," the bartender echoed.

"Uh huh." The mutant thought for a moment, then hit on something. "The sorta stuff yer friend Worf might cozy up to."

"Ah," Guinan said. "You want a warrior's drink."

Wolverine grunted. "Yer catchin' on."

The bartender leaned forward, crooked her finger and beckoned her guest with it—as if she wanted to tell him a secret. He leaned forward as well.

"I don't want to embarass you," Guinan said, in a voice so soft only the two of them could hear it, "especially in front of all these Starfleet types. But I don't think you could *handle* the kind of stuff Worf cozies up to."

The mutant looked at her and smiled. "That sounds like a challenge, darlin'."

"Maybe it is. Do you accept?" Guinan asked, returning his smile.

"Y'see, I got this mutant healin' factor goin' for me. Ask Dr. Crusher, if ya don't believe me. Whatever kind o' punishment I take, my body bounces back."

"How about that."

"I get beat to a pulp," he told her, "I'm good as new before y'can rustle up some band aids."

"Impressive," Guinan responded. "You can slug down a warrior's drink and still feel fine—because of your healing factor."

Wolverine merely nodded.

Reaching under her bar again, she produced a ceramic mug the size of her head and set it before the mutant. Then she made her way to the refrigeration unit, took out a jug of Worf's favorite drink, and opened the top of it.

Guinan poured the dark, pungent liquid into the mug, filling the thing all the way to the top. Then she replaced the top on the jug and watched her guest's nose wrinkle up.

He peered into the glass. "What *is* it?" he demanded.

"Prune juice," Guinan said, smiling. "A warrior's drink." She looked at Wolverine, feigning surprise. "Unless, of course, you're not the warrior you say you are."

The mutant considered the stuff, then looked up. "You *are* feisty," he told her, with just a hint of admiration.

"Takes one to know one," the bartender noted.

She half expected Wolverine to mutter a curse and walk away. After all, a mug of prune juice was a mug of prune juice. But to his credit, he didn't back off from his promise.

Picking up the mug, he drained the whole thing, right down to the dregs. When he was done, he wiped his mouth with the back of his gloved hand.

"Hit the spot," he rasped, unwilling to give even an inch.

"It sure will," Guinan agreed.

"Yeah," said Wolverine. "Well, see ya."

His responsibility fulfilled, he pushed back from the bar and made his exit from the lounge.

Guinan shrugged. Then she collected the mutant's empty mug, took another swipe at the bar with her cloth and surveyed the place. As she had predicted, it was starting to fill up.

It wasn't Ten-Forward, Guinan mused. But it was beginning to feel like home nonetheless.

Chapter Fourteen

CHANCELLOR AMON TURNED in his chair and stared out the oval window behind him. It was a remarkably clear day. He could see the fortress above Verdeen in the distance, cradled in the Obrig Mountains.

But not well enough, apparently. Not *nearly* well enough.

Turning back to the rounded monitor on his desk, Amon considered the strained visage of his security minister. "Could you say that again?" he asked in the calmest voice he could manage.

Tollit frowned. "The transformed have escaped, Chancellor. Every last one of them."

Amon shook his head. "How can this be?"

"They were more powerful than we imagined," the other man explained. "Sometime before dusk, they overpowered Osan and his garrison and left the fortress a shambles." His frown deepened. "If you could *see* this place, Chancellor . . ."

Amon held up a hand, not wanting to hear the details. He had sincerely believed himself past the worldwide emergency. With almost every reported case of transformation plucked from society and segregated, he had seen himself—and Xhaldia—well on the road to a solution.

Now it seemed he had only made the problem worse.

"Fortunately," said Tollit, "one of the guards managed to slip his bonds and get to a communication station. Otherwise, we might still not know what took place here."

The chancellor heaved a sigh. Perhaps it was time to let others take the lead in this area. "What do you suggest we do?" he asked.

His minister stroked his chin. "The challenge, of course, is to find the transformed and recapture them. Mind you, they've had nearly a day to hide themselves, and they've probably split up in a dozen different directions. However, we've had no reports of stolen hovercraft, so they may still be in the vicinity."

"Near Verdeen?" Amon suggested.

"Perhaps *in* Verdeen," said Tollit. "Some of them, at least—though we haven't gotten word of any sightings."

The chancellor nodded. "Do whatever you have to. And keep in mind, we are no longer dealing with a group of innocents. They have become capable of violence—even if it is we who are responsible for that change in them—and they must be treated accordingly."

The minister understood. "We will consider them dangerous."

Amon sat back in his chair. "Keep me informed of developments as they occur, all right?"

Tollit agreed that he would do that. Then he signed off.

The chancellor massaged the bridge of his nose with the fingers of one hand. *Blood of the ancients,* he thought. *I hope Minister Tollit has better luck with the transformed than I did.*

Captain Picard had meant to visit Dr. Crusher for the last several hours. However, it had taken him longer than he had expected—or wished—to record his latest round of captain's logs.

Now, his duties done, he emerged from the turbolift closest to sickbay and followed the bend in the corridor. Because of that bend, he failed to see Storm coming from the other direction until the silver-haired woman was almost on top of him.

She appeared to be as surprised as he was. "Captain Picard," she said, smiling pleasantly.

"Stor " he began to say in response . . . then remembered that she preferred he call her Ororo. "I take it you're just coming from your appointment with Dr. Crusher?"

The mutant nodded. "That is correct. Mine was the last such appointment."

"And did her studies turn up anything useful?" Picard asked.

Storm shrugged. "Perhaps. The doctor told me it is difficult to say until she has had a chance to go over the data."

"Of course," he said. "I just thought she might have—"

Suddenly, the captain heard something—a loud *whoosh,* getting closer and closer at an alarming rate.

He spun around just in time to see a red-and-white missile headed straight for him. By the time he realized it was Archangel, he had already ducked and watched the mutant sweep past him.

"Stop right there!" Picard bellowed after his guest, his voice echoing commandingly from bulkhead to bulkhead.

Archangel didn't seem to have heard him at first. He simply continued on his way, speeding almost effortlessly down the hallway.

Then, with a splaying of his large, white wings, the mutant slowed himself. Turning gracefully despite the tight quarters presented by the corridor, he came speeding back in the captain's direction.

This time, Picard resolved, he would not flinch. He would stand his ground, no matter how much it looked as if Archangel would plow right into him.

As it turned out, the captain need not have been concerned. Before the mutant had covered half the space between them, he spread his wings again and landed on the floor.

Picard felt a surge of anger. He tried to throttle it, but it resisted his best efforts.

"You asked to see me?" Archangel inquired, a superior-looking smirk on his face.

Picard regarded him. "You have been drawing attention to yourself with your antics since you set foot on this ship. And before that, you did the same on Starbase 88. I have seen enough of it," he said. "I want it to stop!"

The mutant looked at him as if he had just grown wings of his own. Then he turned to Storm.

"Is he serious?" Archangel asked her.

"You are having this conversation with *me*," the captain declared. "And since you asked, I am *very* serious. Shadowcat and Nightcrawler don't use their powers on the *Enterprise*—why must you?"

The mutant shook his head. "Kitty and Kurt don't have wings, Captain Picard. Do you know how it feels to be confined to this . . . ," his mouth twisted, "this *ship* of yours, when everything inside you yearns for a place to soar? To be free?"

"That's what holodecks are for," Picard told him—more coldly, perhaps, than he had intended.

"Holodecks?" Archangel echoed scornfully. "Do you think—"

"Warren!" snapped Storm.

He looked at her, his eyes wide with indignation. "Ororo, I can't—"

"You *can*," she insisted, "and you *will*. We are guests here. You must not forget that."

Archangel continued to stare at her for what seemed like a long time. Then he glanced at Picard, as if measuring the man's resolve.

Finally, he moved away. And in accordance with Storm's wishes, he didn't take to the air again. He *walked*.

The captain watched him go. Part of him sympathized with the mutant's point of view. However, another part of him remained stubbornly opposed to Archangel's thoughtless behavior.

And yet another part, he realized, simply didn't like the man. He couldn't deny it. Sometimes, a person just rubbed one the wrong way—and Archangel was such a person.

Storm turned to Picard. "You were harsh on him," she noted.

He took a breath, then let it out. "Perhaps."

"If you understood Warren a little better . . ." she began.

"I understand him all too well," the captain told her—again, more dispassionately than he would have liked.

"I do not think so," the woman persisted. "You believe he flies about your vessel because he hates confinement. And that is true—he hates it with a passion. But that is not the reason he flies."

Picard pulled down on the front of his uniform. "Then why *does* he fly? Why does he go around startling my crew at every opportunity?"

"What he's doing," Storm explained, "is pushing the envelope."

The captain turned to her. "Pushing . . . ?"

"The envelope," she repeated. "Trying to see how far he can go."

"I'm familiar with the phrase," Picard told her. "What I'm having trouble with is the application."

Storm frowned. "You have to understand something about the world we come from, Captain. As long as any of us can remember, we have been hunted and feared by so-called 'normal' human beings. Being accepted for what we are . . . it has always been a dream to us, a goal we could hold up but never realistically hope to attain."

"So I've been apprised," said the captain.

"Yet in your reality," she continued, "prejudice and race-hatred seem to have been eliminated. Had we not

114

seen it with our own eyes, we would never have believed it. And yet, here it is."

Storm's voice trembled ever so slightly. Her eyes took on a surprisingly liquid cast, as if they looked upon something precious and holy.

"We wield powers your people have never heard of. In our world, we would have been cast out for that—purged mercilessly from society. But no one here has tried to purge us. On the contrary—they have done everything in their power to embrace us."

Picard nodded. "I see," he said softly.

The mutant heaved a sigh. "I hope so. I hope you comprehend the wonder of a society that judges each being on his or her merits. More than your technological advances, more than the great distances you have traveled in search of knowledge . . . this is the true miracle of your Federation, Captain. This is your greatest achievement."

She fell silent then, overcome with emotion, and the captain didn't dare break that silence. He waited until Storm herself decided to go on.

"What does this have to do with Warren?" she asked. She smiled wistfully. "Deep down, my friend, he does not trust this world of yours—its generosity or its willingness to accept him for what he is. And, insofar as you are a symbol of your world, he does not trust *you.*"

Picard tried to follow her. "He wants to see if there is a limit to my acceptance of him."

Storm nodded. "That is correct. Like a child deprived of his parents at an early age, it is difficult for him to feel loved by anyone. So he probes. He tests. He attempts to prove to himself, over and over again, that a place like this can be *real.*"

The captain regarded her. "What would you have me do, Ororo? Ignore his behavior? Allow him to run roughshod over my crew?"

She shook her head, her silver tresses glinting in the overhead illumination. "I only ask you to feel what

Warren is feeling. See the situation with his eyes. Then do as you see fit."

It wasn't an unreasonable request. Picard was about to tell her that when a voice came to him over the intercom.

"Captain," said Riker, "I have a Priority One communication for you. It's Admiral Kashiwada at Starbase 88."

Picard wondered if this was a response to Geordi's request for additional information. If so, it was a quick one.

"I'll be right up," he told Riker.

"Aye, sir," said the first officer.

The captain looked at Storm. "I would like to continue this conversation after I speak with the admiral."

"It would be my pleasure," she told him.

Reluctantly, Picard tore himself away from the woman and went to see to Kashiwada's call.

Chapter Fifteen

ENTERING HIS READY room, Captain Picard sat down behind his desk and faced his monitor. Then he activated it.

Immediately, Admiral Kashiwada's wizened features filled the screen. The man seemed a tad less serene than usual—even though he had already been relieved of the X-Men's company.

"Admiral," said Picard. "Am I to understand you've already sent the information Commander La Forge requested?"

Kashiwada waved the subject away. "Not yet," he said. "As it happens, there's a matter of considerably greater urgency at hand."

No niceties this time, the captain noted. And the communication was Priority One. Clearly, something was afoot.

"You're familiar with a world called Xhaldia in the Antiacus system?" asked the admiral.

"Certainly. A Federation ally, though not a member."

"That's the one," the admiral confirmed. "Its government sent out a distress call recently. It seems there's a rather volatile situation on the planet's surface. They've attempted to deal with it themselves, but it's too much for them to handle with their meager planetary security forces."

Kashiwada went on to tell the captain about it. The man hadn't lied; it was volatile, all right.

"And you would like the *Enterprise* to respond?" Picard asked.

"You're the one nearest Antiacus at the moment, Jean-Luc—less than a day's travel at warp nine." The admiral shrugged. "It's only a matter of luck you're *that* close; normally, there aren't any starships in light years of your position."

The captain leaned back in his chair. "We will attend to it."

Kashiwada smiled. "Best of luck, Jean-Luc. I trust I will see you again soon." And with that, his image vanished from the monitor.

Picard sighed. Apparently, the planning session at Starbase 42 would have to wait a while. And so would any attempt to return the X-Men to their own frame of reference.

He looked up at the intercom grid hidden in the ceiling. "This is the captain, Number One. We have a new destination."

There was silence for a moment. "A new destination, sir?"

"That's correct," said Picard. "Have Lt. Rager set a course for Xhaldia in the Antiacus system. Warp nine."

The Enterprise seldom traveled at speeds higher than warp five. However, this was an emergency.

"Aye, sir," Riker replied.

The captain turned from his monitor and sought a view of the stars through one of his observation ports. Before long, he saw them wheeling about, as his officer implemented the course change.

"Computer," he said, "tell me about Xhaldia."

* * *

Sovar felt his mouth go dry.

This can't be, the security officer told himself. I must have heard the captain incorrectly.

Using his tactical controls, he established a link with Lt. Rager's control panel. Instantly, one of his screens showed him a chart of the sector where the Antiacus system was located.

Just as Captain Picard had requested, Rager was setting a course for the planet Xhaldia. And she was accelerating to warp nine.

When scientists discovered that high-warp travel wore out the barrier between space and subspace, Starfleet had prohibited anything faster than warp five. Except, Sovar added silently, in emergencies.

Dire emergencies.

And now the *Enterprise* was headed for Xhaldia at warp nine! The lieutenant clenched his teeth and wanted to know why.

Suddenly, he realized Commander Riker was coming around the command center. The first officer stopped beside Sovar.

"Xhaldia's your homeworld," he said.

The lieutenant nodded. "Yes, sir. It is."

Riker frowned. "If I can tell you what's going on, I will," he said.

Sovar looked at him. "Thank you, sir."

The first officer clapped him on the shoulder. Then he returned to his seat in the command center.

The security officer sighed. At warp nine, it wouldn't take them long to reach Xhaldia. A day, at most. For the moment, he would have to embrace that small consolation . . .

And hope the emergency drawing the *Enterprise* there wasn't as dire as it might have seemed.

Chancellor Amon considered the image of his security minister on his monitor. "I think you made the right decision," he said.

Tollit frowned. "Albeit reluctantly. I truly believed we

would be able to find and recapture the transformed—in Verdeen, at least, if nowhere else."

"But they have proven elusive," Amon noted, "difficult to pin down. And on those occasions when you *have* managed to corner one, it has been an unhappy experience for your guardsmen."

The minister nodded. "As you say, it was the right decision to bring in Starfleet. I only hope they will be gentle with the transformed. After all, they are still children, powerful as—"

Suddenly, Tollit's image disappeared—to be replaced with the corpulent visage of Morna, Xhaldia's minister of global communications. Morna looked as worried as the chancellor had ever seen him.

What now? Amon asked himself. *What* else *can go wrong?*

"We have a problem," said the communications minister, dabbing perspiration from his forehead with a pocket cloth.

The chancellor leaned forward again. "A problem of what nature?"

Morna scowled. "I believe we are under attack."

Amon looked at the man, dumbfounded. "Attack?" he echoed. "But why would anyone attack Xhaldia?"

In the twenty-eight years since the chancellor's people had ventured into space, Xhaldia had never had anything but friendly relations with its neighbors—and for good reason. The planet wasn't strategically important to anyone, and none of its resources were in great demand. The Xhaldians had never even built a defense fleet, relying instead on their world's natural defenses and their alignment with the Federation to keep troublemakers at bay.

"I don't *know* why," said Morna. "But a little while ago—ten minutes, perhaps—our sensor net picked up the approach of a large, unidentified vessel, previously concealed from us by the moon. We hailed them, in accordance with regulations. At first, there was no response."

The minister dabbed at his forehead again. He was doing his best to remain calm, but it wasn't working very well.

"And then?" Amon prodded.

"Then they responded after all—by destroying one of our booster satellites."

The chancellor was aghast. Because of the naturally occurring energy fields permeating Xhaldia's atmosphere, his people had constructed a series of satellites to facilitate communications with entities in space. Without those satellites, they would be cut off from the Federation and anyone else capable of speaking with them.

In short, they would be *alone.*

"Song of the ancients!" Morna breathed. He was looking wide-eyed at one of his monitors.

"What is it?" asked Amon.

The minister turned to him again. "They've destroyed two more satellites. That leaves only *one.*"

The chancellor bit his lip. One thing was clear—they would have to get off another message to the Federation before the last of the satellites was destroyed. They would have to let their friends know that the situation had become more urgent.

"Send out another distress call," he told Morna. "Tell the Federation that we are under attack from alien invaders. Do it *now!*"

The minister did as he was told, sweat pouring down both sides of his face. Like Amon, he was hoping desperately that his efforts were in time.

Suddenly, Morna's mouth fell open.

"What is it?" Amon demanded.

The minister swallowed hard. "They've destroyed the last satellite," he reported miserably.

"What about the message?" the chancellor asked. "Did it get through?"

Morna looked at him. "I . . . I don't think so."

Amon swallowed back his fear. "Send out a message

planetside, Morna. Whatever our enemy has in mind, we've got to mobilize against it."

The minister nodded. "As you say, Chancellor. Only . . ."

"What is it, Morna?"

The heavyset man looked at him helplessly. "What do they want from us?" he wondered.

Amon shook his head. "I wish I knew."

With that, Morna cut off the communication.

The chancellor slumped forward on his desk, burying his face in his hands. What did they want indeed?

Then he reminded himself that he didn't have the luxury of sitting there and groaning. He had a great deal to do. He had to call a conference of his ministers and map out a plan of action . . . see to his world's defense.

If he could stave off the enemy for just a while—a few days, at least—it might be enough time for Starfleet to respond to their first distress call. Certainly, it was a goal worth aiming for.

Amon grunted softly at the way things had turned out. A few minutes earlier, he had believed the escape of the transformed was the worst problem he would face that day. Now he knew how wrong he had been.

And then it struck him—the unlikeliness of it all. First, the discovery of the transformed. Then, the appearance of an alien ship. There had to be a connection between the two.

But what was it? he asked himself . . . knowing he hadn't even the semblance of an answer.

Chapter Sixteen

ERID WAS AT home, eating dinner with his parents. They were glad and grateful to have been reunited with their younger son, though their faces still showed the pain of not knowing where he was or what had happened to him.

"It must have been terrible," said his mother.

Erid looked down at his plate of spiced tubers. "Words don't begin to do it justice," he told her.

"The fortress . . ." said his father. "I can't even imagine what that was like. And that wasn't the worst of it, was it?"

Erid shook his head. "I felt like a freak. And I was always afraid of what I carried inside me."

"The power," said his mother.

"Yes. Even after I learned to control it, I was scared that it would come out when I didn't want it to and hurt someone."

"Someone innocent," his father suggested.

Erid nodded. "Someone innocent."

"And you say you looked . . . different?" his mother asked. There was concern in her eyes—concern for *him*.

"*Very* different," he told her. "My hair was all gone. And my blood vessels had become big and swollen, and the flesh around them had turned purple." He managed a smile. "I can tell you, I wasn't pleasant to look at."

Both his mother and his father were silent for a moment. It couldn't have been easy for them to hear what Erid was saying. No parent wanted his or her child to experience such horror.

"But it's over now," his father said at last. "You're normal again. And you're home with us."

Erid's mother put her hand on top of his. "You don't have to worry about any of those awful things anymore."

He nodded. "I know. As time goes on, it's beginning to seem more and more like a bad dream. And—"

Suddenly, he felt a heaviness in his arms and legs—a heaviness he remembered all too well. His mouth went dry with fear.

No, he thought. *This can't be happening. It's supposed to be over.*

Still, the heaviness didn't go away. It got worse. And as he looked on, terrified, his veins began to grow under his skin.

"What is it?" asked his mother. "What's the matter?"

Erid got to his feet, tipping the dinner table over, smashing the dishes on the floor. His father took hold of his arm.

"What's happening?" he wanted to know.

But Erid couldn't tell him. His mouth was too full of panic to make words come out. All he could do was watch as his blood vessels became high, hard ridges and the skin turned purple around them.

Except for the vessels in his hands. Those remained strangely, hideously normal. A glow began to come from his fingers.

Erid knew what came next. "Run!" he told his parents. "Get away from me!"

"No!" his mother insisted. "You need us!"

"You can't stay with me!" he tried to explain. "Not when I'm like this! You'll die!"

Erid's father shook his head. "We're your parents! We can't just leave you like this!"

Suddenly, a brilliant beam of energy shot out from one of his fingertips and struck his mother in the shoulder. She cried out in agony and fell spinning to the floor, where her blood began to pool around her.

Erid wanted to reach out to her, to help her, but he couldn't—because more of the bright, blazing beams were springing into existence. More and more and more . . .

"No!" he screamed.

. . . and realized he wasn't in his parents' house anymore. He was somewhere else. In a bed somewhere. And someone was embracing him, looking needfully into his eyes.

Corba, he thought. *I'm with Corba. The beams . . . my hurting my mother . . . it was just a nightmare.*

But something was wrong in the real world, too—he could see it in Corba's expression. She seemed frightened by something, and Erid knew she didn't frighten easily.

"What is it?" he asked, blinking away the last vestiges of sleep.

She pointed to the window. "Look."

Erid pulled away his covers and made his way to the window. It was still dark out, but as he got closer, he could see a flash of light. It blinded him for a moment.

When his vision cleared, he was greeted by a sight that made all his experiences to that point seem commonplace and mundane. A large vehicle of some kind was blocking half the street. Nearby, three bulky, alien figures in battle armor seemed to be standing guard while two others carried unconscious Xhaldians toward the vehicle.

Erid recognized the unconscious ones. They were two of the transformed who had escaped from the fortress with him—the woman who turned invisible and the man who could grow twelve feet tall.

125

He didn't understand. What was happening? Who were the aliens?

Suddenly, he heard Paldul's words in his head. They throbbed with urgency, forcing Erid to hold his head in pain.

"Someone's found us," thought the telepath. "They've broken into the first building and dragged our comrades out. The rest of us have to get away while we still can."

"Can't we fight them?" Erid wondered back, his heart beating hard against his ribs.

"You don't understand," Paldul thought, his anxiety coming through in waves. "They've got stun weapons that put to shame those we saw in the fortress. We've got no choice but to run."

Erid opened his eyes and saw that Corba had been subjected to the same painful announcement. She looked at him.

"Wehavetogo," she rasped.

"Yes," he said.

They pulled on their clothes as quickly as they could, then ran down the hallway and found the stairs. Erid's legs felt heavy, unresponsive. Corba could have sped ahead of him if she had wanted, but she lingered so she wouldn't leave him behind.

On the stair, they found two of the other transformed—Inarh and the woman who drew energy from things around her. They glanced at Erid and Corba, but they didn't say anything. They just made it down the stairs as quickly as they possibly could.

When they reached the ground floor, they crossed the common area and headed for the building's back door. Corba got to it first. She peeked through the oval window set into it, then turned to the rest of them.

"It'sclearbackhere," she said.

That was all they needed to hear. The four of them burst out of the door, followed the alley behind it to a perpendicular alley, and got as far away from the building as they could.

Erid wondered what had happened to Leyden and

Denara. For all he knew, they had been among the first contacted by Paldul, since they were among Rahatan's favorites. If that were so, they were out on the streets already, concealing themselves from the aliens.

In any case, he couldn't worry about them at the moment. Not when he had his hands full worrying about himself and Corba.

Propelled by fear, Erid ran as quickly as he could on his leaden legs—and he didn't look back. Not even once.

Chapter Seventeen

THE MOMENT SOVAR'S shift ended, he went looking for Robinson. He felt he had to share what he had learned with someone, and the transporter operator *was* his closest friend on the *Enterprise*.

As it happened, his search took him to Holodeck Two, where Robinson had booked an hour's worth of time. When he got there, he found out her program was already in progress.

Sovar stood outside the interlocking doors for a moment, wondering whether or not to interrupt his friend. After all, it might have been a personal fantasy Robinson was pursuing in the holodeck, and he didn't want to intrude on something like that.

On the other hand, he didn't think he could wait an hour. He had to talk to someone *now.*

Accessing the holodeck controls, the security officer opened the jigsaw-puzzle doors. As they slid apart, he caught a glimpse of a figure standing with her back to him.

She was wrapped in a purple cloak, the hem of which

moved in a gentle wind. Beyond the figure, framed by columns of shadow-blue marble, distant peaks blazed in the fierce, golden light of sunset.

A scent of flowers and honey came floating out to Sovar on the breeze. Drawn by it, he took a step forward into the holoscene and realized it wasn't just the columns ahead of him that were made of blue marble. So were the floor under his feet and the peaked ceiling above him.

The holodeck doors closed behind him, wrapping him completely in the illusion. Here, a simple, stringed instrument rested on a wooden stand. There, a silver pitcher and two silver goblets stood on a table. And in a third place, a dark velvet divan stretched like a Terran cat.

The figure in the cloak turned and reacted to his presence. It was Robinson, of course. She smiled at him, looking a little embarassed.

"Marble halls," she said, as if that were explanation enough.

Suddenly, Sovar understood. His friend had created the place from the words of Banshee's song—minus the vassals and the serfs, apparently. What's more, she had done a breathtaking job of it.

But he hadn't come here to admire her skill with a holodeck. He had something much more pressing on his mind.

"B.G.," he said, "I did not wish to interrupt your scenario, but something has happened on my homeworld. Something almost . . ." He tried to find the right word. ". . . unimaginable."

Robinson's brow creased. "What is it?"

He told her about the development of strange abilities in young people all over Xhaldia. He talked about the fear that had gripped the planet's people when they discovered superbeings in their midst. And he spoke of the reaction of their leaders.

"The government must have become frightened, too," Sovar related, "because it incarcerated these beings.

They said it was for the protection of the transformed, but—"

"The transformed?" asked Robinson.

"It is what the superbeings are being called," he explained. "In any case, the government's action backfired. The transformed broke out of the fortress at Verdeen and disappeared."

"I don't blame them," said his friend.

"No," said the security officer. He took a step toward her. "You don't understand, B.G. There are thousands of people in the vicinity who are neither superbeings nor armed guardsmen, but ordinary Xhaldians—people whose lives are at risk."

Robinson nodded. "And you're afraid for them."

"Yes." He sighed. "The government has called for assistance from the Federation. Though Xhaldia is not a member planet, it has ties—"

"I know," she said gently.

Of course, he thought. He had described them to her himself.

"The *Enterprise,*" he said, "was the vessel closest to my homeworld. We are on our way to Xhaldia now . . . to see if we can accomplish what Verdeen's guardsmen cannot."

"To round up the superbeings?" Robinson asked.

"Yes. And to re-establish order."

His friend came closer and held him by the arms. "How did you find all this out, Relda?"

He sighed. "Commander Riker told me—with the captain's permission, of course. Captain Picard will inform the rest of the crew in a little while, but he wanted me to know first."

His friend nodded. "That was—"

Before she could finish her statement, there was a flash of blown diodes, and an entire section of the sunset-painted mountains behind Robinson blinked out of existence. In its place, Sovar could see a naked portion of the black and gold hologrid.

The transporter operator shook her head. "What the—?"

Suddenly, someone stepped out of the disabled grid section. Someone who, after Sovar got over his surprise, looked a lot like Shadowcat.

Looking a little puzzled, the mutant gazed at the two officers. Then she turned around and studied the place where the scenery was missing. At last, she turned back to Sovar and Robinson.

"Sorry about that," Shadowcat said. "I was on my way to Deck Eleven. Lt. Barclay was going to show me the computer core—I'm kind of interested in computers— and . . ." She shrugged. "I guess I got lost and blew a few circuits. I mean, I do that when I pass through a system that uses electricity, so usually I'm really—"

Sovar held up his hand. He was filled with anger. After all, the mutant had intruded on a very personal conversation—whether by accident, as she claimed, or by design.

"We have heard your explanation," he told her. "Now leave us."

Shadowcat frowned. "Okay," she said. *"Be* that way about it." Without another word, she melted back through the section of exposed hologrid.

The security officer turned to his friend. "Do you think she overheard what I said about our mission?"

Robinson shook her head. "Hard to say. But I wouldn't worry about it too much. The captain's going to tell the whole crew soon, right? So it's not exactly as if she uncovered a secret."

Sovar thought about it. "I suppose you're right."

"Besides," his friend said sympathetically, "it sounds like you've got enough to worry about "

Captain Picard touched a pad on his keyboard and eyed the monitor just above it. Instantly, the screen displayed the shuttle diagnostics he had ordered several minutes earlier.

Right on time, he thought. But then, he had served with Commander La Forge for a long time, and he knew no one was more punctual.

Normally, Picard wouldn't have been quite so concerned about shuttlecraft readiness. However, according to the information he had received from the *Enterprise*'s computer, Xhaldia's atmosphere was rife with energy fields which would disrupt normal transporter operation—or subspace radio waves, for that matter.

The shuttles were by no means as efficient an option as the transporters would have been. The captain would be limited in terms of how many security officers he could deploy to the planet's surface, and how quickly. However, he would have to make do.

Just then, he heard the chimes that signified the presence of a visitor outside his ready room. He leaned back in his chair and faced the door.

"Come," Picard said.

A moment later, the door opened, revealing Commander Riker. But as the first officer entered the room, Picard saw the man wasn't alone.

Storm walked in after him. Then came Banshee and Wolverine. One by one, the X-Men took up positions on the opposite side of Picard's desk, each with the same determined expression on his or her face.

"They wanted to see you, sir," said Riker.

The captain nodded. "Thank you, Number One." He turned to the mutants. "Would any of you like a seat?"

Storm shook her head. "No. Thank you."

Resting his elbows on the armrests of his chair, Picard made a steeple of his fingers. "All right, then. What can I do for you?"

Banshee looked to Storm. So did Wolverine.

"Go ahead, 'Ro," said the mutant in the mask.

Storm regarded the captain. "It is very simple," she said. "We would like to help."

Picard didn't understand. "Help . . . ?" he replied.

"On Xhaldia," said Banshee.

132

The captain nodded. "I see."

However, it wasn't clear to him how his guests had gotten wind of the situation there. His orders to the crew wouldn't be posted for half an hour.

Riker looked at him. Obviously, he had the same question on his mind.

The first officer turned to the X-Men. "Tell me," he said, "how did you know about that?"

Storm shrugged. "Shadowcat was on her way somewhere when she overheard two of your officers in conversation. However, she told me she was not eavesdropping and I am inclined to believe her."

"What's it *matter* how we know?" asked Wolverine. "Like Ororo says, we wanna lend a hand."

"Y'see," Banshee explained, "these transformed . . . we feel a kinship with 'em. We were like 'em once, changin' in ways we did nae understand."

"Fortunately for us," Shadowcat added, "we had Professor Xavier. He gave us a direction."

Storm nodded. "But it is unlikely that there is a Charles Xavier on Xhaldia. The transformed will be scared, confused . . . and, unless I am very mistaken, hated and feared for what they have become."

"Someone needs t' reach out to 'em," Banshee elaborated. "I know I'm doing it back home." He smiled in his charming, homey way. "Someone needs t' give these kids a leg up, before they hurt someone or get hurt themselves. An' since we're here, it'd be a shame t' give anyone else th' job."

"In other words," Picard replied, "you would like to offer your services in dealing with the transformed on Xhaldia."

"In other words," said Wolverine, "yer darn tootin' we would."

The captain weighed the request. "You know," he replied at last, "I generally depend on Counselor Troi in matters of empathy, and she has yet to fail me in that regard."

133

Storm frowned. "No doubt. But there is a difference between knowing how someone feels and how someone is *going* to feel."

"Tell 'im, 'Ro," said Wolverine.

"We can deal with the transformed based on years of experience," the silver-haired woman went on. "Your counselor may sense their initial shock, but she cannot know the despair that is likely to follow in its wake. Or the self-loathing. Or the bitterness."

"And, the transformed could be dangerous," Wolverine pointed out. "In a way yer not used ta dealin' with. But *we* are."

"That's a fact," Banshee agreed.

As Picard considered the X-Men's comments, he eyed his first officer. "What do you think, Number One?"

"You know," said Riker, "they have a point, sir. In all deference to Counselor Troi and our security team, they *do* have more experience with this sort of thing."

The captain regarded the mutants. "Normally, I don't allow my guests to take part in Starfleet business. In this case, however, you appear to have a genuinely unique insight into the condition of the transformed."

"Just like I was tellin' ya," said Wolverine.

"Also," said Picard, "I have seen you and your comrades in action—and in a situation as serious as this one, I would be foolish not to arm myself every way possible."

Banshee grinned. "Then we're partners?"

Picard shook his head. "Not nearly."

Wolverine's eyes narrowed. "But you said—"

"I will call on you," the captain told him, "only if and when I deem it necessary—and even in that event, you will obey my every directive."

The mutant didn't look at all happy with Picard's answer.

But Wolverine's reaction didn't faze the captain in the least. "I command this vessel," he continued evenly, "and I will brook no other arrangement."

Banshee's smile faded a bit. "We're used t' operatin'

on our own, y'know. That's th' way we're most effective."

Picard nodded. "I understand completely—but it doesn't change anything. If you hope to participate in our mission, you must take your cue from me. There is no alternative."

The muscles worked in Wolverine's temples. Banshee's smile disappeared altogether. But it was Storm who finally replied.

"If those are your terms," she said with equanimity, "we accept."

Chapter Eighteen

PICARD CONSIDERED THE tiny, blue-green sphere pictured on the viewscreen in front of him. The planet was hardly bigger than the pinpricks of light that served as a backdrop for it.

"Xhaldia," said Riker, who was sitting in his customary position on the captain's right.

Picard nodded. Then he looked to his left, where Counselor Troi was leaning forward in her seat, a tiny knot of concentration at the bridge of her delicately chiseled nose.

With the planet still a good several hours away at full impulse, the Betazoid would be unable to sense anything about the Xhaldians or their current situation. Her empathic talents simply didn't extend that far.

Nonetheless, Troi remained intent on the forward viewscreen. Despite the vast distance between the *Enterprise* and her destination, the counselor instinctively continued to reach out, attempting to feel what the embattled Xhaldians were feeling.

Fortunately, subspace radio wasn't nearly as limited as

Troi's empathic abilities. At this distance, it would only take a few seconds for a message to reach Xhaldia.

"Lt. Sovar," said the captain. "Open a channel to Chancellor Amon."

"Aye, sir," the security officer replied.

Data, who was seated at Ops, turned to face Picard. He had a puzzled expression on his face.

"Sir," he said, "there appears to be a vessel in orbit around Xhaldia."

"A vessel?" Picard repeated. He eyed the viewscreen with new interest. "Why have we only now discovered this, Commander?"

"Judging from its position and the likelihood of a geosynchronous orbit," said the android, "it was probably hidden from us by the planet."

The captain frowned. This was an unanticipated complication.

"Maybe the Xhaldians requested assistance from someone else," Riker suggested.

Picard shook his head. "Not likely, Will. The Breen are the only other presence in this part of space—and I don't think the Xhaldians called on *them* for help."

His exec grunted. "Good point, sir."

The captain turned to his android second officer again. "Maximum magnification, Mr. Data."

A moment later, the image on the viewscreen seemed to jump closer to them—close enough to display a huge, rust-colored ship against a cloud-covered sweep of the planet's surface.

Picard scrutinized the vessel. It was wide and relatively flat, with long, boxlike nacelles above and below it on either side, and its topsides were rife with a variety of impressive-looking weapon clusters.

It was possible the ship's crew wasn't especially warlike. But in the captain's experience, vessels didn't bristle with weaponry unless their occupants were eager to use it.

Picard glanced at Riker. "I've never seen this design before, Number One. Have you?"

"No, sir," said his first officer.

Data worked his Ops controls. "I am unable to find a match for it in our computer files."

"Captain," said Sovar, "I cannot seem to raise Chancellor Amon. There appears to be a malfunction in the communications booster satellite."

"Try another one," Picard told him.

"I have, sir," the Xhaldian assured him, an undercurrent of concern in his voice. *"None* of them seems to be working."

The captain sat back in his seat and considered the evidence. An unexpected and hostile-looking ship in orbit around the planet. A malfunction in its only link to the outside universe. And all at a time when Xhaldian civilization was wracked by unprecedented chaos.

It could hardly have been a coincidence. The more Picard thought about it, the more it sounded like a premeditated act of aggression.

But how could the aggressors have known this would be a propitious time to attack? Did they have some insight into the emergence of the transformed? Or had they simply been scanning Xhaldia, waiting for the right moment—and seen the opportunity handed to them on a platter?

So many questions. So few answers.

The captain stroked his chin. "Yellow alert," he said at last. "Shields up, Mr. Sovar."

"Aye, sir," came the response.

All over the ship, crewmen would be reporting to their section chiefs. Tactical systems would be checked. Silent glances would be exchanged by friends and colleagues.

But nothing would happen for several hours. After all, they had only recently passed the outermost world in the Antiacus system.

Picard wanted desperately to hurry, to come to the Xhaldians' assistance just a little sooner. He could have managed that by activating the *Enterprise*'s warp drive—but it was too dangerous to go to warp so close to a star and its planets.

Normally, the captain would have sat there as patiently as he could, while the *Enterprise* homed in on beleaguered Xhaldia. However, he had some business to attend to.

"You've got the bridge," he told Riker. "I believe our guests will want to know what is going on."

Chapter Nineteen

PICARD LOOKED AROUND the lounge, one of the smaller ones on Deck Seven. The X-Men were all present.

"Since you have offered to help with the situation on Xhaldia," he said, "I thought you should know that it has changed. There is a vessel in orbit around the planet."

"A vessel fulla *who?*" asked Wolverine. "Friends or enemies?"

"We don't know who they are," the captain replied. "Nor do we know why they are there. But the evidence suggests they are not on a humanitarian mission."

"What'll you do?" Shadowcat asked.

"Whatever we have to," he told her. "If they are invaders, we will oppose them. If they are something else, we will deal with them as seems appropriate. However, the one thing we will *not* do is act precipitously."

"In other words," said Nightcrawler, "we're taking it slow until we know what's going on. Sounds right to me."

"And what about us?" asked Colossus. "What can we do?"

Picard shrugged. "Nothing, really—other than remain prepared to face the situation around Verdeen. Of course, if I see a use for your talents before that time, I will not hesitate to let you know."

Storm frowned. "I would like to come up to your bridge later on, to see this vessel with my own eyes."

The captain couldn't see any reason to forbid it. The silver-haired mutant wasn't the type to get in the way.

"As you wish," he responded.

"Thank you," Storm replied.

Picard scanned the X-Men's faces. They seemed to have taken the information he had given them in stride. Then again, these were seasoned warriors, unlikely to flinch at the prospect of adversity.

"If there are no other questions . . ." he said.

"I have one," Colossus told him. "How are Dr. Crusher and Commander La Forge faring with their research?"

The captain sighed. "They have yet to come up with anything conclusive, I'm afraid. But if I were you, I would trust in their abilities. Neither of them has failed me yet."

On that note, he rose and left the room, leaving the X-Men to ponder what he had told them. The difficult part for them, Picard knew, would be the waiting.

But then, that was the difficult part for him as well.

Ruugh Isadjo, High Implementor of the Draa'kon vessel *Connharakt,* leaned forward in his command pod and eyed the vessel imaged on the scanplate in front of him.

He didn't know where the ship had come from. However, he was reasonably certain it was not native to Xhaldia. His people had been monitoring the planet on and off for nearly thirty cycles, and they had never seen such a vessel in its vicinity.

Isadjo turned his dark, massive head to gaze at

Mynaagh, his second-in-command. "Who is this?" he demanded. "Why are they here?"

Mynaagh's gill-flaps fluttered, knowing her wisdom was being tested. "Their arrival at this juncture reeks too much to be a coincidence. We must assume they have come to defend Xhaldia against us."

The Implementor's leathery-skinned hands balled into fists. "But we destroyed the planet's means of contacting void-going entities. And according to our instruments, we did it *before* they could send for help."

His second-in-command scowled, her slitted, yellow eyes sliding toward the scanplate. "So we did," she agreed reluctantly, shamed by her inability to shed light on the situation.

"That is all you can say?" he rasped.

Mynaggh's lips pulled back from her several rows of teeth. "It is all," she spat, knowing the significance of such an admission.

Isadjo's eyes slid toward the ship on the scanplate as well. It seemed small, but he knew from long experience that appearances could be deceiving. He made a sound of disgust in his cranial cavities.

This was supposed to have been a quick and easy mission, assuring his political faction on the Draa'kon homeworld the prominence it had long deserved. Now, the matter had become complicated.

Still, it wasn't Mynaagh's fault that this had happened. At least, it didn't *seem* to be. Therefore, Isadjo had no reason to inflict unnecessary pain on her.

"Submit yourself to the recycling facility," he told his second-in-command. "But first, sever your primary nerve linkages."

Mynaagh gazed at him with gratitude in her eyes. "I am pleased to serve so wise an Implementor," she hissed. Then she lumbered out of the command chamber and went to carry out his order.

Isadjo grunted at her departure. "Ettojh," he barked.

His third-in-command advanced to his side. "Implementor?"

"You are now second," said Isadjo. "Serve well."

Ettojh bowed his dark, rounded head. "While you permit it," he replied, completing the ritual.

That done, the Implementor returned his attention to the scanplate. He tried to decide whether it would be better to go after the interloper now or wait for it to come closer.

Normally, he would have gone after it and would have relished the encounter. However, he had forces on the planet's surface to take into account. Under the circumstances, it seemed the better choice was to remain in orbit.

Isadjo was not known for his patience. Quite the contrary, in fact. But in the long run, he reminded himself, it hardly mattered *when* he destroyed the interloper . . .

Only that he *did.*

Even before the captain uttered the words, the counselor felt the rush of urgency that always preceded them.

"Red alert," said Picard.

The bridge was bathed in a lurid red light, signaling a new level of preparedness all over the ship. Weapons were powered up and shields were reinforced. Even the captain moved forward to the edge of his chair.

Troi knew it was only a matter of minutes before she would be able to sense the psyches of the alien aggressors—if they *were* aggressors. She was so focused on that eventuality, she almost failed to notice as the lift doors opened behind her—or as someone emerged from them who was hardly a member of the crew.

Then she felt the inner calm of the newcomer, the remarkable air of self-possession, and even without looking she knew exactly who had joined them. It could only be the mutant known as Storm.

Captain Picard, who was seated to the counselor's right, turned to look at the X-Man. So did Commander Riker. However, their emotional reactions to Storm's presence were quite different, Troi mused.

143

The first officer clearly didn't quite approve of the situation. To him, the bridge was a place for uniformed officers only, except in those rare instances when a civilian had been recruited for his or her expertise. As far as he was concerned, the mutant didn't fit that bill.

Picard, on the other hand, wasn't at all perturbed by Storm's entrance. On the contrary, he seemed to welcome it.

In fact . . .

Suddenly, Troi realized she was in danger of crossing a boundary she had set for herself a long time ago. As a ship's counselor, her job was to monitor the feelings of her colleagues, to make sure they were sailing on an even keel—not to pry into their personal lives.

And yet, without meaning to, she had read a very personal emotion in the captain. An emotion she had no business knowing about.

The Betazoid couldn't undo what she had done. She couldn't erase the knowledge from her mind. She could only keep it to herself and make sure no one else found out about it.

As she thought this, Storm took up a position beside her and examined the viewscreen. "Ah," the mutant said evenly. "We are almost upon them now."

"Almost," the captain confirmed.

"I see now why we couldn't contact Xhaldia," Sovar noted sourly from his place at the tactical station. "The communications booster satellites have all been destroyed."

Troi frowned. More and more, she wished she could get inside the aliens' heads. Perhaps there was a reason for their actions.

"Three hundred thousand kilometers and closing," reported Rager, who was manning the Conn station.

"We should be close enough to scan them," said Riker.

"Aye, sir," replied Sovar. "I'm trying that now."

After a moment, the counselor saw Picard look back over his shoulder. "Results, Lieutenant?"

Sovar grunted. "Their shields are making it difficult, sir. But I'm picking up some four hundred life forms. A single species, as far as I can tell . . . one we've never encountered before."

The captain appeared to digest the information. "What about their tactical capabilities? Weapons and so on?"

The Xhaldian studied his monitors. "Their weapons are based on disruption technology—not unlike that used by the Klingons and the Romulans. They have no tractor emitters that I can see, but they're built for battle. Nearly sixty percent of their power is permanently channeled to their weapons ports."

"Two hundred thousand kilometers," Rager announced.

"Their propulsion systems?" asked Riker.

"Much like ours," said Sovar. "Maybe a little less efficient. And if they're a lower power priority, they can't proceed at high speeds for any length of time."

"Unfortunately," Picard observed, "that won't be a disadvantage in close quarters. In fact, we should channel extra power to shields and weapons ourselves—just in case."

The tactical officer followed the captain's suggestion. "Done, sir."

Rager spoke up again. "One hundred fifty thousand kilometers."

Soon, Troi thought, they would be face to face with the aliens. By then, she would have found out the truth.

Abruptly, Data turned to face Picard. "Captain, I have managed to penetrate Xhaldia's energy fields with long-range sensors."

Picard nodded. "Excellent, Commander."

The android returned his attention to his Ops monitors. "There is a great deal of interference, but . . ."

"Yes?" the captain prodded.

Troi was eager to hear his findings as well.

"It appears," said Data, "there are several smaller

versions of the orbiting vessel already in evidence on the planet's surface. Eight of them, to be precise. What is more, they seem to be clustered in a particular area."

Picard digested the report. "What area is that?" he asked.

The answer didn't come from the android. It came from the station directly behind them.

"The vicinity of Vordoon," said Lt. Sovar, his voice trembling ever so slightly.

"The transformed," Storm gasped, with a certainty that seemed to go beyond logic. "Whoever these people are, they are after the transformed."

Riker scowled. "It seems that way, all right."

"But why?" asked the X-Man. "And how did they know about the transformed in the first place?"

"A good question," said the captain.

"Eighty thousand kilometers," Rager told them.

"In any case, it's not an invasion," the first officer observed. "At least, not the kind we anticipated."

"That's true," Picard agreed. "One can hardly conquer an entire world on the strength of a few landing parties."

"Captain," said Sovar, breaking into the exchange. "We are being scanned by the alien vessel."

Of course, the counselor thought. If the *Enterprise* could scan the aliens, the aliens could scan *them.*

"I guess we're even now," said Riker.

Suddenly, Troi felt something on the fringes of her consciousness—something that made her skin crawl. Her every instinct told her to break the connection. But she knew how important it might be, so she opened herself up to it even more.

"Counselor?" said Picard.

Troi groaned. "I . . . sense the aliens. They are . . . brutal . . . belligerent. All they care about is power."

Storm put her hands on the counselor's shoulders. "Easy," she said. "Do not seek to do too much, child."

But Troi wasn't finished. "They have . . . nothing but

contempt for the people on the planet . . . for the Xhaldians. They consider them . . . consider *all* other species . . . unworthy of their concern."

The counselor writhed in her seat. She had never felt such arrogance, such hunger for havoc and destruction. Up until then, she had been willing to give the aliens the benefit of the doubt; she could do so no longer.

"They are conquerors," she whispered. "But they have not come here to conquer. There is something else . . . something they covet . . ."

The transformed, she thought. Just as Storm had said.

Satisfied that she had gleaned all she could, Troi severed the empathic link. Overwhelmed by a wave of relief, she slumped sideways in her chair, her skin bathed in a cold sweat.

"Are you all right?" Picard asked her.

The counselor nodded. But her fears had been confirmed—and then some.

"Twenty thousand kilometers," Rager said.

Storm knelt at Troi's side. "By the goddess," she said admiringly. "Those aliens are tens of thousands of miles away. And yet, you can see what is in their hearts?"

"The counselor's talents are most impressive," Picard agreed. He gazed at Troi, still concerned about her. "Are you *certain* you're all right?"

"I'm fine," the Betazoid told him. "Really."

"Impressive is not the word for it," the mutant said. "Professor Xavier is the most powerful telepath on Earth, and even he requires mechanical aids to detect minds miles away."

On the screen, the alien vessel loomed larger and larger. The counselor only had to look at it to be reminded of the brutality within.

"Five thousand kilometers," Rager said dutifully. "Four thousand. Three thousand. Two—"

"All stop," Picard commanded.

As Rager cut power to the impulse engines, the *Enterprise* came to a halt. According to the monitor in Troi's armrest, they were a mere five hundred kilometers from the alien vessel—and no further from Xhaldia than her solitary moon.

The captain sat back in his seat. "Hail them, Mr. Sovar."

The Xhaldian looked surprised, but he did as he was told.

For a moment or two, there was no response. Then Sovar looked up from his control console.

"Their Implementor wishes to speak with you," he told Picard.

The captain stood and approached the viewscreen. "Put him through," he told the lieutenant.

In the next instant, a dark and formidable-looking visage confronted them. The alien's head was round and massive with bulblike structures protruding from its forehead, and it lacked anything even vaguely resembling a neck. Its skin was leathery, its yellow eyes long and slitted like a lizard's.

The counselor swallowed. There was no pity in the alien's expression, no inclination toward compromise. Still, she knew Picard had to attempt to achieve a peaceful solution.

"I am Captain Jean-Luc Picard," he said, "commanding the *U.S.S Enterprise*. I've come in response to—"

"I am Isadjo," the alien growled, showing a maw full of short, sharp teeth, "High Implementor of the Draa'kon vessel *Connharakt*. You will go back where you came from, or we will most certainly destroy you."

Chapter Twenty

Picard considered High Implementor Isadjo. Obviously, the Draa'kon wasn't one to beat around the bush.

But then, neither was the captain of the *Enterprise*.

"We have no intention of going back where we came from," he replied almost matter-of-factly. "Not until we have assured ourselves that Xhaldia is safe and secure again."

The High Implementor made a derisive sound. "You will have reason to wish you had decided otherwise, Captain Jean-Luc Picard."

Then he cut off the communication. Immediately, his image was replaced by that of his ship.

"Sir!" said Sovar. "They're firing at us!"

"Evasive maneuvers," the captain told Rager. "Picard delta—"

Before he could get the rest of it out, the deck pitched wildly beneath him. It sent him staggering into Data. As he disengaged himself from the android, the ship lurched again—even worse than before.

"Picard delta theta!" the captain barked, completing

Rager's instructions. Then he turned to his tactical officer. "Mr. Sovar, report!"

The Xhaldian studied his monitors. "We've taken hits to decks seven, eight, thirteen, and seventeen, sir. Shields down . . ." His eyes narrowed in disbelief. ". . . eighty-eight percent!"

The captain swore beneath his breath. Eighty-eight percent with two volleys? *At five hundred kilometers?* It was unheard of. But, obviously, that was the kind of firepower they were up against.

As Rager took them through one twisting turn after another, the *Connharakt* broke orbit and came after them. Its weapon ports seething with power, it looked for all the world like a predator moving in for the kill.

Picard had other ideas, however. "Target phasers and photon torpedoes," he told Sovar.

"Targeted," said the Xhaldian.

The captain eyed the viewscreen, where the Draa'kon vessel loomed like an alien leviathan. "Fire!"

The *Connharakt* was wracked with phaser fire and photon explosions. But it kept coming, undaunted, as if hadn't been hit at all.

"Several direct hits," Sovar reported. "But they don't seem to have had much effect. We barely put a dent in their shields."

Picard was tempted to fire again, but decided against it. His resources were limited, after all.

He turned to Data. "Run an analysis of their shielding, Commander. Let's see if there are any weak spots."

As the android got to work, the captain glanced at Rager. "Let's give them a different look to contend with. Picard delta omega, Lieutenant."

"Aye, sir," said the Conn officer.

Rager began a new set of maneuvers . . . just as the Draa'kon unleashed another savage barrage. Most of it slid by them into the void, but a blast caught the edge of the saucer section.

Suddenly, the bridge skewed hard to port, forcing

Picard to grab Rager's chair or be thrown to the floor. At the same time, one of the aft control panels erupted in a geyser of sparks. Immediately, a crewman grabbed a fire extinguisher and played it over the panel.

"Shields are gone, sir!" Sovar called out.

Feeling his jaw muscles flutter, Picard turned and eyed the viewscreen with renewed resolve. "Where's my analysis, Mr. Data?"

"I am almost finished," the android replied. A moment later, he swiveled around in his chair. "As you suspected, sir, the overall toughness of the *Connharakt*'s shields comes at the expense of some weak spots elsewhere. These can be found behind all four of the vessel's warp nacelles."

Picard clapped Data on the shoulder. "Good work, Commander."

"Thank you, Captain," said the android.

Picard turned to Rager. "We need to get behind them, Lieutenant."

"I understand, sir."

Without hesitation, the conn officer brought their nose up and avoided another Draa'kon volley—one that would have gashed them from stem to stern. What's more, Rager stayed with the maneuver, bringing them directly behind the monstrous *Connharakt*.

The captain could see the flares of cold blue fire lodged in the enemy's nacelles. If Data's analysis was accurate, they had an opportunity to turn the tide of battle.

But it wouldn't be there for long. "Target phasers!"

"Targeted," said Sovar.

Picard gritted his teeth. "Fire!"

Four ruby-red beams lanced out, two striking the nacelle on the upper right and the others striking the upper left. Both structures exploded in clouds of blue fury.

But the captain wasn't about to let up. Not when the Draa'kon's next barrage might be the one that destroyed the *Enterprise*.

"Fire!" he commanded.

Again, four phaser beams pierced the enemy's shields. Again, they elicited twin energy outbursts. But when the viewscreen cleared, Picard could see that only one of the remaining nacelles had exploded. The other was badly charred, but intact.

Which meant the Draa'kon juggernaut could still move. And if it could move, it could *hunt*.

Even as that thought crossed the captain's mind, he saw weapons ports swivel on top of the *Connharakt*. "Get us out of here," he told Rager. "Picard delta omicron."

But the Draa'kon were already striking back. A fierce, green light blanched out the viewscreen for a moment. Then the *Enterprise* was punished with the most devastating barrage yet.

The captain was catapulted forward, flipping end over end. He hit a bulkhead with such force he felt himself black out for a moment. When he came to, the taste of blood strong in his mouth, he took stock of his bridge.

The lights, still tinted by the red alert, were flickering on and off almost hypnotically. Two more of the aft consoles had exploded and were spewing sparks. And his people were strewn all over the place.

With the exception of Data. Somehow, the android had managed to remain at his post. As Picard looked on, his second officer's artificial fingers flew over his control board in a blur of speed.

The captain knew what Data was doing, too. Having taken over the helm function, he was trying to keep the *Enterprise* in one piece despite the enemy's intentions to the contrary.

Dragging himself to his feet as his officers and Storm did likewise, Picard ignored his bruises and abrasions and glanced back at the viewscreen. It showed him the *Connharakt*, still dogging their heels, still unleashing volley after fiery, green volley.

But for the time being, the android was eluding them.

Taking advantage of the respite, the captain helped a shaken Lt. Rager to her feet and saw her back to her conn station. Then he turned to Sovar, who had only a moment earlier regained his position at Tactical.

"Report," Picard told him, as his first officer came to stand beside him.

The Xhaldian glanced soberly at his monitors. "Weapons are offline," he told the captain. "So's the warp drive. The impulse engines have been damaged as well—there's no saying how long they'll last."

Picard scowled. Without shields, weapons, or the ability to go to warp, they were defenseless. The only thing keeping them from annihilation was their impulse drive, and that might abandon them at any moment.

He needed to pull a rabbit out of his hat. And *quickly.*

Suddenly, a voice rang out over the intercom system. "Captain, this is Commander La Forge. I've got an idea."

At that point, Picard was willing to grasp at any straw at all. "What is it, Commander?"

"It's Nightcrawler, sir," said Geordi. "He may be able to teleport us onto the Draa'kon ship."

An intriguing idea, the captain conceded. But . . . "They still have shields," he replied.

"That's just it," the engineer told him. "Nightcrawler's teleportation abilities don't work the way our transporters do. He circumvents normal space by entering some other dimension."

The captain saw Geordi's point. "If that's so, he can get past the Draa'kon ship's defenses—"

"And perform a mission of sabotage," Riker finished. "Maybe even bring their shields down, so we can get other personnel aboard."

Picard turned to Storm. "A possibility?"

She didn't look optimistic. "Kurt is no expert on alien technology. He would hardly know what to wreck. And even if he did," she said grimly, "what you're suggesting would be extremely dangerous for him."

"In what way?" Picard asked.

"Kurt can only teleport over a distance of a couple of miles," Storm explained. "And normally, he only aims for a destination he's familiar with. Otherwise, he runs the risk of materializing inside something solid." Her nostrils flared. "Or in this case, materializing out in space."

"Don't forget," Riker added, "the *Connharakt* will be a moving target. We'll have to match her course and speed if Nightcrawler's to have a chance."

Abruptly, the deck lurched under their feet. Apparently, the Draa'kon had found them with another barrage.

"Hull breaches on decks nineteen and twenty," Sovar reported. "Commander Worf is coordinating repair teams."

"If there is any other way . . ." Storm began.

"Storm . . . Ororo, please this may be our only chance," Nightcrawler insisted over the intercom link. "I can do it, Captain. And someone can come with me to handle the technical end of it."

Storm eyed Picard. "You must understand," she said, "Kurt and whomever he takes along may be adversely affected by the process."

"Adversely . . .?" the captain asked.

"Sickened," she said. "Exhausted. Perhaps to the extent that they will not be able to carry out their mission."

The first officer looked at Picard. "Not if it's Data who goes along. He doesn't get sickened *or* exhausted. And he's got all the technical expertise we could ask for."

The android cast a glance at them, having overheard their conversation. "I would be more than happy to accompany Nightcrawler, Captain. That is, if you deem it advisable."

The captain considered it. The maneuver would require split-second timing, of course. And if it didn't work, he would be dooming two good men. But if he *didn't* try it, he might be dooming his entire vessel and its crew.

"Very well," he said at last. "If it is all right with your leader, I'll take you up on your offer, Nightcrawler. You and Commander Data will attempt to disable the *Connharakt*'s shield generators." He glanced at Storm and she nodded.

"Aye, sir," the android responded.

As Data got up and was replaced by another officer at Conn, the captain turned to Riker. "Assemble some boarding teams, Number One—with a couple of X-Men present in each of them."

He gave Storm a moment to object to the idea. She didn't. In fact, she seemed pleased.

"I'll want to lead a team myself," said the first officer.

"I expected no less," Picard admitted. "See to it that each team targets a different tactical system. When I see the *Connharakt*'s shields drop, I will give the order to transport."

Riker nodded, then headed for the turbolift with Data in his wake. With a glance at the captain, Storm went with them.

Picard almost asked her to stay behind, to continue as his advisor with regard to her compatriots. But then, as perhaps the most powerful being in their midst, she would be infinitely more useful as a member of one of the boarding parties.

As the first officer passed the tactical station, he said, "You're with me, Mr. Sovar."

The Xhaldian hesitated only long enough for another officer to take his post. Then he joined Riker, Data, and Storm as they entered the lift.

"Captain," said Nightcrawler, still speaking over the ship's intercom, "if this is going to work, I'll need a moment to familiarize myself with the *Connharakt*'s layout."

Again, the bridge staggered under the weight of a Draa'kon barrage. Picard glanced at the new tactical officer.

"Additional breaches on decks thirty-one through thirty-three," the man told him.

The *Enterprise* couldn't take much more of this, the captain thought. He looked to the intercom grid again.

"Commander La Forge will show you our sensor data," he told Nightcrawler. "Will that be enough?"

The mutant grunted. "It will have to be, nicht wahr."

Chapter Twenty-one

DATA ENTERED ENGINEERING with a phaser in each hand. He found Nightcrawler and Geordi bent over the free-standing situations monitor.

Halfway there, the deck pitched beneath the android, spilling him into a bulkhead. In fact, everyone in engineering was thrown off their feet.

No doubt, the Draa'kon have breached the hull again, Data thought. He could smell the smoky odor of distant circuitry fires. It gave them all the more reason to hurry.

"Data," said Nightcrawler, helping Geordi to his feet, "I'm as ready as I will ever be."

"Good," said the android, handing the mutant his phaser. "I, too, have assimilated all our information on Draa'kon ship design. Therefore, even if we do not materialize in the immediate vicinity of the shield generators, I am confident I will be able to find them."

Nightcrawler patted him on the back. "I like an optimist."

Data smiled. "Thank you."

"Commander La Forge," came the captain's voice over the intercom. "How much longer need we wait?"

Geordi looked at Nightcrawler, then at the android. "We're ready when you are, sir."

"Excellent," said Picard. "Stand by. We are attempting a maneuver which will allow us to match the *Connharakt*'s course and speed."

Data didn't know what that maneuver might be, but he was certain it entailed a great deal of risk. As Storm had said, Nightcrawler's maximum range was only a couple of miles. At that distance, a direct hit would turn the ship into a blazing scattering of debris.

"Ten seconds," the captain warned them.

Their timing would have to be excruciatingly precise, the android reflected. The slightest miscalculation . . .

"Nine," said Picard. "Eight. Seven. Six."

The android took up a position next to the mutant, who put his hand on Data's shoulder.

"Five. Four. Three," the captain continued.

Nightcrawler cleared his throat. "Here goes nothing."

Data sincerely hoped it was a joke.

"Two," said Picard. "One . . ."

There was no sensation attached to the experience of teleporting alongside the mutant. At least, none that the android could discern.

He simply found himself in a wide, high-ceilinged corridor he had never seen before, made of a dark metal he couldn't identify. The place was illuminated with lurid, red lighting strips.

And there was a smell of sulfur, of course—Nightcrawler's trademark, apparently.

Data turned to the mutant just in time to see his eyes roll back in his head, his powers having been taxed to their very limits. As Nightcrawler's knees buckled, the android caught him and slung him over his shoulder as gently as possible.

Then he headed down the corridor, hoping to get his

bearings. After all, the mutant had done *his* job. Now it was up to Data to do the same.

His nerves taut, Riker stood alongside Storm, Shadowcat, Sovar, and a couple of other security officers and awaited word from the captain that the *Connharakt*'s shields were down.

But with each passing second, the first officer's hopes fell a little more. After all, Data and Nightcrawler had popped out of engineering almost three minutes earlier. The longer it took to hear from them, the less likely it was that they had accomplished their mission.

Or even survived.

It was easy to catalog all the bad things that might have happened to them, beginning with their never having reached the *Connharakt* in the first place and ending with a disastrous firefight in the shadow of the shield generators. Nor could he rule out any of those possibilities.

Still, Riker chose to think positively. In all the years he had known Data, the android had never let him down—never failed to come through. With any luck, his record would hold this time as well.

Suddenly, the captain's voice broke the silence. "Captain Picard to transporter rooms one, two, and three. Effect transports immediately."

Inwardly, the first officer cheered. Data and Nightcrawler had worked their miracle, it seemed. The enemy's shields had been stripped away, leaving them vulnerable to the *Enterprise*'s away teams.

Standing at the transporter console, Lt. Demeter worked his controls quickly and efficiently. Riker braced himself for whatever he might encounter when he materialized on the *Connharakt*.

But after a moment, nothing had happened. Cursing to himself, the first officer watched Demeter frown and try the transport a second time.

"What's the matter?" Riker asked.

The transporter operator shook his head, then looked

up at the first officer. "Their shields are back up, sir," Demeter reported miserably.

No, thought Riker. *It can't be! Not after Data and Nightcrawler risked their lives for this. Not after they succeeded, for godsakes!*

What in blazes had gone wrong?

Worf looked around. He found himself in a wide, high corridor made of some dark metal, lit with blood-red strips. Banshee, Archangel, and the three security officers assigned to him stood alongside him.

In accordance with his orders, the Klingon tapped the communicator on his chest. "Worf to Commander Riker," he said.

There was no answer.

"Try again," Banshee advised him.

The Klingon did that. He obtained the same results.

Then he tried the other team leader. "Worf to Commander Troi."

No answer there either.

The Klingon didn't like it. Riker had put together *three* teams so the Draa'kon would have several problems to deal with at once. If only Worf's had gotten through . . .

Then it occurred to him that it might simply be a communications problem. The Klingon tested the theory by attempting to contact Data.

"Worf to Commander Data."

"I am here," came the response. "Unfortunately, I believe our two parties are the only ones on board. Apparently, the Draa'kon have a redundant system of shield generators. Almost as soon as we disabled the primary generators, a secondary set took over."

The Klingon scowled at the way events had unfolded. Nonetheless, he resolved to make the best of it.

"We will proceed according to plan," he said.

"Likewise," the android replied.

"Lovely," said Banshee.

Ignoring him, Worf studied the corridor in both directions. If he and his team had been beamed to the right location, his objective was down the passage to his right. At its end, there was a perpendicular passageway, right where he had expected to find it.

"This way," he said.

Without comment, his comrades came along—with one exception. Archangel flew up ahead, no doubt to reconnoiter. A moment later, he came to the end of the hallway and veered out of sight.

The Klingon didn't object. In fact, he approved of the mutant's scouting-out their prospects.

It made sense for each of them to use his or her talents to their best advantage. That was why Commander Riker had assigned each team a couple of X-Men, wasn't it? So they could draw on the mutants' strengths?

Suddenly, Worf heard a shout of surprise, followed by another—cries so guttural even a Klingon couldn't have made them. Then he saw a beam of green energy scald the bulkhead up ahead of them, its source the corridor Archangel had invaded.

Before Worf could hiss a warning to his comrades, the winged mutant came whipping around the corner, frantically waving his arms at them. "Watch out!" he shouted.

As his warning echoed from bulkhead to bulkhead, a squad of seven or eight Draa'kon flooded the junction ahead of them—their weapons spitting vicious, green energy bolts that filled the corridor with their fury. The Klingon shoved Banshee in one direction and threw himself in the other, narrowly avoiding the barrage.

One of the *Enterprise* security officers wasn't so lucky. Caught in one of the enemy's bursts, Lt. Wayne was lifted off his feet and thrown backward four or five meters. By the time he landed, the man was dead, his chest a wet, smoking ruin.

Cursing under his breath, Worf took aim and returned the Draa'kon's fire. Kirby and Ditko, the surviving security officers, followed suit.

So did Archangel, but from an entirely different angle. As the others stood their ground, he launched himself into the air and performed a devastating strafing run with his borrowed phaser.

Obviously unprepared for an adversary who could fly, the Draa'kon raised their weapon barrels too late to hit the mutant with their energy bolts. All they could do was scar the metal ceiling in his wake.

Archangel, on the other hand, was more successful. By the time he wheeled about on the far side of them, he had taken out one Draa'kon with a well-placed phaser shot and was zeroing in on the others.

Banshee didn't even pull his phaser from his jacket pocket. Instead, he opened his mouth . . . and let out a shriek so loud that even Worf could barely stand it.

Instantly, one of the Draa'kon's weapons exploded in his meaty hands. And a fraction of a second later, his comrade's weapon did the same.

As Archangel forced the enemy to turn and deal with him, the Klingon took down another Draa'kon with his phaser. A beam from Kirby sent yet another one slamming into a bulkhead, and Ditko dispatched one as well.

Ignoring the chaos around him, a Draa'kon nearly burned a hole in Archangel's wing. Fortunately, the mutant was quick enough to rise out of harm's way. Then he released a beam of his own, striking his adversary in the forehead and dropping him where he stood.

That left only one armed Draa'kon. Lips pulled back in a wolfish grin, Worf cut him down. Then, for good measure, he turned his phaser on the two whom Banshee had disarmed, stunning them.

In the silence that followed, those still standing listened for signs of other Draa'kon. For the time being, there weren't any.

Taking advantage of the respite, Kirby went to check on Wayne. Kneeling beside the man, he felt Lee's neck for a pulse. Then he looked at Worf and shook his head.

Klingons believed the body to be nothing more than a

162

shell for the spirit. Since Wayne's spirit had clearly been released, Worf felt no responsibility regarding it.

Gesturing for Kirby and the others to follow him, he advanced along the corridor. One by one, they fell into line behind him.

Again, with a single airborne exception.

Chapter Twenty-two

STILL IRKED that he had not been able to beam over to the enemy ship, Riker settled into the pilot's seat in the shuttle. He tapped a stud on the craft's control console. Instantly, the captain's image appeared on one of the console's monitors.

"Number One," said Picard.

"We'll be ready to depart in a moment, sir," the first officer responded. "We're just waiting for the medical tricorders the doctor wanted us to bring."

The muscles worked in the captain's jaw. "Don't worry, Will—we'll take care of the Draa'kon up here. You just concern yourselves with the Draa'kon down *there.*"

Riker nodded, knowing Picard wasn't half as confident as he sounded. "I'll do that, sir."

Then the captain's image blinked out, to be replaced by a darkened screen. The first officer understood. After all, they were still being pursued by the Draa'kon, though in the last few minutes the captain's maneuvers had bought them a respite.

"Commander?" said a feminine voice.

Riker turned and saw Dr. Crusher depositing a container on the deck of the shuttle. "Your tricorders," she noted.

Crusher looked harried, her copper hair in disarray. But then, sickbay had been brimming with casualties in the last few minutes.

"Here," Sovar told her, "I'll take that." Bending to the task, he lifted the doctor's container and stowed it in a place designed for such cargo.

Crusher eyed the first officer. "Getting me that blood information is as important as anything you'll do down there."

"I don't doubt it," said Riker.

He turned in his seat and surveyed his squad. Storm, Shadowcat, and his four security officers were already seated. As the first officer watched, Sovar joined them.

The doctor sighed. "Good luck, Will."

Riker gave her a reassuring smile. "Thanks. Now if you'll excuse us, we've got some work to do."

As Crusher withdrew from the shuttle, the first officer touched the hatch control. A moment later, the metal plate slid closed, rendering the craft airtight and spaceworthy.

Leaning forward and glancing out his observation port, Riker could see the next shuttle over. It was piloted by Lt. Kane, one of the officers on Troi's away team and a fine pilot in his own right.

The first officer couldn't see the counselor herself or the others who accompanied her. But he found some comfort in the knowledge that Wolverine, Colossus, and some of the ship's best security people were with her.

Not that Troi couldn't take care of herself. But when one was entering what amounted to a war zone, one needed all the help one could get.

As he thought this, the shuttlebay's doors slid apart. Only an invisible barrier still held the atmosphere inside the ship.

Riker powered up his engines. "Clear for departure?"

he asked the officer in charge of the bay, who was standing at his control panel off to the side.

Suddenly, a shudder ran through the ship and the shuttledeck tilted wildly, sending men and women skidding across its surface. Fortunately, the shuttles themselves stayed put for the most part. Only one pod tipped over and lay on its side like a wounded beast.

It was a grim reminder of how vulnerable the *Enterprise* was in her damaged state. Riker almost hated to leave her—but like Troi, she was in the best hands he could imagine.

It didn't take long before order was restored and personnel returned to their posts. But it seemed to the first officer that Dr. Crusher would have some new casualties to deal with.

"Clear for departure," came the response, at last, from the officer in charge of the shuttlebay.

Riker worked his controls, lifting his shuttle off the deck while he still could, and nudged it forward toward the bay's transparent energy barrier. Then he activated the thrusters and slid the craft right through it.

A moment later, the first officer found himself free of the ship. He could see the immense, dark form of the *Connharakt* bearing down on the *Enterprise*—but with a burst of impulse speed, he powered himself clear of the alien warship. After all, with the Draa'kons' warp drive damaged, the shuttle could move every bit as fast as they could.

Riker's next stop was Verdeen. Still, he lingered for a few seconds to make sure the other shuttle made it out of the Enterprise all right. When he saw it emerge through the barrier and dart clear of the *Connharakt* just as he had, he nodded approvingly.

Then he headed for the planet's surface.

Worf and his team made their way down the dimly lit corridor, eyeing the juncture up ahead of them. They had to be getting close to their objective, the Klingon observed.

Not that it had been easy. They had run into squads of powerful Draa'kon defenders no less than three times since beaming aboard. And while Lt. Lee remained their only real casualty, they had all been battered and bloodied in hand to hand fighting.

Archangel was no exception. As usual, he was scouting up ahead, out of sight of the away team, though it made him more vulnerable than the rest of them. If not for his uncanny speed in close quarters, the mutant's pinions would have been clipped a long time ago.

Abruptly, the winged man came hurtling around the corner at them. Worf tensed. To this point, Archangel's retreats had meant a firefight was in the offing. But something about the mutant's expression made the Klingon suspect otherwise.

"We made it," Archangel told him. Alighting in front of them, he jerked his thumb over his shoulder. "Their engine room is just around the bend."

Encouraged, Worf picked up the pace. When he got to the juncture, he peeked around the corner at the corridor to his right.

It was empty. But the Klingon could see a grey, heavy-looking archway at the end of it, and beyond the archway there was something that looked very much like an engine room.

"You see?" asked Archangel.

Worf nodded. "I see."

He considered the contingent of armed guards that stood just inside the arch, illuminated by the glare from unseen light sources. The Klingon estimated that there were half a dozen of the Draa'kon. And, of course, there would be engineers and such further within, who might also have access to weapons in an emergency.

Worf turned to Ditko and Kirby. "It will be up to you," he said, "to disable the power transfer mechanisms. Though I do not know for certain, I imagine they will be similar to those you have seen on the Enterprise."

The security officers nodded and rechecked their phasers.

"And what're we t' do?" asked Banshee. "In other words, you, me, and our wee friend with th' wings on his back?"

The Klingon grunted. "We will *fight.*"

The mutant smiled. "Sounds like a plan."

Peeking into the corridor again, Worf raised his left hand—a signal for everyone to get ready. A couple of seconds later, he let it drop. Then he charged down the passageway, phaser held before him.

It took a moment or two for the Draa'kon to realize they were under attack. The two nearest guards whirled and took aim at the away team, their shots burning streaks in the bulkheads on either side of the Klingon.

Then it was the intruders' turn. Worf sent one of the guards flying with a ruby-red phaser burst, and Archangel swept the other one's feet out from under him. Two more Draa'kon stepped up to take their places, but Banshee opened his mouth and knocked them senseless.

Chaos erupted as the away team spilled into the cavernous, grey engine room. Green and crimson beams leaped back and forth, the faces of friend and foe alike illuminated in the crossfire.

The Klingon rolled to elude a point-blank blast and cut down his adversary with one of his own. A moment later, he saw his winged ally drive a Draa'kon into a bulkhead face first, then twist up and back along the ceiling to set his sights on another victim.

Banshee was driven to his knees by a two-handed blow from behind. But before his assailant could finish him off, Kirby skewered the Draa'kon with a well-placed phaser beam.

And so it went.

The engine room echoed wildly with their bellows and their grunts, with the thud of bodies hitting each other and then hitting the deck. Worf fired, ducked, and fired again, trying desperately to make out his adversaries in the midst of flickering chaos.

Finally, he saw a sizable flash out of the corner of his

eye, and knew by that sign that either Ditko or Kirby had gotten to the power transfer mechanisms. As circuitry sputtered and plasma conduits exploded, the Klingon collapsed another Draa'kon with a phaser shot to his midsection. Then he gestured for his team to withdraw from the engine room.

Laying down cover fire, Worf watched Ditko and Kirby race him to the exit. Banshee joined them a moment later. Last of all came Archangel, half his face bathed in blood from a cut to his temple.

Still, they were all alive, all in one piece. It was the best the Klingon could have hoped for.

Releasing a few last shots into the fireshot confusion in which they had left the engine room, Worf herded his charges down the corridor. After all, his mission wasn't over yet.

And it wouldn't be until he got his team home again.

Through narrowed eyes, High Implementor Isadjo watched the interlopers make their way along a corridor, leaving a scattering of fallen Draa'kon in their wake. Enraged, he cursed in the sacred tongue of his ancestors.

So these were the invaders who had destroyed the remainder of his mighty propulsion capabilities. Isadjo's gill-flaps fluttered. Had the *Connharakt*'s internal sensor net not been damaged in its battle with the Enterprise, he would have gotten a look at them a good deal sooner.

And now that he *had* gotten a look at them, his mind raced with a multitude of questions. Who were these beings that they could cut down his soldiers like stands of marsh grass? Could it be that someone else had seeded a world as the Draa'kon had long ago seeded Xhaldia?

Isadjo was loathe to throw any more of his forces at the intruders, as it barely seemed to slow them down. Yet neither could he allow them to continue on their path of destruction.

Fortunately, he still had another option. "Ettojh," he snapped, "in which section are the invaders?"

169

His second-in-command consulted his scansurfaces. "Level three, section twenty-two, Implementor. Moving toward section twenty-three."

Isadjo's lips pulled back, exposing his many rows of teeth. "Activate the fire barriers ahead and behind them," he rumbled. "Then remove the air from their corridor."

As far as he had been able to tell, the intruders carried no personal oxygen supplies. With nothing to breathe, even the most formidable of them would turn weak and die.

Of that, at least, he was certain.

Chapter Twenty-three

WORF PELTED DOWN the corridor, Kirby and Ditko close behind. Archangel circled up ahead, having already scouted the next corridor.

If the Klingon's memory of the *Connharakt*'s schematics served, Worf and his team were swiftly approaching the transporter facility. That was where they would find Data and Nightcrawler, whose orders had been to precede the other teams there and prepare the place.

And if Data and Nightcrawler hadn't made it? If the Draa'kon had captured or destroyed them, and perhaps even set a trap for the other teams in the transporter room?

The Klingon would worry about that when the time came. At the moment, he was busy enough trying to get them to the rendezvous point.

Suddenly, he saw a flicker of yellow light up ahead. Knowing what it might mean, Worf cried out a warning. But before Archangel could heed it, he passed straight through the center of an intensifying energy field.

The mutant jerked and twisted in supreme agony, his momentum carrying him through the barrier and out the other side. Fortunately for him, his pain didn't last long. He went limp and lost consciousness well before he hit the deck and rolled to a halt.

By that time, the energy field had stretched from one bulkhead to the other. It reached as high as the dark, rounded ceiling and as low as the floor, and it looked to be airtight into the bargain.

Banshee uttered a curse and tried to go after his fellow X-man, but the Klingon restrained him. "You must not touch that barrier," he grated. "It may knock you out as well."

"We can't just let Warren lie there," the mutant insisted. "Can ye nae see the lad needs help?"

Glancing back over his shoulder, Worf saw that a similar barrier had been erected in back of them. Realizing the nature of their trap, he shook his shaggy head.

"What is it?" Banshee demanded.

"It is a response to the outbreak of fire," the Klingon replied, "not unlike those one finds on Starfleet vessels. Force fields drop on either side of the blaze. Then vents in the bulkheads draw the air out of the enclosure."

The skin at the bridge of the mutant's nose gathered in a knot. "You mean they're gonna try to suffocate us?"

Worf nodded. "I believe so."

Ditko looked up at the ceiling, then aimed his phaser at it and unleashed a bright red beam. It didn't even leave a char mark on the metal.

Turning to the Klingon, the officer shrugged. "The field is everywhere, sir. There doesn't seem to be any way out."

"Now that's where ye're wrong, lad," said Banshee. He eyed the barrier in front of them as if it were a living adversary, standing between him and his fallen comrade. "There's *always* a way out."

Throwing his redhaired head back and opening his mouth, he unleashed a high-pitched shriek. The force field sizzled and sputtered at the point where his sonic blast made contact with it, but remained stable otherwise. And when the mutant stopped shrieking, the barrier looked no different than when he had begun.

What was worse, Worf could hear the hiss of air as it began to leave their prison. The Draa'kon intended to suffocate them, all right. He clenched his teeth, wishing he had guessed wrong for a change.

"Wait a minute," said Banshee. He regarded the Klingon. "What if we were t' work together? My sonic blast and yer phaser, in th' same wee spot? Maybe we could find a ventilation shaft or somethin'."

It wouldn't hurt to try, Worf told himself. He reset his weapon and aimed it at the bulkhead, just to the left of the barrier. "Here," he decided.

"Whatever ye say," the mutant replied.

Again, he unleashed a blast, forcing the field to desolidify in that one particular spot. A moment later, the Klingon fired his phaser right into the heart of Banshee's handiwork.

And it did the trick.

The phaser beam cut through the barrier and dug a hole in the metal bulkhead beneath it. But before long, the mutant had to stop and take a breath.

"It's th' blessed oxygen," he gasped. "We're losin' it, Worf."

The Klingon could hardly disagree. He was getting lightheaded, weak in the knees, and he was by far the hardiest of them.

"We must try it again," he told Banshee.

The mutant nodded, gathered his resources and delivered another blast in the same spot. As before, the barrier grew muddled. And as before, Worf applied his phaser beam to the center of it.

This time, they dug even deeper, exposing circuitry and power conduits. But eventually, Banshee had to stop, plant his hands on his knees and suck down a breath. And the oxygen was still running out of their enclosure.

Ditko and Kirby sat down to save their strength. But the mutant and the Klingon didn't have that luxury.

"We don't have much time left," Worf wheezed, knowing it was an understatement.

Banshee eyed him. "One more time, then," he panted, "with feelin', now." And he directed yet another sonic blast at the bulkhead.

At the same time, Worf activated his phaser. Thanks to the mutant's valiant effort, it probed beyond circuitry and power conduits, delving deeper and deeper with each passing moment.

Banshee screamed a scream of defiance, as if he were daring the Draa'kon's trap to beat them. He dripped perspiration and turned a dangerously dark shade of red, but he refused to give up. And he kept screaming until his eyes rolled back in his head and he slumped to the deck, half-unconscious.

When the mutant's sonic blast stopped, the Klingon's phaser beam became useless against the barrier. Worf muttered a curse and sank to his knees, hating the idea of defeat even more than he hated the idea of death—though both of them seemed unavoidable at that point.

Suddenly, there was a massive pop and the Klingon felt a breeze wash over him. Wondering how that could be, he looked at the barrier ahead of them and saw that it was gone.

But how . . . ?

And then it came to him. The energy field had to have been projected from somewhere in the bulkhead. Their digging must have damaged one of the projectors.

Taking deep, laborious breaths, Banshee rose to his knees beside Worf. Then he staggered to his feet and lurched forward until he was able to sink beside Archangel and check his vital signs.

"The lad's alive," the mutant said of his teammate, "but his breathin' is shallow, and I d' nae think his color's all it should be."

By then, Ditko and Kirby were on their feet as well,

shrugging off the effects like the others. The Klingon tossed Archangel over his shoulder, wings and all.

Then they continued down the corridor, hoping they didn't meet another squad of Draa'kon before they reached their destination.

As Riker dropped his shuttle through a dense layer of clouds, he got his first glimpse of Verdeen.

It was a small city by Terran standards, nestled in the foothills of a high, sprawling mountain range. Continuing his descent, the first officer could see that the place was laid out in a simple grid, every street at right angles to those that crossed it. There were spots where a tall, steep hill interrupted the pattern, but those were few and far between.

In most parts of the city, the streets were choked with people and vehicles. But not in the northwest section. It seemed that portion of Verdeen was deserted.

No, the first officer thought, his attention drawn to a series of bright, green flashes. *Not* completely *deserted.*

Looking more closely at one of the wider thoroughfares, he spied a squad of invaders pursuing a small group of Xhaldians—*more than likely,* he thought, *some of the transformed.*

Convinced he had found his "war zone," Riker looked for a place to put down. Finally, he located a plaza big enough and swung his shuttle into a position directly above it. Then he switched to reverse thrusters and eased the craft to the ground below.

None of the buildings surrounding him was more than a dozen stories tall. They were utilitarian, to say the least, each of them displaying the same oval windows and grey, unadorned facade.

The first officer waited until he was certain the shuttle was on firm ground. Then he got out of his seat and addressed his team of eight, which included Lt. Sovar and four other security officers as well as Storm and Shadowcat.

"Remember," he said, "there's nothing subtle about this. The idea is to take out as many Draa'kon as we can before they realize they've got a fight on their hands."

Storm looked at Riker skeptically. "They already *have* a fight on their hands, Commander. They have the transformed."

The first officer dismissed the idea with a gesture. "I heard the report about the prison, too," he reminded her. "But you're not going to tell me a gaggle of kids with untested abilities is going to stand up to a trained, alien invasion force."

The mutant frowned. "I have seen such youngsters stand up to greater adversity," she said. "And though I grant you that this is not my world, I would not be surprised if the transformed were the more serious threat before this day is over—not only to the populace, but to themselves."

Riker considered her advice. "Maybe that'll be the case," he conceded. "But for now, we'll hit the Draa'kon with everything we've got and worry about the transformed later."

"You are in charge of this mission," Storm told him. "I assured your captain that I would follow your instructions and I will."

That's all right, the first officer mused. She'll be a lot happier when the Xhaldians are safe from these predators.

"All right," he told his team. "Split up into pairs, as Captain Picard recommended. But stay in contact as much as possible. If you're injured, don't try to make it back to the shuttle—the Draa'kon may be watching it. Just remain where you are and we'll get you some help." He looked around. "Any questions?"

There weren't any.

Riker nodded. "Good."

Tapping a command into his helm console, he slid open the hatch door. Then he led the way outside. A few moments later, after everyone was out, the door closed again.

The first officer looked around. Half a dozen streets radiated from the plaza. Down one, he saw a glint of green light—evidence of the Draa'kon.

"You're with me," he told Storm, taking out his phaser and heading for the street in question.

The mutant didn't answer. She just followed.

Hearing footfalls in the corridor outside, Data looked up from the Draa'kon transporter console. Nightcrawler, who was standing by the door near a couple of stunned adversaries, gestured for the android not to worry.

"It's Worf's team," he said, remarkably enthusiastic despite his extreme fatigue. "They made it, Data!"

As the footfalls grew closer, the mutant showed himself and gestured for the others to hurry. A few moments later, the Klingon and his comrades burst into the room.

The android noticed that Archangel was injured. Also, one member of the team was missing. "Lt. Wayne?" he asked.

"Dead," said Worf.

"I am sorry to hear that," Data told him.

"An' we'll nae be much better off ourselves," Banshee noted, "unless we get a move on, lads."

Acknowledging the wisdom of the remark, the android returned his attention to the aliens' transporter console. "We can beam only four at a time," he said. "Mr. Ditko, you and Mr. Kirby will be in the first group. Also, Nightcrawler and Archangel."

No one argued. Everyone knew the Draa'kon might come charging into the room at any moment, at which point their opportunity would be lost.

The Draa'kon transporter grid, which was divided neatly into pie-shaped quadrants, stood only a meter or so from Data. Worf carried the winged man to it and placed him in the arms of the slender and still weak Nightcrawler, who was left to hold up his teammate as best he could. At the same time, Ditko and Kirby got on.

Nightcrawler grinned at the android. "See you back on the ship," he said.

Data nodded. "Back on the ship."

Then he dropped the *Connharakt*'s forward shields— a trick he had prepared in advance—and activated the Draa'kon transporter. The *Enterprise*'s shields weren't a problem, of course, as they weren't functioning.

A couple of seconds later, Ditko, Kirby, Nightcrawler, and Archangel were surrounded by ascending circles of neon blue. Then, with an abrupt burst of energy, they disappeared.

A few seconds later, the *Connharakt*'s shields went up again, as the ship's redundancies kicked in. However, the android had had enough time to beam his comrades back to the *Enterprise.*

Now came the slightly trickier part. After all, Data himself would be departing with the second group.

As Worf and Banshee took their places on the transporter grid, the android preset as many controls as he could and waited. Finally, he saw an indication that the *Connharakt*'s shields had dropped again.

Taking advantage of the opening, Data activated the transporter's delay function and stepped over the prone figure of the Draa'kon transporter operator, joining the others on the grid.

Turning to the room's entrance, he took out his phaser. Worf had his weapon in hand as well.

"How long?" Banshee asked.

"Only a few seconds," the android told him.

No sooner had he uttered his reply than he heard the sound of heavy footsteps outside the transporter room. It seemed their departure would not be a smooth one after all.

As soon as the Draa'kon showed themselves, Data used his phaser to level one of them and send another spinning into a bulkhead. Worf caused a third one to double over.

But there was still one more. Making his way through the phaser barrage, he took aim at Banshee and fired. As the mutant cried out, the android tried to shove him out of harm's way.

But he had a feeling he wouldn't be in time.

Suddenly, he found himself standing on an *Enterprise* transporter platform. To his surprise, Banshee was all right after all. And so was Worf.

Nightcrawler, Kirby and Ditko were waiting for them alongside Lt. Robinson, the transporter operator on duty. Archangel was present as well, though Dr. Crusher and her people were in the process of spiriting him off to sickbay.

Data turned to Banshee. "I believed you had been struck by a Draa'kon energy bolt," he said. "I am glad I was mistaken."

Banshee smiled a grim smile. "Fortunately, I had a moment t' show that bloody Draa'kon th' error of his ways. Or did ye think I was soundin' off merely for the fun of it?"

The android recalled the mutant's cry and understood. But then, after what he had seen Nightcrawler accomplish, he should have known better than to underestimate the resourcefulness of an X-Man.

Chapter Twenty-four

CAPTAIN'S LOG, SUPPLEMENTAL. *As we race to effect repairs to the* Enterprise, *I find myself locked in a stalemate with High Implementor Isadjo of the brutal Draa'kon.*

While our weapons and our deflector shields are useless at the moment, we still retain some mobility at impulse speeds. The Connharakt, *on the other hand, still boasts the use of her shields and some of her weapon batteries— but thanks to the success of our saboteurs, she sits dead in the water, incapable of offering pursuit.*

A message has been sent to the nearest starbase, notifying it of our predicament. Xhaldia is, therefore, assured of assistance, regardless of what happens to the Enterprise—*though I do not know when that assistance will arrive or in what form.*

In the meantime, I have ordered the dispatch of a third shuttle to the city of Verdeen on Xhaldia's northern continent. After all, our efforts will have availed us

180

*nothing if we cannot stop the Draa'kon from carrying out
their agenda on the planet's surface . . .*
  Whatever that agenda may be.

Crusher approached Archangel's biobed, where he lay
unconscious, recovering from his bout with a coalescing
force barrier. At least, that was how Worf had described
it.

Gazing at her patient, the doctor decided that Deanna
was right. The mutant *was* too handsome for his own
good.

Suddenly, Archangel's eyes opened wide, startling her
with their naked fury. His hand shot out and grabbed her
wrist, twisting it painfully.

"Where . . . ?" he gasped.

"The *Enterprise*," she told him gently, pulling her
hand back with an effort. "Sickbay. You were injured on
the Draa'kon ship . . . remember?"

Slowly, understanding began to dawn. "The *Enterprise*," he echoed.

"You suffered a considerable jolt to your nervous
system," the doctor explained, checking his vital signs
on the bed's readout. "With the help of our cell regenerators, you'll eventually be as good as new—but it'll take a
little time."

What she saw on the readout surprised her. Quickly,
she ran a diagnostic, which came up negative. Then she
scanned the biodata again, with exactly the same results.

It seemed Archangel was doing a lot better than she
had expected. In a couple of hours, he had made a full
day's worth of progress.

He frowned. "Where are my teammates?"

"They've gone down to the planet's surface," Crusher
told him. "To try to deal with the Draa'kon."

The mutant cursed and tried to sit up. Remarkably, he
succeeded.

"I should be with them," he said. "Storm and the
others . . ."

He tried to slide off the bed, but she restrained him. It

wasn't easy, either. Obviously, he had regained a good deal of his strength.

"They'll be all right," she told him.

Disgusted with his weakness, he allowed her to move him back again. "Are you sure about that?" he said.

Crusher wasn't, of course. Not any more than she could have been sure Lt. Wayne would survive the boarding of the *Connharalat*.

"I didn't think so," Archangel said. He turned away, no doubt imagining the worst.

"You feel responsible for them," she observed. "Even though you're not the one in charge."

Her patient turned to her again. "That's right. Storm's our leader . . . but I'm the one who's been around the longest." His eyes lost their focus for a moment. "I was one of the first, you know."

"The first . . . ?"

"X-Men," he told her. "A member of the original team formed by Professor Xavier, before the world had even heard of mutants."

"Professor Xavier," said the doctor. "He's your . . . leader?"

"Leader, mentor, father figure . . . all of that. Professor X was the one with the vision. He saw that a clash was coming between *homo sapiens* and *homo superior.* And he wanted the world to survive that clash—to see a day when mutants and normal humans could live together in peace."

"Sounds like a worthwhile goal," the doctor said.

Her patient shrugged. "Worthwhile—and maybe impossible."

"Things haven't worked out the way the professor planned?"

"Not so far," Archangel conceded.

His eyes glazed over, as if with memories he didn't feel like talking about. Then they brightened a bit.

"But the situation on Xhaldia is still new," the mutant told her. "It's still taking shape. The transformed have a better chance to lead normal lives than we did."

Crusher saw where he was going with this. "We'll help them," she reassured him. "And we'll do fine, with or without you."

He grunted. "You're just saying that to keep me from leaping out of bed."

"If you could leap out of bed," she countered, "I'd be the first to give you my blessing. But you can't, and we both know it."

Archangel scowled, his frustration showing. "Then at least let me sit on the bridge. I know my teammates, Doctor. At any given moment, I know what they'll do and how they'll do it. I can't imagine your captain wouldn't want to know it, too."

Crusher considered the mutant's request. Certainly, there was a big difference between sitting on the bridge and going into combat—and it would be a big help to have an X-Man at the captain's side.

"I'll ask the captain," she promised. "After that, it's in his hands."

"Fair enough," Archangel said.

The doctor started to move away—but he grabbed her hand. And while he didn't quite have the strength to hold her there, he was a lot closer to it than he had a right to be.

"Thank you," he told her.

She looked into the mutant's face and saw the determination there—the need to be a part of what was happening on Xhaldia. She would try to communicate that to the captain as well.

Still, there were no guarantees. "Don't thank me yet," the doctor said.

With a thrust of his arms, Sovar muscled himself up onto the roof. Then he reached back for Shadowcat, only to find her already floating up to him.

Together on the roof, they looked around at the surrounding area, all of it blanketed in a premature twilight by the dense cloud cover overhead.

A green flash from off to the north caught Sovar's eye. He turned that way and saw another one.

At the far end of a narrow, twisting alley, the lieutenant spotted what he was looking for—a handful of young Xhaldians. Perhaps four or five of them, running for their lives from a half-dozen well-armed Draa'kon.

At this distance, the Xhaldians looked as normal as he was, though the invaders' interest in them plainly suggested otherwise. Then Sovar got a glimpse of one particular youth, and his suspicion was confirmed.

He pointed for Shadowcat's benefit. "Look," he said, wincing in sympathy. "The poor boy."

The mutant looked, her hazel eyes narrowing at the sight. "I wonder if it hurts."

Sovar wondered, too. After all, the Xhaldian's bare arms, visible through large rips in his sleeves, were ridged over with huge, purple blood vessels. His legs seemed so heavy he could hardly run and there was barely any brush left on his head.

Then the lieutenant saw another directed-energy flash and remembered what he was doing there. His job was to stop the Draa'kon and he was determined to do that.

"None of those kids seem to be using their powers," Shadowcat commented. "They're too scared or they don't know how."

Sovar nodded in agreement. He could easily imagine their being frightened. If he had been transformed, persecuted, and hunted as they were, he would have been scared half out of his wits.

Unfortunately, the Draa'kon outnumbered the lieutenant and his partner, so it wouldn't do much good to go toe-to-toe with the brutes. Clearly, they had to take a different tack.

One thing was in their favor, Sovar noticed. The alley seemed to work its way around a row of buildings and return on the other side of the roof he was standing on. With a little luck, he might be able to plant himself there and pick off the Draa'kon as they went by.

Of course, the transformed had to elude the invaders

for another minute or so for the trap to work. And even then, there was no guarantee Sovar wouldn't be spotted after his first shot and destroyed. But in his line of work, there was *never* a guarantee.

The lieutenant turned to Shadowcat to tell her his plan—and realized he was standing on the rooftop all alone. He glanced this way and that, wondering what could have happened to her. Then he heard shouts and realized the chase was coming his way sooner than he'd thought.

Sovar couldn't afford to worry about the mutant anymore. He had to duck or take a chance on being detected prematurely.

Getting down on his belly, he inched over to the edge of the roof and scanned the labyrinthine alley in the direction of the transformed. No sign of them yet—or their pursuers either. But they were coming, all right.

Finally, he got the glimpse of them he needed. As far as Sovar could tell, the Draa'kon hadn't taken down any of the transformed yet.

It was as if they were herding the young people rather than hunting them. Driving them toward a particular place, where the Draa'kon were perhaps better equipped to capture them.

The one with the purple veins seemed to have the hardest time keeping up the pace. He stumbled and lurched as Sovar looked on. If the youth had ever been built for speed, he wasn't any longer. The lieutenant's heart went out to him.

"A little further," he whispered. "A little further."

Suddenly, he felt something grab him by the wrist. Instinctively, he wrenched it free—and was startled to see he'd been in the grasp of a hand reaching right out of the rooftop.

A moment later, a head floated up to join it—Shadowcat's head.

Sovar took a breath, let it out. "What are you doing?" he rasped.

"Sorry," she said. "I forgot who I'm dealing with."

She jerked a thumb in the direction of the alley. "Had to scout around a little. Get the lay of the land and so on."

Slowly, so he could see what she was doing, she took hold of the lieutenant's wrist again. "Just trust me," she told him. "Okay?"

He swallowed. "Okay."

A moment later, he began sinking through the roof, drawn by Shadowcat's gentle pull—though to him, it seemed as if the roof was rising all around him. It was a frightening, claustrophobic feeling. Something like falling through still water, except he had no trouble breathing.

When the roof rose to the level of his eyes, he began seeing the inside of the materials that made up the building—not a cross-section, exactly, but the way it looked within. Unfortunately, it was too dark for him to make out much in the way of details.

Then the darkness lifted and he could see again. He and Shadowcat were in a room—a dining alcove. But only for a moment. That slid past as well, as did another layer of floor.

Finally, Sovar found himself in another dining alcove—but this one was on the ground floor, just outside the alley. His companion let go of his hand and pointed to a broken window.

"You're on your own now," she told him.

"What about you?" the lieutenant asked.

"I'm not big on ray guns," she quipped, "but I'll find a way to make myself useful." And with that, she sank through the floor as if it were the easiest and most natural thing in the world.

"Good luck," he breathed, and took up a position by the window.

In a moment or two, the transformed went by, gathered in a tightly knit group—as if staying so close together would make them more secure somehow. Of course, it did just the opposite, making one big target out of them.

186

But Sovar wasn't really concentrating on the pursued. He was concentrating on their pursuers.

A heartbeat later, the Draa'kon went by his window as well. There were six of them—the number the lieutenant had counted earlier. All were armed. And all were making good speed, despite their lumbering gait.

Sovar took aim at the Draa'kon in the lead. But before he could press the trigger on his phaser, he saw the invader stumble and fall on his face. And when he went down, it forced his comrades to lurch to one side or the other in an effort not to trample him.

Had he never met Shadowcat, the lieutenant wouldn't have thought to glance at the ground in the Draa'kons' wake. But he *had* met her, so he looked for her telltale hand sticking up from the street.

And found it.

In the meantime, the Draa'kon were in disarray, and the mutant's interference had enabled the transformed to open a bigger lead. But none of it would mean anything unless Sovar took advantage of the situation.

Aiming along the body of his phaser, he triggered its crimson beam and watched one of the Draa'kon hit the ground. Since none of the enemy had seen the source of the beam, the lieutenant took another shot. A second invader staggered and collapsed.

By then, they had figured out where the phaser assault was coming from. Seeing the Draa'kon take aim at his broken window, Sovar ducked.

A moment later, both the window and the casing around it blew back into the room, propelled by a storm of emerald fury. Afraid the wall would be the victim of the next barrage, the security officer rolled sideways over tiny pieces of glass and debris to get out of the way.

But there *wasn't* any next barrage. Instead, Sovar heard a series of guttural shouts and saw a flash of pale light through the windowless opening. Crawling back to see what was happening in the street, he peered out just in time to watch a Draa'kon get hammered with a bolt of white energy.

For a second or so, the lieutenant didn't know where the bolt had come from. Then he saw the transformed with the ridged, purple veins lumber back into view on his right, the youth's fingers extended in the Draa'kons' direction.

Both of his hands were glowing like small suns.

But, strangely, that wasn't the quality about the transformed that surprised Sovar the most. The thing that stole his breath and left him numb in the knees was his realization that he *knew* the poor fellow. Knew him well, in fact. For he saw now that the wretch he had pitied earlier was his own younger *brother*.

Spurred by a new sense of urgency, the lieutenant fired at another Draa'kon and sent him sprawling. He didn't take cover again, either. He simply fired again, folding another of the invaders.

The last Draa'kon took careful aim and probably would have killed him with an energy blast, except he found something was grabbing his ankle. Looking down, the invader saw a pair of slender hands tugging at him.

Quite possibly, Shadowcat would have dragged the brute below the level of the street and left him there, but that wasn't Sovar's style. Before the mutant could carry out whatever scheme she had in mind, he stunned the Draa'kon with a burst from his phaser.

As if that were her cue, Shadowcat floated up through the surface of the street, brushing her hands against one another. The lieutenant recognized it as a human gesture of accomplishment.

"We came, we saw, we conquered," the mutant quipped.

However, Sovar wasn't in a jesting mood. Climbing through the opening where his window had been, he regarded the transformed who had been his brother—who was now kneeling in the street, attending to a comrade suffering from exhaustion. It made the lieutenant's stomach tighten to see his kin in such a hideous state.

"Erid . . . ?" he said tentatively.

Surprised by the use of his name, the younger Sovar looked up and found its source. For a moment, he stared at his older sibling, as if finding it hard to believe he was standing there.

Then his mouth twisted with hatred. "Get out of here!" he bellowed. "Leave us alone!"

The lieutenant winced at the venom in his brother's words. The Draa'kon's blasts couldn't have hurt much worse, he told himself.

"You need help," he told Erid. *"All* of you."

"We need *nothing* from the likes of *you!*" his brother rasped.

Then, as the security officer watched, his brother picked his friend up in his arms and started to walk away with her.

Chapter Twenty-five

CRUSHER FOUND PICARD on the bridge. He was sitting in the command center, gazing warily at the image of the Draa'kon vessel on the viewscreen.

With Riker and Troi gone, the seats on either side of the captain were empty. As the doctor sat down in one of them, Picard glanced at her.

"They're all stable," she said, answering his unspoken question. "Except Archangel, of course."

That drew the captain's interest. "Oh?"

"I'm not sure why," Crusher told him, "but he's recuperating a lot more quickly than I expected." She paused. "Did you read my report on him?"

"I did," Picard replied, turning back to the screen.

"Then you know Archangel has something unusual in his blood. Not a healing factor, like Wolverine's, but some kind of techno-organic material."

The muscles in the captain's jaw rippled. "And you think it may be the reason for his rapid recovery?"

"I'm starting to," the doctor told him. "Remember,

the Borg can repair themselves fairly quickly. Maybe he can as well."

"An interesting theory," he conceded, "but why hasn't Archangel displayed this propensity before?"

She shook her head. "Maybe it has something to do with the type of injury he sustained. Maybe it had to be goosed by the bioregeneration process. All I know is he should still be lying there, unconscious, and he's almost back to normal."

Picard gave Crusher a sidelong glance. "Why do I get the feeling you're about to ask me something I won't like?"

She smiled. "Archangel asked me to speak with you on his behalf. He thinks he can be useful here on the bridge, providing insights into the actions of his teammates."

The captain frowned. "Insights, indeed."

"Those are his friends down there," the doctor noted. "He wants desperately to help."

Picard didn't respond right away. "You're certain he's sound?" he inquired at last.

"Sound *enough,*" she answered. "And getting sounder all the time."

Again, the captain took some time before he spoke. "Very well," he said. "Tell him he's welcome here."

Crusher nodded. "Thank you, sir."

Picard sighed. "Thank *you.*"

Leaving the captain to his grim watch, she got up and headed for the turbolift. Archangel would be pleased, she thought. And perhaps he *would* be useful, if it came to that.

As the lift doors opened, the doctor entered the compartment and turned around. "Sickbay," she said. A moment later, the lift began to take her to her destination.

Halfway there, an idea struck her. A bizarre idea, she had to admit—but one that might prove exceedingly helpful to her. Maybe Archangel wasn't the *only* mutant on the ship who could provide some insights . . .

* * *

With the towering form of Colossus at her side, Troi walked slowly down the dismal, empty street, unaccustomed to the phaser in her hand. Her Betazoid senses reached out methodically in every direction, seeking friend and foe alike. However, this part of Verdeen was as abandoned as it had looked during their descent.

Anyway, that was how it seemed at first.

Then something registered in the counselor's mind—something brutal and bloodthirsty, gratified by the prospect of violence. Inwardly, she cringed, knowing that emotional terrain all too well.

She had made contact with a Draa'kon soldier. No—two of them, she told herself. And they weren't alone. There were gentler beings with them—beings wracked with fear, focused at the moment on self-preservation to the exclusion of all else.

Xhaldians, Troi noted. And they were in danger.

Grabbing the mutant's metallic arm, she pulled him toward the intersection ahead of them. "Come on," she said.

"You've found some Draa'kon?" he asked.

"Yes," the counselor told him, "Draa'kon—and Xhaldians as well. And if we don't hurry, the Xhaldians may not survive much longer."

Hearing that, Colossus picked up the pace, too. For someone who seemed to be made of metal he moved rather quickly, eating the ground ahead of them with long, loping strides. In fact, Troi was hard pressed to keep up.

At the end of the street, she turned right and the mutant followed. When they came to the end of that street, they turned left and kept running.

"How much further?" Colossus asked.

"Not much," the counselor told him, panting a little. "It feels like they're around the next corner."

As they approached the building at the end of the block, she slowed down and gestured for her partner to do the same. After all, she thought, she might be able to incapacitate the Draa'kon without exposing Colossus and herself to any danger. That was what phasers were for.

Finally, they reached the corner of the building. By then, Troi could hear voices. Apparently, the Draa'kon were interrogating the Xhaldians.

Lowering herself to one knee, she leaned forward and took a peek. She could see the Draa'kon, all right. And a couple of Xhaldians, too. The aliens had backed the natives up against a wall and were pointing their energy weapons at them with obvious intent.

". . . by the vegetable market," one of the Xhaldians was saying. "Just a couple of blocks from here. There are five or six of them."

"You will show us," one of the Draa'kon insisted.

"Be glad to," the Xhaldian told him. "You'll be doing us a favor, taking those monsters away with you."

"That's right," said one of the other Xhaldians. "They're freaks. They don't belong among decent people."

"And we're not the only ones who think so," the third Xhaldian added.

It wasn't just their fear talking, the counselor realized. They really felt that way about the transformed.

Colossus's brow knotted and he swore beneath his breath. "I have heard enough of such talk to last me a lifetime," he whispered.

Troi pulled her head back. "We've still got to help them," she told the mutant. "That's what we came here for."

He grunted, his expression still heavy with indignation. "It is always that way, is it not? They hate us, they revile us, and yet we help them anyway."

The Betazoid felt his pain. She felt his deep, abiding bitterness. But she also felt his resolve to see their mission carried out.

"You will have difficulty getting close to the Draa'kon," she said. "Perhaps I can stun them from here."

Colossus shook his head. "That will not be necessary," he replied.

Then he dug his metallic fingers into the wall in front of them. When he withdrew them, he had wrestled two chunks of it free.

"I, too, can operate at a distance," the mutant told her.

Troi looked at the chunks of building material in his hands and nodded appreciatively. "Yes," she said, "I suppose you can."

"What are we waiting for?" Colossus asked her.

The counselor shook her head. "Nothing at all."

Then they turned the corner and went after the Draa'kon together.

Crouched behind a pile of disruptor-blasted rubble, Data picked his head up for a moment, took aim, and squeezed off a shot. He saw his phaser beam miss a Draa'kon and strike a surviving wall beside him instead, showering the android's intended target with tiny fragments.

A moment later, the enemy returned his fire, destroying half of the debris protecting him. Before they could destroy the rest of it, Data gathered his legs underneath him and dove full-length for a bigger pile nearby.

Again, he drew a barrage of green disruptor bolts, but none of them hit his artificial body. Rolling to a stop, he waited until the barrage was discontinued. Then he raised his head again and reconnoitered.

Perhaps twenty of the Draa'kon had hunkered in the ruins of a couple of buildings they had all but leveled earlier. Beyond them, penned in by the aliens on one side and a sudden, steep hillside on the other, was a structure that sheltered an indeterminate number of Xhaldians—more than likely, some of the transformed.

From what the android had seen since his arrival planetside, the Draa'kons' perferred tactic was to herd the transformed—driving them from street to street or building to building—and then to capture the youths en masse. Their objective, as Storm had speculated on the *Enterprise,* seemed to be to take the transformed back with them to the *Connharakt.*

Why? Data had had a few moments to contemplate the question while his shuttle was descending, and he believed he had come up with some answers. However, there was no time to refine his theories at the moment. He and his comrades, under the leadership of Commander Worf, were too busy attempting to spoil the Draa'kons' kidnapping plans.

On the android's right, Banshee opened his mouth and blasted the remnants of a wall, exposing a pair of surprised Draa'kon soldiers. Without hesitation, Data skewered one with a discharge from his phaser. But several other beams failed to hit the second invader, and he lumbered to safety.

Then, as if the attack had annoyed them, the enemy emerged from cover all together and hammered the Starfleet officers' positions. The resulting volley was nothing short of devastating. What's more, it caught two of the android's comrades by surprise.

Jerking and spinning under the influence of the Draa'kons' disruptor bolts, Saffron and Bertaina fell and lay still. Data didn't have to feel their pulses to know they were dead. And now that he had emotions of his own, he was able to regret their passing as deeply as anyone.

"Himmel," came a cry from the pile of debris on his right.

Turning, he saw that it had come from Nightcrawler. "What is it?" the android asked the mutant.

"We're not getting anywhere this way," said Nightcrawler. "And if we run out of ammunition before they do . . ."

He didn't have to finish his sentence. Data knew well enough what would transpire at that point. He and his comrades would be forced to withdraw, leaving the transformed at the mercy of the Draa'kon.

To the android, that wasn't a viable option.

"How are you feeling?" he asked the mutant.

Nightcrawler looked at him, his golden eyes locked on Data's. "Not as bad as I thought I would after that jump to the Draa'kon ship." His eyes narrowed suspiciously. "Why do you ask?"

The android smiled. "I believe you know why. It might save some lives if we can get into that building and spirit the transformed out of it."

The mutant took a breath and let it out. "You ask a lot of me, my friend. It's a good thing I like you."

"Then you will do it?" Data pressed.

"Have I a choice?" Nightcrawler asked in return.

The android regarded him for a moment. "That is a rhetorical question," he concluded.

Covering the distance in a single bound, the mutant was beside him.

Unfortunately, the debris didn't offer sufficient cover for both of them. "Stay down," Data advised him, putting a firm hand on the mutant's shoulder.

"Don't distract me," came the reply. "When I'm tired, I need to concentrate even harder."

The android studied Nightcrawler's face, watching as his companion composed himself. After all, Data's positronic brain allowed him to catch nuances the human mind could not.

Still, he failed to pin down the precise moment at which the mutant effected the teleport. He simply came to the abrupt realization that he was no longer outside the beleaguered building, looking in. He was *inside* it. So was Nightcrawler. And they were standing in the midst of the transformed who had hidden themselves there.

"Someone's here!" cried one of the transformed.

"Please do not be alarmed," Data said calmly. "I assure you, we are not here to hurt you. In fact—"

"Liar!" shouted another of the youths.

"No!" the mutant yelled back. "We're not with the Draa'kon. We're—"

Before he could finish his disclaimer, the air around his head turned into a solid crystal. Unable to breathe, the already weakened Nightcrawler fell to the ground, his eyes staring and filled with horror.

The android knelt and took the crystal in his hands, hoping he could break it without harming his friend. But before he could make the attempt, someone raised her fist and pierced him with a bolt of charged plasma.

Data writhed uncontrollably, flopping around as if he had lost control of his limbs. And of course, he had.

His artificial body had always enabled him to tolerate a considerable degree of physical punishment. But when it came to a high-powered plasma charge, he was as vulnerable as anyone else.

"You do not . . . understand," the android told the transformed, trying to make their faces stop swimming in front of him. "We are not . . . not your enemies. We came here to . . . to offer . . ."

Before he could finish, he shut down.

Chapter Twenty-six

D<small>R</small>. C<small>RUSHER</small> <small>ENTERED</small> the holodeck and saw what she had created. It was a large room with hardwood walls and furnishings, where tall windows framed in heavy, red velvet drapes let in shafts of moonlight.

The place spoke eloquently of comfort and old-fashioned charm, not unlike her grandmother's house in the Caldos Colony. Comfort and charm and a quiet, stolid strength.

Here, a potted plant lent grace to an otherwise bare corner. There, an Oriental vase contributed a delicate beauty. And still elsewhere, a brick fireplace held the glow of burning embers.

Caught in that glow was a heavy, mahogany desk, the darkened computer monitor that sat on it, and what looked at first glance like a golden egg. A second look told the doctor that it was a chair of some kind, positioned with its back to her.

Then her gaze was drawn to the window beyond it, and she saw the reflection there. *His* reflection.

"Professor?" she ventured.

There was no answer—at least, not at first. But a moment later, the chair pulled back from the desk into the center of the room, where there was more room for it to maneuver. Then it turned around a hundred and eighty degrees, gradually revealing the man inside it.

The mutants were right, she thought. There was something of a resemblance after all. Crusher found herself smiling.

Xavier didn't smile back. In fact, he didn't seem to exhibit any expression at all. He merely made a pyramid of his fingers, as if that were a statement in itself.

"I find myself at a disadvantage," he told her.

"I'm sorry," the doctor said, remembering her manners. She came forward and offered the man her hand. "My name is Beverly Crusher. I'm the chief medical officer here."

The professor grasped her hand politely. "Here?" he echoed skeptically. "You mean in Salem Center? Pardon me for saying so, but I don't know any medical doctors who dress as you do."

She nodded. "I know you'll find this hard to believe, but we're not *in* Salem Center. We're on a starship. And . . ." She took a breath and let it out. ". . . you're not Charles Xavier."

He almost smiled, his eyes sparkling with firelight. "I'm not?"

"Not really," the doctor told him. "You're a holographic representation of Charles Xavier. I created you with data uploaded from your computer files when this ship was in your reality."

The professor regarded her intently. After a moment, he began to look concerned. "I can't enter your mind to verify your statements. I wonder why that would be."

"Because," she said, "there's no way to simulate your mental powers here in the holodeck."

Xavier's brow creased. "Holodeck? I thought you said we were on a ship of some kind."

"We are," Crusher replied patiently.

After all, she needed the man's help. They *all* did.

"The holodeck is a facility on our ship," the doctor explained. "In fact, there are several such facilities. They employ electromagnetic fields and omnidirectional image projectors to simulate objects, environments, . . . and even living beings."

The professor's eyes narrowed beneath his upswept eyebrows. "How interesting," he said.

"You bolievo mo, thon?"

"For the moment," he responded, "I'll accept your explanation as the truth—if only as an excercise in logic. Now, if I may ask . . . for what purpose did you create this simulation?"

Crusher found herself grateful for the man's intellect. Not every twentieth-century Earthman would have been able to accept what she had told him, even on a provisional basis.

"It seems," she said, "we have a problem on our hands."

She told him about the situation on Xhaldia. Then she told him about the X-Men's involvement in it.

"I understand you're a geneticist," the doctor went on. "One of the foremost geneticists on Earth, in fact."

"That's correct," Xavier said.

He didn't take any obvious pride in the description. He might as well have been discussing someone else's achievements as his own.

"And you've had extensive experience with mutations," she pointed out. "A great deal more than I have, certainly."

The professor nodded. "I see what you're getting at. You'd like me to assist you in understanding the Xhaldians' transformations . . . perhaps even contribute to an attempt to reverse them."

"Exactly right," Crusher confirmed. "I've asked our away teams to obtain information on the genetic makeup of the transformed. With any luck, they'll be bringing it back to me in the next several hours."

Xavier placed his forefinger against his temple. "And you expect a mere simulacrum—a collection of projected images and electromagnetic fields—to be helpful in this regard?"

"That depends," she said.

He tilted his head slightly. "On what?"

"On whether you're as good as they say you are."

For a second or two, the professor seemed to ponder her remark, examining it from one angle and then another. Finally, he spoke.

"I'm ready when you are," he told her.

As Data regained his senses and opened his eyes, he had one thought: *Nightcrawler.*

The last time he had seen the mutant, his fuzzy, blue head had been encased in a solid piece of crystal, which was preventing him from drawing a life-sustaining breath. If Nightcrawler had remained in such a condition for more than a few minutes, he had surely suffered brain death.

Leaping to his feet, the android scanned the room in which he found himself. It was tiny—more like a large closet, actually, a wan sliver of light coming through under its door. And he was alone, though his supersensitive hearing could pick up the sounds of not-so-distant battle.

Obviously, he was still in the building where he had lost consciousness. And if the fight outside was still going on, hardly any time could have elapsed. Unfortunately, his internal chronometer couldn't shed any light on that question; the electrical charge he had sustained had caused it to stop functioning temporarily.

In fact, *all* of him had stopped functioning. But as far as Data could tell, he was back in working order again.

Finding the door, he didn't bother to determine if it was locked. He simply straight-armed it and walked outside, ready for anything.

A couple of transformed whirled at the sight of him. One was the young woman who had shocked him into insensibility; however, the android didn't give her the chance this time. He crossed the room with inhuman

201

quickness and administered a nerve pinch he had learned years earlier.

The Xhaldian collapsed in his arms, providing a fortuitous shield against the powers of her companion. It was just as well, considering Data didn't know what the other transformed was capable of.

Whatever his abilities, he must not have considered them equal to the task. Instead of going after the android, he turned and ran into the next room, shouting a warning.

"The other one's awake!" he roared.

Relying on the element of surprise, Data burst into the room—the same one he and Nightcrawler had teleported into earlier. The transformed whirled, looking cornered and determined to defend themselves.

The mutant was there as well, lying against a wall in a pool of shadows. The crystal casing was gone from his head, but his eyes were closed and he wasn't moving.

The android moved to his comrade's side and checked his pulse. It was weak but detectable, and he was breathing on his own—a good sign. Still, he guessed Nightcrawler had been subjected to more than a lack of oxygen.

As Data got to his feet, one of the transformed pointed at him. "Stay where you are!" he warned him, "or we'll do to you what we did to your friend!"

The android shook his head sadly. "I tried to tell you before . . . we are not your enemies. In fact, we may be your only prospect of salvation."

"Don't listen to him," one of the transformed told the others.

Data turned to him. Unlike some of the youths, this one looked like any normal Xhaldian.

"Once our guards are down," the transformed went on, "he'll turn us over to the aliens! Do we want that?"

His companions answered him with a resounding: "No!"

The android held his hands out and moved out of the

shadows. "Why do you mistrust me so? Can you not see that I am like you?"

The transformed looked at him askance. "You're *nothing* like us," one of them railed.

"Nor am I like anyone else," Data replied evenly. "In fact, I am unlike any other creature in the entire galaxy."

He pushed up his uniform sleeve and opened the access compartment in his forearm. The display of circuitry inside him brought a gasp of surprise from the transformed.

"You see?" the android asked them. "I *am* like you. I am different. And because of that, I have been treated unfairly on occasion. I have even been ignored, which is sometimes worse than being treated unfairly. But despite everything, I still trust."

Having demonstrated his artificial nature, he closed the compartment in his arm and pulled his sleeve down. The transformed looked at him, still wary but apparently willing to hear him out.

Data looked down at Nightcrawler. "He, too, is different. On his world, he is shunned and even feared merely because he does not look and act the way normal people do."

"Would you do to Nightcrawler what others have done to him? What others have done to *you?*" the android asked. "Would you shun him and fear him without cause, simply because he is unfamiliar to you? Because he is . . . different?"

The Xhaldians looked at one another. There was no pride in their expressions, no righteous anger. There was only regret.

"If you were going to trust someone," Data continued, "would you not trust someone who had experienced what you are experiencing now? Someone like myself, perhaps . . . or Nightcrawler here?"

He had barely finished speaking when one of the transformed—a tall, almost gangly young man—got up and went over to the mutant. Bending down, he touched

Nightcrawler on the shoulder. Then he looked up at the android.

"It was a toxin," he said, by way of an explanation. "I make them. It kept him quiet."

"I see," Data responded. "And now you have neutralized it?"

The youth nodded. "He'll be all right in a moment or two."

His prediction was an accurate one. Within seconds, the mutant began to stir, then blink and sit up. He looked around wonderingly—first at Data and then at the transformed.

"Unh . . . ?" he began. Then he must have remembered, because he felt his face. "That crystal thing . . ."

"Is gone," the android assured him. "So are the toxins that kept you unconscious."

Nightcrawler digested the information, then glanced at the transformed. "You've convinced them we're not the enemy, obviously."

Data considered the Xhaldians. "I believe I have," he agreed.

"Tell us what you want us to do," said the youth who had been guarding the android in the other room.

"Just revive your friend—the one who was able to disable me with her electrical powers," Data advised him. "After that, Nightcrawler and I will do all the work. If all goes as we hope it will, you'll be somewhere safe in a matter of a few minutes."

"I'll go get her," the transformed responded.

As the youth left the room, the mutant placed his hand on the android's shoulder. "Good going, my friend. But what did you tell them?"

Data shrugged. "The truth."

Chapter Twenty-seven

"IT IS NOT going well," Isadjo muttered.

Ettojh, his second-in-command, slid his eyes toward him. "Did you say something, High Implementor?"

Isadjo considered his scanplate. He could see the *Enterprise* hanging in space against a backdrop of stars, no less a spikefly in his fleshfolds than when it arrived.

And yet, this spikefly—this mere annoyance, as it had seemed at first—had wrought havoc with his mission. And if it continued to do so, his faction's long-cherished hope of preeminence would die stillborn—a galling prospect, but one the Implementor couldn't ignore.

"It is not going well," Isadjo repeated, this time with more venom in his voice. "We have yet to complete our repairs, Ettojh. And the harvesting parties should have been on their way back by now."

"No doubt," said his second-in-command, "the teams from the *Enterprise* are impeding their efforts."

"Or stopping them altogether," Isadjo noted. "One thing is certain—we cannot give them much more time.

Not when Captain Picard has no doubt sent for reinforcements, which could arrive at any moment—and discover what we created on Xhaldia."

His second's gill-flaps fluttered uncomfortably. "The harvest has been so long anticipated, Implementor . . ."

Isadjo whirled on him, baring his several rows of teeth. "You think I don't *know* that, Ettojh? You think I don't feel the shame of ''

He stopped short of admitting his failure out loud. But clearly, that was what it was turning out to be—a failure. And yet, were there not *degrees* of failure? *Degrees* of shame?

If Picard's people had an opportunity to study the Xhaldians who had been transformed, they might be able to create a harvest of their own—which would make them a much more formidable enemy in the future. The Implementor couldn't allow that to happen; one never knew where the homeworld would turn for its next conquest.

"Our path is clear," he told Ettojh. "If our soldiers cannot bring in the harvest, we will have to make certain no one else receives it either."

His second didn't answer. He just made a sound of obedience in his cranial cavities and awaited Isadjo's orders.

Turning to his scanplate again, the Implementor wished he could reach out and crush the *Enterprise* in his big, leathery fist. But as long as the *Connharakt*'s propulsion systems were in disrepair, he couldn't mount any kind of offensive whatsoever.

Isadjo's mouth twisted. "This is what we will do . . ." he began.

Picard was standing in front of his command center, eyeing the Draa'kon vessel as if that alone would turn it to dust.

Behind him, at one of the stations rendered unusable by the Draa'kon attack, Archangel was no doubt regarding the *Connharakt* as well. He seemed even fitter than the captain had expected after his conversation with Dr. Crusher. In fact, one would scarcely guess what sort of injuries the mutant had sustained. However, if he had any "insights" regarding his teammates, he had yet to share them with anyone.

Picard sighed. He should have known Archangel's presence would be less than productive. The man was reckless, irresponsible—

Suddenly, Ensign Suttles called out his name.

Picard glanced at the tactical officer, who had taken over in Sovar's absence. "Yes, Mr. Suttles?"

"Sir, the Draa'kon are powering up another hull port. But it doesn't seem to be a directed-energy device."

The captain returned his attention to the screen. If the enemy wasn't bringing another weapon to bear, what *were* they doing?

Suddenly, he got his answer—as a cluster of linked black spheres shot out from the *Connharakt* and headed for Xhaldia. "What *is* that?" he asked.

"Scanning," said Suttles. "Sir, it's some kind of explosive device." He tapped out a command and read another monitor. "It's headed for—"

Picard knew the answer even before the ensign uttered it.

"—Verdeen!" Suttles gasped.

The captain cursed himself for not having seen it in advance. With the transformed denied to the Draa'kon, the aggressors had decided no one else would have the uniquely talented youths either.

Of course, the enemy's directed-energy weapons couldn't penetrate the planet's energy barrier. So they had to try a different tack—an explosive device powerful enough to kill the transformed and everyone else in the vicinity. And if the device boasted its own guidance system—which was no doubt the case, since its target was deep in Xhaldia's atmosphere—even the Draa'kon couldn't call it back anymore.

"How long do you estimate until detonation?" Picard asked.

Suttles didn't hesitate. "Twelve minutes and thirty-five seconds, sir."

The captain bit his lip. There was still time to do something about the device. But *what?*

With the *Enterprise*'s weapons systems off-line, he couldn't destroy the missile from where he sat. And without any of the Xhaldians' booster satellites to help him, he couldn't contact his personnel on the surface either.

Picard's only chance to defuse the threat was to take another shuttle and go after it. But even then, it seemed, his options were extremely limited.

If he destroyed the device in the planet's atmosphere, the ensuing blast would likely kill him. Nor could he beam the missile aboard his shuttle, since the transport process might detonate it as well.

Seize control of the device with a tractor beam? The captain doubted he would be able to pilot a shuttle through Xhaldia's energy-laden atmosphere and perform such a delicate tractor operation at the same time—even if he had help from one of his remaining officers.

In the end, he told himself, there was really only one course of action open to him. He would have to catch up with the device and set it off with a phaser beam. If his life was the price he had to pay to save Verdeen from destruction, he would do so—and do it gladly.

Picard turned to Rager. "You have the bridge," he told her. Then he headed for the turbolift.

Suddenly, he found Archangel barring his way. "Where are you going?" the mutant asked him.

"To a shuttle bay," the captain responded, though he need not have said a thing. Then he gave Archangel a look that made him move out of the way.

The lift doors opened and Picard got inside. But he didn't get inside alone. The mutant came with him.

As the doors closed, Archangel turned to him. "You're going after that cluster missile, aren't you?"

The captain didn't return the winged man's scrutiny. "As it happens," he said, "I am. Computer—Shuttlebay One."

The lift began to move.

"Take me with you," said Archangel.

Finally, Picard looked at him—his expression a skeptical one. "Why would I do that?"

"Because I can help," the mutant told him. "I may not be a hundred percent, but I can probably fly at peak efficiency for a short period of time. With a little luck, I can make it to the missile and disarm it."

The captain shook his head. "We don't know anything about the technology that went into it."

"But we *will*," Archangel insisted. "When we're up close and personal with it, you'll scan it with those high-powered, sophisticated instruments of yours and figure out what makes it tick."

"Even so," said Picard, "the friction created by its passage through the atmosphere will render it too hot to handle."

"Can you slow it down?" the mutant asked.

Picard glared at him. "Yes, with a tractor beam. But if you make a mistake? And the device explodes in your face?"

Archangel smiled a taut smile. "Then you'll have one less annoying X-Man flying around your ship."

"This is not a laughing matter," said the captain.

His eyes blazing, the mutant pounded his fist against the side of the lift. "Listen to me," he demanded. "I know we've had our differences. And believe me, I'm not apologizing for anything. But we both know there's liable to be fallout from that cluster. Even if you detonate it in the air, every Xhaldian within a hundred miles could be caught in its drift."

Picard wished Archangel was wrong about that. But there was a chance that what he was describing would come to pass.

There *could* be fallout. In that case, the captain's

sacrifice would have been for nothing. And the worst part was, he would never know if he had succeeded in saving Verdeen.

As he regarded the winged man, the muscles rippled in Picard's temples. "We *have* had our differences—you're right about that. Unfortunately, I don't have so many options that I can afford to turn one down."

"Then you'll accept my offer?" asked Archangel.

The captain grunted. "Don't make me regret it."

The lift doors opened a moment later, revealing Shuttlebay One. Together, Picard and the mutant headed for the nearest pod.

Chapter Twenty-eight

SOVAR WATCHED HIS brother walk away under the silver-gray sky. For just a moment, he was tempted to let Erid have his way. Then he realized he couldn't do that.

Overtaking his brother, he placed himself in the youth's path. "Blood of the ancients," he pleaded, "just listen to me for a moment."

"Go away," said Erid.

"I won't," the lieutenant insisted.

"You had no trouble going away before," his brother reminded him, shifting the weight of the half-conscious woman in his arms.

"That was different," said Sovar. "It was something I had to do. But I can't leave you here like this, at the mercy of those Draa'kon. Come with me, brother. I can help you."

Erid shook his head. "I don't need your help."

"You *do,*" the security officer insisted. "You don't know what you're up against in these aliens."

"Don't you think I've seen what they can do?" his

brother railed at him. "Don't you think I've seen the transformed they've dragged into their vehicles?"

"Then what are you waiting for?" Sovar wondered. "Let me take you someplace safe. Let me—"

"There *is* no place safe for me," Erid spat.

He held his chin up, displaying the purple veins popping out of his neck. He wriggled the fingers that were glowing with a soft, yellow light.

"I'm a freak, can't you see that?" he demanded. "I'm a monster. Just ask the government that put me in a prison when I hadn't done anything wrong, or the guards who looked at me from their battlements with pity and disgust . . ."

"No," said the lieutenant. "You're Erid Sovar. You're blood of my blood. And for the ancients' sake, you've got to—"

Before Sovar could finish his plea, he saw his brother's eyes grow wide. He watched Erid drop his friend's legs with one hand, then raise his glowing fingers and point them in the lieutenant's direction. And he saw the burst of deadly white light that sprang from those fingers.

Sovar closed his eyes, certain that his brother had decided to destroy him after all in a fit of rage and resentment. But as it turned out, he was wrong about that.

The bolt of energy never touched him. Instead, it leaped right past him . . . and struck a Draa'kon soldier who had recovered his weapon, sending him sprawling backward in the street.

The invader didn't move. And for a moment, neither did the security officer, as he realized how close he had come to death. Turning, he looked at his brother again.

"He was going to blast you in the back," Erid said, still holding his friend in his arms. He shook his head, tears welling in his eyes. "I couldn't let him do that."

"Of course you couldn't," Sovar replied. "No more than I could let anyone hurt *you*. You're my brother, after all—no matter what's happened to either one of us."

212

Neither of them said anything for a moment. Then the lieutenant held out his hand. Erid clasped it.

"Come on," Sovar told him, clapping him on the shoulder. "We've got to get you someplace safe."

His brother picked up his friend's legs and turned to the other transformed standing in the street with them. "You've got to get us *all* someplace safe," he said.

"Amen to that," remarked Shadowcat.

Taking the lead, Sovar showed them the way to his shuttle.

Troi walked down yet another gray, abandoned street, listening to the sound of shouts in the distance, probing past the oval windows on either side of her for evidence of a Draa'kon trap.

Colossus walked beside her, doing his best to remain wary also. But his emotions were still roiling over the three Xhaldians they had rescued minutes earlier—or more to the point, what the Xhaldians had *said*.

About the transformed being monsters—freaks—who didn't belong among decent people. About them not being the only ones who thought so.

Naturally, Colossus had taken offense at their remarks. After all, in his mind, there wasn't much difference between the transformed and the mutants of his Earth.

The counselor recalled the looks on the Xhaldians' faces when they saw who had rescued them. Without saying a word of thanks, they had taken off—no doubt afraid they had exchanged one captor for another.

It was just as well, Troi thought. Colossus had been filled with so much heartache, so much animosity, he might have done something to the Xhaldians he would regret later on.

Suddenly, her thoughts were interrupted by another set of cries—more immediate than any of the others they had heard. Instinctively, the counselor broke into a run, her destination the intersection ahead of them. The

213

mutant caught up with her after a moment or two, then forged ahead.

When they reached the cross-street, Troi's attention was drawn to the next intersection on her right. A handful of the transformed had stopped dead in their tracks there—apparently, to pick up one of their number who had fallen.

But as they pulled their comrade to her feet, a barrage of energy beams sliced the air around them. What's more, they weren't the green disruptor bolts of the Draa'kon. They were blue in color and a lot narrower.

But who . . . ?

A moment later, the counselor got her answer. The transformed ran away and left Troi's line of sight. But they were replaced by a large mob of Xhaldians, many of them wearing blue uniforms—and all of them armed with energy weapons.

The city guards, the counselor thought, and some citizens who had rallied around them. And they were firing at the transformed, when the Draa'kon were the real threat.

Troi could feel the Xhaldians' fear and hatred burning themselves into her consciousness. The civilians in the group, more wide-eyed than the others, brandished their weapons and yelled for their enemies to go back where they came from.

It alarmed and annoyed the counselor to see it. But as she found out, Colossus was *more* than annoyed . . . he was *livid.*

As the mutant had told her, he had seen crowds react this way against his kind before. It was no wonder he was full of anger and resentment at seeing it now.

Suddenly, his outrage rose to a crescendo. "No!" he bellowed at the top of his lungs.

And with unmitigated disgust for those who would persecute society's outcasts, the mutant raced down the street. His fury was so great, so terrible, Troi was rooted to the ground.

But only for a second. Then she went after him, not

knowing whether she should fire her phaser at the Xhaldians or at Colossus.

With his long strides, the mutant reached the intersection before the mob had completely passed through it. By then, he had drawn the attention of the city guards, who pointed their weapons at him and ordered him to stop.

They might as well have asked a sun not to blaze. Condemning the Xhaldians for their narrow-minded stupidity, Colossus plowed into their midst.

Grabbing the barrel of a weapon, he ripped it from a guard's grasp and hurled it down the street. Then he grabbed another weapon and did the same with it.

Some of the Xhaldians tried to batter him or bear him to the ground, but the mutant took hold of them and tossed them away. Before long, five or six of them lay in the street, stunned and disarmed.

"That's enough!" Troi cried as she arrived on the scene, worried that someone might get killed in the melee.

Of course, the transformed had been running that risk at the hands of the guards all along, but she had to face one problem at a time.

Suddenly, she saw the transformed who had fled the guards before. But they weren't running away anymore. They were rushing *into* the guards' midst.

As if for . . . protection? Troi thought.

More confusing yet, the guards were still firing their weapons. But, as the counselor realized in the next instant, they weren't aiming at the transformed. They were aiming *past* them—at a squadron of Draa'kon.

The invaders were their targets all along, Troi told herself. The transformed had only been caught between the mob and its adversaries.

"Colossus!" she cried, seeing him wrench yet another weapon from its owner's grasp. "Stop and look around—they're not the enemy!"

Hearing the counselor's voice cut through the din, the mutant turned and saw her point to something. Following her gesture, he caught sight of the Draa'kon just in time to avoid a bright green energy bolt.

It wasn't the only one, either. The invaders were unleashing a barrage calculated to bring the Xhaldians to their knees.

Colossus was open-mouthed with surprise and embarrassment, but he wasn't the type to give up so easily—and neither was Troi. As she leveled blast after blast at the Draa'kon, the mutant picked up one of the guards' weapons and squeezed off an energy burst of his own.

The guards untouched by Colossus continued to fire as well. But one after the other, they went down, unconscious, under the weight of the invaders' attack. The tide was turning against the retreating Xhaldians—in part because of the mutant's costly blunder.

In effect, the counselor thought, Colossus was guilty of the same kind of rash judgment he had always detested in others. It was an irony he seemed destined to regret.

However, just as it appeared the Draa'kon would overrun them, a phaser barrage struck the aliens from behind. Two of them went down, then two more.

Before the Draa'kon could whirl and return fire, a blue and yellow dervish was among them, kicking and striking and slicing with long, sharp claws. Ignoring the Xhaldians, they attended to this new threat.

But attending to Wolverine and stopping him were two different things.

The mutant displayed none of the bluster that had gotten him in trouble at Starbase 88. He conducted himself like a warrior, as devastatingly efficient as Worf on his best days, and Troi was unutterably pleased he was on their side.

Then, just in case the Draa'kon weren't beleaguered enough, the gargantuan Colossus waded into them as well. That gave the rest of them—the counselor, the security officers, and the city guards—the luxury of picking off the enemy almost at will.

It wasn't long before the Draa'kon succumbed.

Standing knee-deep in fallen adversaries, Wolverine retracted his claws and tossed a grin in Troi's direction. "Thanks fer leavin' a few fer *me,* Darlin'."

She chuckled wearily. "My pleasure."

However, Colossus was feeling anything but pleased. Finding a couple of the city guards, he made a point of apologizing to them for his mistake.

No doubt, the counselor thought, it would be a long time before the mutant forgot this lesson.

Picard plunged through Xhaldia's upper atmosphere at the controls of his shuttlepod, making adjustments every few seconds as the vessel bucked another wave of energy-laced turbulence.

Archangel was hanging on to the back of the captain's seat, as intent on Picard's monitor screens as he was. No doubt, he could see the red blip on the one that tracked the cluster missile's progress.

"How are we doing?" the mutant asked.

"So far, so good," the captain told him without turning around. "At this rate, we will overtake our target in slightly more than a minute."

What he didn't say was that they were proceeding at a speed faster than the pod was designed for. But then, even after they caught up with the missile, Archangel would need time to reach it and disarm it.

"It's getting warm in here," the mutant noted.

"So it is," Picard confirmed.

That was what happened when one pushed the limits of one's shielding against the increasing friction of descent. The physics were simple—the denser the atmosphere, the more quickly a vehicle would burn up. Or at the very least, bake anyone inside it to a crisp.

The pod shuddered and threatened to veer off course, so the captain directed more power to the stabilizers. A bead of perspiration traced a path down the side of his face. He wiped it away with the back of his hand.

Archangel pointed to the screen with the red blip. Another blip had joined it and was approaching it steadily, though its progress belied the difficulty of piloting the pod.

"Looks like we're in the ballpark," the mutant observed.

Picard wasn't a fan of 20th-century sports, but he understood the reference. Seeing no need to reply, he tried scanning the cluster missile. After all, Archangel couldn't disarm it if the captain couldn't determine how it worked.

Unfortunately, his sensors couldn't tell him much about the missile's inner workings yet. The energy permeating the atmosphere was getting in the way, giving Picard a distorted and incomplete picture.

And it was getting hotter. *Much* hotter.

The captain could feel the sweat trickling down both sides of his face now. His uniform was wet, too. He desperately wanted to remove his tunic, but didn't dare—not with the pod jumping and quivering the way it was.

Worse, their deflectors were starting to buckle under the strain. Even with the shields in working order, the temperature in the cabin had risen thirty degrees. If the deflectors deserted them at this speed, they wouldn't survive long enough to *see* the missile, much less disarm it.

But on the monitor screen, at least, there was good news. One red blip was swiftly overtaking the other.

"Get ready," Picard said.

Archangel moved to the hatch in the side of the pod. "You still haven't told me what to do when I get there," he pointed out.

"I will," the captain assured him.

Little by little, his sensors delivered a more intelligible insight into the mechanics of the cluster. Picard studied them, queried the onboard computer, studied them some more, and queried again.

At last, he got the answer he was looking for. Keeping his eyes on his controls, he described out loud what the mutant would have to do.

"It won't be easy," the captain finished. "But then, you knew that when you volunteered for this."

Like Picard, Archangel was sweating profusely. "At least I won't have to stay here and wilt," he quipped.

Indeed, the heat was getting unbearable. And it wasn't likely to get any better when the captain tried to slow the missile's descent.

A moment later, the red blips on his screen converged. Picard looked out his observation port and glimpsed the cluster through ragged layers of high clouds. The device wasn't more than a hundred meters away.

He decelerated to match its speed. Then, confirming that he had dropped below the altitude of Xhaldia's energy bands, he reached for another set of controls.

"I'm extending tractor beams," he said, wiping heavy drops of perspiration from his eyes.

It was hotter in the pod than the hottest desert the captain had ever known. But in his youth, he had been a marathon runner. He could stand it, he told himself. He *would* stand it.

With infinite care, he locked the tractors onto the cluster. Then, when he was certain the connection was secure, he began to apply reverse thrusters—not in the hopes of stopping the missile altogether, but to diminish its surface temperature so the mutant could handle it.

Immediately, Picard felt a jolt—an indication of the extra load imposed on his thrusters. The cabin temperature began to climb at a terrifying rate.

However, both the missile and the pod were slowing down. Glancing at his monitors, the captain saw the change in their rate of descent. Four hundred kilometers per hour . . . three hundred and fifty . . . three hundred . . .

"Go," he rasped, fighting to keep from succumbing to the heat.

"I'm gone," Archangel responded.

Picard touched a pad on his panel and opened the hatch, exposing the pod's interior to a blast of frigid wind. Glancing over his shoulder, he saw the mutant spread his wings and corkscrew his way out of the cabin.

Godspeed, the captain thought. Then he pushed the pad again and saw the hatch slide closed.

Chapter Twenty-nine

RIKER KNELT BESIDE the Draa'kon.

The invader was covered with earth and fragments of pavement, one of which had caved his skull in. His eyes were staring, a rivulet of green blood drying in the corner of his wide, lipless mouth.

The first officer looked up at his companion. Storm's hair lifted in the breeze as she gazed at the other Draa'kon in the vicinity. All of them were dead, all partially buried beneath a shattered landscape of dirt and rubble that stretched for a hundred meters in either direction.

"If we dig around," she said bleakly, "we will no doubt find a great many more of them."

"That may be," Riker allowed. He got to his feet. "The question is . . . who did this?"

The mutant looked at him pointedly. "Who do you think?"

"You're going to tell me it was the transformed?" he asked.

"Who else could it have been, Commander? The city

guards? Do they have weapons capable of creating such upheavals?" With a gesture, she indicated the buildings on either side of the street. "Can they wreak this kind of havoc without breaking a single fragile window?"

The first officer shook his head. He had seen the X-Men in action. He knew people like them could have unusual abilities. But to ascribe such monumental destruction to beings who had barely come to know what talents they possessed . . .

Then he recalled what it was like when Q endowed him with virtual omnipotence, and his perspective changed. He had been in control of his powers from the get-go. Suddenly, it didn't seem quite so far-fetched for even a neophyte to tear up a street.

He was about to admit that Storm might have been right when he heard a series of distant cries, followed by a rumbling and an unsettling vibration beneath their feet. Riker's instincts told him an earthquake was underway, but his mind insisted otherwise.

Storm shot into the air, her garments fluttering in a wind that appeared to have come from nowhere. She seemed bent on tracking the thunder in the earth to its source.

"Hey!" he shouted at her. "What about me?"

Glancing back at him over her shoulder, the mutant weighed his question for a moment. Then she executed a tight turn and zeroed in on him.

The next thing the first officer knew, he was soaring in the direction of the dense, gray sky, Storm's slender but strong fingers locked around his wrist. His senses reeled, but he kept his eyes open, not wanting to miss a single moment of it.

When he had had the powers of a Q at his disposal, Riker had never thought of using them to fly. Now, as he and the mutant rose higher than the highest building in Verdeen, he regretted the oversight.

Just a little while earlier, he had sailed over the city in a shuttle. But this was different, he told himself. *Very* different.

In a matter of seconds, he spotted the scene of confusion and chaos where the cries and the vibrations had come from. So did Storm, apparently, because she changed direction and swooped like a bird.

They bore down on the place with breathtaking speed, slipping past a rooftop and landing on ground that was still level and whole. Then they sized up the challenge ahead of them.

As in the last place they had come across, there were plenty of Draa'kon corpses strewn about, half-buried under earth and debris. But here, there were other corpses as well—the twisted, broken bodies of blue-suited city guards, civilians, and even what appeared to be some of the transformed.

At the center of it all, standing on a high mound of earth that seemed to have risen straight through the pavement, stood a single figure—a tall, slender Xhaldian with a crooked smile on his face.

He wasn't alone, either. Four others, who appeared to be his accomplices, were standing at the base of the mound with Draa'kon disruptors in their hands. Judging by their appearances, at least two had come from the ranks of the transformed.

A little further off, half a dozen plainly terrified Xhaldians were huddled in the lee of an uprooted chunk of pavement. When they saw Riker and Storm approach the scene, hope illuminated their expressions.

"And who have we here?" asked the Xhaldian on the mound, his tone a cruel and disdainful one.

More than likely, he was the one who had caused all this destruction—hard as that was for the first officer to believe. He came forward.

"I'm Commander William Riker of the *U.S.S. Enterprise.*" He pointed to the heavens. "The ship that's fighting for the life of your world up there."

"How helpful," the Xhaldian responded. "Though, as you can see, we freaks are perfectly capable of handling the invaders on our own."

He has a point, the first officer told himself. It was just as Storm had predicted. The transformed had become a bigger threat than the Draa'kon.

"Who *are* you?" asked the mutant, taking her place beside the first officer.

The Xhaldian's smile turned hard. "My name is Rahatan. I'm the one in charge around here—in case you hadn't noticed."

Her eyes narrowed. "By whose authority are you in charge?"

The Xhaldian glared at her. "By my own."

Suddenly, one of his allies on the ground put his hands to his head and shouted a warning. Whirling, Rahatan found himself eyeing a pair of *Enterprise* security officers, their phasers extended in his direction.

Wilkes and Calderon, Riker thought. Two of the men from his shuttle.

"Come down from that mound," Calderon told Rahatan.

The Xhaldian shook his head. "Come here and get me."

"Stay where you are," Riker yelled.

Wilkes and Calderon froze, awaiting further orders. But to the first officer's dismay, it didn't save them.

The ground exploded underneath them, flinging them high in the air. By the time they came back to earth, they were too broken and bloody to still be alive.

Riker's resolve sharpened in the heat of his anger; he took advantage of the distraction to fire at Rahatan himself. But something protected him from hitting the Xhaldian—some kind of translucent shielding that deflected the force of the phaser beam.

Looking at the foot of the mound, he could see where it had come from. One of Rahatan's lackeys had reached up and used her power to protect him.

The Xhaldian turned around again to face the first officer. "That was ill-advised," he said in a strangely reasonable tone. Then he began to point in Riker's direction.

"Stop!" shouted Storm.

Intrigued, Rahatan glanced at her. "Why should I?"

"Because you cannot kill *him* until you have killed me first. And that is something you will never accomplish."

A smile returned to the Xhaldian's face. "Is that a challenge?"

The mutant shrugged. "If you like."

"You've made a mistake."

"Have I?" Storm asked.

"A big mistake," Rahatan told her, reeking of confidence. "You don't know what you're dealing with here."

"I see," she said. "I am overmatched?"

"That's one way to put it."

"I am taking my life in my hands?"

"That would be another way."

Storm's eyes narrowed. "Under the circumstances, what do you propose I do? Give up?"

He shrugged, his expression becoming almost playful. "You're a handsome woman. I think I could find a place for you. Next to me, maybe."

"You are too kind," she told him, her voice free of hostility. "But I think I will take my chances against you rather than alongside you. You see, I have faced your kind before."

"My *kind?*" he echoed.

Storm nodded. "You are powerful, no doubt. But what you have gained in power, you have lost in visual acuity."

His forehead creased. "What are you talking about? My eyes are as good as they ever were."

She shook her head. "You only see the things your power can obtain for you. You've lost the ability to look into your heart . . . and discern right from wrong."

His eyes blazed, and he gestured to the corpses he had buried. "You think it's wrong to kill someone who's trying to kill *you?*"

"I think it's wrong to kill *anyone,*" Storm insisted. "There is always another way, if one tries hard enough to find it."

His mouth twisted. "I can only think of *one* way to deal with insects—and that's to crush them underfoot!"

She didn't lose her composure. "Then perhaps you are not as powerful as you have come to believe."

A cry of rage tore from him—and with a sound like thunder, the earth cracked open between Storm's feet. In a heartbeat, the crack became a fissure and the fissure became a gaping crevasse, causing the mutant to lose her footing and slip into the widening hole.

No! thought Riker.

But there was nothing he could do to save her.

"That will teach you to question my power," the earth-mover bellowed, shaking a fist at the departed Storm.

Suddenly, Riker saw Rahatan forced back from the edge of the fissure—not by anything solid, but rather by a lusty, howling wind that seemed to emerge from its depths.

The first officer knew it didn't make any sense for a wind to be rising out of newly cracked earth. Still, he wasn't complaining—because a moment later, that same wind lifted Storm into sight, her uniform and silver hair whipping all about her, her head held high.

She's alive! Riker realized. Alive and whole—or at least, no more injured than she had been when this started.

Surprised and frustrated, Rahatan gave voice to his fury. Then he brought his arms up as if he were lifting weights. The ground around him shuddered and groaned miserably, and two large chunks of earth and masonry tore loose from their foundations.

The Xhaldian gestured again, flinging the fingers of one hand in Storm's direction. Instantly, one of the chunks of earth went hurtling at her.

But as Riker had learned, the mutant knew how to take care of herself. She countered with a gesture of her own, destroying the missile with an explosive flash of blue-white lightning.

Even before all the debris had fallen to the ground,

Rahatan hurled the other chunk of earth. But Storm created another lightning bolt and demolished that one as well.

By then, Rahatan's allies must have decided the combat wasn't going their way. One of them, a specimen with luminous eyes, raised his Draa'kon disruptor rifle and took aim at the airborne mutant.

But before he could press the trigger, Riker nailed him with a phaser beam. The transformed slammed into the mound of earth behind him, his weapon sliding out of his hands.

Turning to Rahatan's other supporters, the first officer fired at each of them in quick succession. The one with the green pocks on his forehead was knocked senseless, while the female's shielding protected her from a second beam.

She raised her weapon to fire back at him, but Riker wasn't about to stand there and provide an easy target for her. Dropping and rolling, he squeezed off another blast. It caught his adversary in the midsection, doubling her over this time and taking her out of the fray. Apparently, her shielding could only take so much.

But there was one more around, the first officer told himself. A powerful-looking Xhaldian in some kind of natural body armor. Some sixth sense told him to turn around. Whirling, Riker saw Rahatan's last remaining lackey charging at him.

The first officer sidestepped the charge successfully—but in the process, his foot caught on a piece of upturned pavement, causing him to stumble and fall unceremoniously. Even worse, he lost his grip on his phaser. As he watched, it clattered away and fell into a crack in the pavement.

Seeing how vulnerable he was, the strongman dove in an attempt to pin him, but Riker threw himself out of the way and scrambled to his feet.

Unfortunately, he was nowhere near where his phaser had fallen. And without it, he was clearly overmatched.

Or *was* he?

As the Xhaldian in the body armor got up and charged him a second time, the first officer bent and picked up a rock. Then, before the transformed could veer off, Riker reared back and let it fly—striking his adversary square in the forehead.

At first, he thought it might not have been enough. Then the transformed's knees buckled and he fell forward on his face.

The first officer had no time to congratulate himself, however. On the other side of the ruined street, Storm was still facing off with the earth-mover.

By that time, the Xhaldian had to know how badly he had underestimated his opponent. Still, it didn't seem to daunt him a great deal. With a battle oath worthy of a Klingon, Rahatan tossed his head back and raised his hands, which had clenched into white-knuckled fists.

Unbelievably, the ground beneath him began to rise and roll forward, in the manner of a mammoth wave breaking on a seashore. Except the wave had a target, and that target was Storm.

The Xhaldian rode forward on the wave's unchanging crest, legs spread wide for balance, fists clenched at his sides. He had a look of almost maniacal glee on his face.

But Storm didn't move. She simply floated on her updraft above the mighty crevasse, as if she had already resigned herself to her fate. And all the while, Rahatan's wave of earth and debris rolled closer, threatening to bury her under its weight.

Finally, just as her adversary was about to descend on her, the mutant raised a hand to the heavens. As Riker watched, a hail shower seemed to come out of nowhere, pelting the Xhaldian with tiny balls of ice.

Rahatan threw his hands up to protect himself from Storm's onslaught. At first, it looked as if he might be able to stay on his feet and endure it. Then the rain of icy pellets grew heavier and heavier, until the barrage drove the earth-mover to his knees.

But Rahatan wasn't done yet. Though battered and

228

bruised, he still possessed the strength to try one last gambit.

The crest of his earth wave, with him on it, seemed to topple backwards for a moment. Then, like a catapult, it shot forward—flinging the Xhaldian across the gulf between Storm and himself.

And why not? He was bigger than she was, and more powerful. If he could get his hands around her throat, it wouldn't matter that she was a mutant. He would throttle her in no time.

But once again, Storm proved more than equal to the challenge. Before Rahatan could reach her, he was caught in a swirling twist of wind. It wrenched him skyward, spinning him around as he ascended, until he was a hundred meters or more above the ground.

The earth-mover screamed for help, but he didn't get any. His compatriots were all unconscious. So Rahatan kept spinning around, faster and faster, until at last he stopped screaming and went limp in the twister's grasp.

Only then did Storm relent. Gradually, with remark-able gentleness considering how recently the Xhaldian had tried to kill her, she lowered his unconscious form to street level. Finally, when he touched the ground, she put an end to the cylconic winds altogether.

It was over. And, beyond a shadow of a doubt, the mutant had won.

Chapter Thirty

PICARD GRITTED HIS teeth and battled to keep his pod upright as it descended through layers of cloud, its tractor beams locked on the Draa'kons' deadly cluster missile.

His eyes were stinging from heat and perspiration, his uniform soaked through and through, but he wouldn't allow himself to lose his focus. Not when tens of thousands of lives were depending on him.

At the same time, Archangel was contending with the whipping winds and the frustrating lack of visibility to make his way to his objective. As the captain watched, the mutant was buffeted to one side or the other, but over and over again he fought his way back on course.

Picard had seldom seen such courage or determination. It was even more remarkable when one considered that the mutant had been in sickbay less than an hour earlier.

Teeth clenched and bared, wings beating with raw power, Archangel got close enough to the cluster to reach for one of its limbs . . . to close his fingers around it . . .

and finally, folding his wings at just the right moment, to swing himself into the weapon's innermost network.

That done, he found the access plate the captain had told him about. His hair whipping about his head, he took out the phaser Picard had loaned him after they set out. Then he activated it and trained its crimson beam on the plate's lock.

Gently, thought the captain, *gently.* One wrong move by the mutant and they would both be vaporized. Worse, Verdeen would become a city of ghosts.

Fragments of clouds flew up past Archangel, obscuring him for a moment. When the captain caught sight of him again, he was putting away his phaser—*a good sign,* Picard thought.

Then, with the utmost care, the mutant slid open the access plate. The captain cheered inwardly. They were halfway home.

But *only* halfway. The next step would be every bit as tricky as the first. Inside the compartment, Archangel would find the cluster's photon-based power source and its trigger mechanism. His goal would be to deactivate the trigger without disturbing the photon pack.

According to the shuttlepod's sensor readouts, there was only one way to accomplish that—by pressing a single stud. But it was one of several such studs on the body of the trigger mechanism and pressing the wrong one would bring on disaster.

Grimly, the mutant put his hand inside the compartment. Picard watched him work, his throat bone-dry, his eyes feeling as if they had been scraped raw. The heat in the cabin was like a furnace, blistering and unrelenting.

But he still had a mission to perform. If Archangel were to succeed, the captain would have to persevere as well.

Seconds passed, with no relief. On his monitor screens, Picard could see the planet's surface looming closer and closer. What's more, he told himself, the aliens' explosive might have been set to detonate *before* it reached the ground.

Meanwhile, in his perch on the missile, the mutant continued to probe its delicate inner workings. He worked slowly, cautiously, his face a window on his frustration.

The captain glanced at his board again. They were less than five kilometers from Verdeen. Five kilometers and a single minute—at the outside.

If Archangel were to disarm the missile, he would have to do it in the next few seconds. Otherwise, Picard would have to take matters in his own hands and try to wrench the weapon away from its target, as reckless a maneuver as that might be.

Suddenly, the mutant and the alien weapon were lost to Picard's sight, blanketed in clouds. Cursing, the captain tried to make them out again, tried to discern even their outlines through the mask of water vapors.

But he couldn't. And his sensors weren't telling what he needed to know, either.

Grinding his teeth, Picard reached for his thruster controls, intent on veering off to the side and attempting to take the cluster with him. But before he could effect the course change, he saw something loom out of the clouds.

It was a man with wings, headed for the captain like a bird of prey. Struggling against the winds, Archangel reached for the pod's observation port and touched it with one hand.

With the other, he gave made a sign: a thumbs-up. *Mission accomplished,* it seemed to say.

Then, his head lolling to one side, the mutant was ripped from the observation port and lost to Picard's sight.

Fortunately, the captain still had a working transporter. Using his sensors to determine Archangel's coordinates, he compensated for the speed of the mutant's descent and obtained a lock.

Then he activated the transporter beam. A moment later, Archangel materialized in the aft part of the pod, exhausted but alive.

That accomplished, Picard turned his attention back to the missile. After all, it remained something of a threat. Though disarmed, it would crush whatever it hit when it reached the planet's surface.

But now, the captain could drag it off course without fear of detonating its payload—and without having to worry about the friction of descent any longer. With that in mind, he applied his thrusters and set a course for the peaks of a nearby mountain range.

Finally, activating the pod's autopilot, Picard left his seat and went to see to the winged man. As he knelt down beside Archangel, he saw the mutant's eyes latch onto him.

"You . . . had your chance," he breathed, "to get rid of me."

The captain smiled and grasped Archangel's hand. "Perhaps next time," he said reasonably.

The mutant smiled, too.

Strange, Picard thought. A short while earlier, he couldn't have thought less of the headstrong Archangel. Now, he had to count the mutant among the people he admired.

His smile broadened. Strange indeed.

Chapter Thirty-one

Picard leaned forward in his chair. It had been less than a half hour since his return to the bridge, but he could already see his other shuttlecraft emerging from Xhaldia's cloud-swaddled atmosphere.

First came the *Onizuka,* Commander Riker's vessel. Then came the *Pike,* commanded by Counselor Troi. And finally the *Voltaire,* with Worf and his people aboard.

The away teams had done it, the captain acknowledged, with a certain amount of satisfaction. They had stopped the Draa'kon, or they would never have left the planet's surface.

"Open a channel to the *Onizuka,*" Picard commanded.

A moment later, Riker's visage graced the screen. He looked tired and dirty, but he was clearly in one piece.

"Good to see you again, Number One. What is the situation in Verdeen?" the captain asked.

The first officer sighed. "Four dead, sir—Wilkes, Calderon, Saffron, and Bertaina. But the Draa'kon have been stopped, and the transformed have been taken into custody. In most cases, they gave themselves up; in others, they'll have to stand trial."

Picard was willing to wait for the details, of which there would certainly be many. "We are making progress here as well, Will. Shields have been partially restored and Commander La Forge tells me forward phasers will be online momentarily."

"That's good news," said Riker.

"Indeed," the captain replied. "But we can brief each other more fully when you return. I'll alert Shuttle Bay One to expect you."

"Acknowledged, sir. I'll pass that on to—"

Before he could finish, the first officer's shuttle was rocked. Sparks spewed from its control console. And before Picard could determine the cause of it, the viewscreen filled with static.

Automatically, it returned to its previous perspective on Xhaldia and the shuttles. It was enough to tell the captain everything he needed to know.

Before his eyes, the *Connharakt* had begun to stalk the shuttles like a mammoth predator, its propulsion systems at least minimally functional again, and its weapons ports ablaze with destructive energy beams.

Somehow, the Draa'kon ship had powered up its engines without Picard's knowing about it. And if he didn't react quickly, his away teams would be blown out of space.

Even as he thought that, his bridge jerked under the impact of a Draa'kon barrage.

"Transporter Room One," the captain said, his voice taut with urgency. "Prepare to beam our people off those shuttles."

The response came almost instantly—but it wasn't the one Picard had been expecting.

"I can't, sir," replied Lt. Robinson. "That last impact took the transporters offline."

The captain's teeth ground together in frustration. He had to try something else.

"Lt. Rager," he barked, "position us between the *Connharakt* and the *Onizuka!*"

After all, the *Onizuka* had already been hit. And by the look of her, she had been hit hard.

The conn officer did as she was told. A moment later, the *Enterprise* darted into the fray, shielding Riker's shuttle from further fire.

Unfortunately, Picard could protect only one of his craft at a time. And with the state his shields were in, he couldn't do it indefinitely.

A disruptor bolt pounded the *Enterprise,* sending a tremor through the ship. The captain turned to Ensign Suttles.

"Return fire!" he snapped hopefully.

The ensign checked his monitors, then looked up. "We can't, sir. The phasers are still offline."

"Shields down to twenty percent," Rager reported.

On the viewscreen, the two other shuttles were taking advantage of the distraction to escape. But before they could get very far, the *Connharakt* stabbed the *Pike* with a disruptor beam—sending her flying sideways, a trail of plasma emissions in her wake.

"They've crippled her," the captain breathed, accepting what he knew to be a deadly fact.

The *Pike* was easy prey for the *Draa'kon* now—a sitting duck—and even if Picard wanted to leave Riker's craft unprotected, there was no way he could reach her sister shuttle in time.

"Captain," said Suttles, his voice suddenly full of excitement, "we've got forward phasers!"

Without hesitating, Picard pointed to the viewscreen, where the hulking *Connharakt* dwarfed Counselor Troi's tiny shuttlecraft. "Target," he cried, "and fire!"

The taste of blood in her mouth, Troi tried to lift herself off the deck of the *Pike.* Abruptly, she felt a strong pair of hands pull her up the rest of the way.

Turning, she saw that it was Colossus who was providing the assistance. He wasn't just lifting her, either. He was using his metallic body to shield her from a shower of hot sparks.

The shuttle's cabin was in disarray, her control panels sputtering, plumes of smoke wafting forward from the ruin of her propulsion system. However, everyone was still alive.

At least, for the moment.

"Are you all right, Counselor?" asked Lt. Glavin, one of the security officers who had accompanied her to Xhaldia's surface.

"She's just fine," Wolverine interjected. He eyed Lt. Stephenson, the shuttle's helmsman. "Now, if it's okay with you, soldier, I'd just as soon get outta here before those bozos lambaste us a second time."

"I'd be glad to," said Stephenson, "if we still had engines, or even thrusters. But that blast threw everything offline."

Troi peered out the forward observation port, where the Draa'kon vessel blotted out half the stars. In a matter of moments, its disruptor beams would lance out at them again and finish the job they started.

Suddenly, the counselor saw the *Connharakt* raked with blood-red phaser beams. The Draa'kon ship's shields seemed to flicker under the impact.

It gave Troi an idea. It was a longshot, granted, but nothing short of a longshot would save them at that point.

She approached a small secondary console in the aft quarters of the shuttle. Its side was blackened, but it seemed basically intact.

The counselor tried to touch it, but it was too hot for her to handle. She turned to Colossus, whose metallic body seemed capable of withstanding almost anything—including intense heat.

"Hurry!" she told him. "I need you!"

Picard was about to give the order to fire again when the *Connharakt* spat another green disruptor bolt at the *Pike.*

The bolt's energy enveloped the shuttle, obscuring it from the captain's view. Then the craft appeared again—but only long enough for him to watch it explode in a spectacle of white light and antimatter-fueled fury.

My god, thought Picard, his heart sinking in his chest.

He stared at the viewscreen, where all that was left of the *Pike* was a raggedly expanding collection of debris. He tried to come to grips with that fact, to absorb it.

Troi . . . dead? It didn't seem possible.

The counselor had been with him since he took command of the *Enterprise-D* years earlier. She hadn't just been a skilled and respected colleague. She had been a close and valued friend.

And now . . .

The captain swallowed. He felt empty. Numb.

Nor was it only Troi he had lost in the explosion. Wolverine and Colossus had been destroyed along with her—and five of his surviving security officers as well.

"Sir?" said Lt. Yeowell, who was manning Ops in Data's absence. Picard turned to him.

"Yes, Lieutenant?"

Yeowell smiled hopefully at him—a strange thing to do at such a time. "Sir, I picked up evidence of transporter activity just before the shuttle was torn apart."

Picard looked at him, ready to grasp at any straw. "Transporter activity?" he repeated.

"Yes, sir. But the away team didn't transport back to the *Enterprise.*"

The captain looked at him. "Then . . ."

He turned to the viewscreen, where the *Connharakt* seemed to be veering away from the *Enterprise.* Was it possible . . . ?

"They've beamed onto the bridge of the Draa'kon ship," Yeowell reported, confirming Picard's suspicion.

"Hold your fire," the captain told Ensign Suttles.

After all, their own people were at risk on the *Connharakt.* All they could do for the moment was wait and see what happened.

* * *

High Implementor Isadjo grunted as he studied his scanplate, where one of the *Connharakt*'s pale-green disruptor beams had finally stabbed an *Enterprise* shuttle craft.

Before the Implementor's eyes, the scanplate blanched with white light. When it cleared, there was hardly anything left of the enemy craft. Vessel and crew had been destroyed.

It was meager compensation for what Picard and his people had done to the Draa'kon's plans on Xhaldia. However, Isadjo had yet to expend his energy stores. With a little luck, he would yet wreak havoc on—

"Implementor!" roared one of his officers.

Scowling, Isadjo turned in his command pod—and took in a sight he had never imagined he would see, even in his wildest lodge visions. As difficult as it was to believe, his bridge was peppered with Enterprise intruders.

As the Implementor watched, spellbound, the enemy aimed their weapons and fired. His own people did the same. There were shouts of pain and surprise, and a series of thuds as Draa'kon bodies hit the deck.

In the melee, an energy inverter was punctured. It spewed thick, yellow gas across the bridge, making it difficult to see anything—except, of course, the energy bolts that continued to lance in every direction.

Slipping his own weapon free of its sheathe, Isadjo got up from his pod and peered into the hissing, yellow miasma, waiting for an enemy to show himself. None did. But a moment later, one of the Implementor's officers came hurtling out of the fog, his face bleeding freely from four parallel cuts.

Isadjo cursed and took a step forward, trying to catch sight of a likely target. But before he could get very far, another of his officers spun free of the gas cloud, his tunic ripped and bloody.

The Implementor didn't like what was happening. His gill-flaps fluttered uncontrollably. His lips pulled back and a cry of rage filled his cranial cavities.

"Show yourselves!" he demanded of the enemy. "Face me like warriors!"

As if in response to Isadjo's order, a trio emerged from the fog. One was Ettojh, his second-in-command, who was staggering backward under the influence of a powerful blow. Another was Cyggelh, his helmsman.

And the third . . .

The third was a figure clad in yellow and blue, with a mask covering half his face. The invader was grinning, as if he liked nothing better than fighting for his life in close and dangerous quarters.

He wasn't armed with a directed-energy device like his comrades. In fact, all he had in the way of weapons were the long, sharp clawlike things protruding from his knuckles.

Nonetheless, he used them effectively. Before the Implementor's eyes, the yellow-and-blue one slashed Ettojh's disruptor from his grasp and delivered a savage kick to his midsection.

Isadjo's helmsman took advantage of the moment to fire, but the invader ducked and evaded the blast. Then he leaped on the Draa'kon like a ravening beast, sending him slamming into a bulkhead with skull-rattling force.

As the helmsman slumped to the deck, Ettojh tried to grasp the intruder from behind. That too proved to be a mistake, as the yellow-and-blue one flipped Ettojh over his back.

Before Isadjo's second could get to his feet, the invader was on the move again. The Implementor saw a rib-cracking kick, followed by a backhanded swipe of the masked one's claws, and Ettojh went skidding limply across the deck.

Then the invader turned to Isadjo himself. "Hey," he said, "I'll bet you're the creepy crawler in charge. I mean, you *are* the biggest, fattest guy around."

Isadjo trained his weapon on the madman and sent a bolt of green fury at him. A moment later, the masked one was gone, enveloped again by the billowing gas cloud.

There, thought the Implementor. That would teach him to take the Draa'kon lightly.

Suddenly, the invader came flying out of the cloud at him, all feet and claws and savage grin. There was no time to run, no time to fire again. There wasn't even time for Isadjo to brace himself as the enemy's boot heel smashed him right between the eyes.

Captain Picard eyed the image of the *Connharakt* on his viewscreen, waiting for a sign.

"The *Onizuka* is entering Shuttle Bay One," Rager reported. "And the *Voltaire* is hailing us."

"What's the *Voltaire*'s position?" asked Picard.

"Off the port bow," said Rager, "at a distance of half-a-million miles."

"Open a channel," the captain instructed her.

It was Worf's voice that came to them. "How can we help?" he asked.

Picard explained the situation. "Right now," he concluded, "the best any of us can do is stand by."

The Klingon didn't like the idea, but he bowed to it. "Standing by," he agreed.

Almost a minute went by. The captain took a breath, let it out.

Then he heard a small exclamation from Suttles at tactical. "Sir," said the ensign, "I have an audio message from the *Connharakt.*"

The captain frowned, preparing himself for anything. "Put it through," he responded.

For a heartbeat, there was silence. Then Picard heard a familiar voice.

"Captain," it said, "this is Counselor Troi. I'm happy to tell you we have taken control of the *Connharakt.*"

Picard looked at Rager, then at Yeowell. "Taken control?" he repeated, savoring the moment.

"That's correct, sir. High Implementor Isadjo and his bridge officers put up quite a fight, but in the end they were no match for us. Wolverine was particularly persuasive in that regard."

"I see," said the captain, supressing a smile. "May I assume, then, that the *Connharakt* will no longer be attempting to split us like an overripe melon?"

He could imagine the counselor grinning at his gallows humor. "You may indeed make that assumption, sir."

Picard nodded. Once in a while, one of his officers performed a feat that simply astounded him. This was one of those feats

"Good work," he told Troi.

The answer had an undercurrent of pride in it—and fatigue as well. "Thank you, sir."

Chapter Thirty-two

PICARD TOOK NOTE of the tricorder in his chief medical officer's hand as he followed her through the interlocking doors of Holodeck Two. When the doors closed behind them, he found himself in a large, well-lit room with the stark, sterile appearance of a laboratory.

At the far end of the room, hovering in some kind of antigravity unit, a man was peering into a microscope. Taking note of his visitors' entrance, he looked up from his work.

"Dr. Crusher," Xavier said, his voice calm and commanding at the same time. "I've been wondering when you would return."

Then he turned his gaze on the captain, and a flicker of something like amusement crossed his features. Nor was it difficult for Picard to see why. As the doctor had warned him, he and the professor bore a passing resemblance to one another.

Xavier touched a button and his antigravity unit came closer to the captain and his colleague. He stopped it within a meter of them and studied Picard more closely.

"Mon semblable, mon frère," the professor said.

The captain raised an eyebrow. *"The Wasteland,* I believe."

Xavier nodded. "It pleases me that Eliot has survived into your twenty-fourth century. Indeed, now that I think about it, it pleases me that he exists in your continuum at all."

"He and a great many others, I am sure," said Picard. He came forward and extended his hand. "My name is Jean-Luc Picard, Professor. I command the vessel on which this holodeck is located."

"Yes," said Xavier, glancing at Crusher. "The doctor has spoken of you—highly, I might add. However, I imagine you came to speak of something other than poetry."

"That's true," the captain told him. "On the other hand, I'm hardly qualified to assist you and Dr. Crusher in your research."

His curiosity piqued, the professor tilted his head slightly. But he didn't press. He waited for his visitor to go on.

"As Dr. Crusher has no doubt informed you," Picard said, "your X-Men are my guests at the moment. In fact, they proved helpful when complications arose in our dealings with the Xhaldians."

"I am quite pleased with them," Xavier admitted.

"And they with you," the captain replied. "In fact, that was what spurred me to speak with you. Not one of them has missed an opportunity to refer to you in the most glowing and reverent terms—even when the individual in question may not be reverent by nature."

The professor grunted softly. "I believe I know of whom you speak—and, yes, he often surprises people on that count. But . . . ."

"I just wanted to meet you," said Picard. "And applaud what you've done. Given the X-Men's disparate personalities, it cannot have been easy."

Xavier took the praise in stride. "No more difficult, I

imagine, than commanding a starship with more than a thousand people on board."

The captain smiled. *"Touché."* He looked at Crusher. "I suppose I should leave you and the doctor to your work now."

"She tells me it's of some importance," the professor replied, clearly understating the case.

"It was a pleasure making your acquaintance," said Picard. And with that, he turned to go.

"Captain?"

Just short of the doors, Picard stopped and looked back at Xavier.

"If I am truly a creation of your holodeck, as Dr. Crusher seems to think," said the professor, "my program will be in residence here indefinitely. Is that an accurate assessment?"

"It is," the captain confirmed.

"In that case," said Xavier, "I invite you to access my persona whenever the spirit moves you."

Picard smiled. "I will be honored to do so."

Then, with a last glance at the man who fathered the X-Men, he left the holodeck.

Captain's log, supplemental. Captain Stanley and the Venture *have arrived in response to our call for assistance. While they are too late to take part in the conflict, Stanley has volunteered to tow the* Connharakt *to Deep Space Seven, where both ship and crew will await further investigation of the matter by Starfleet Command.*

Meanwhile, we seem to have achieved a victory on another front. As I record this, Chancellor Amon is apprising the transformed of Dr. Crusher's recent breakthrough regarding their condition—a breakthrough with which she had help from an unusual source.

It is the chancellor's belief that this development will help heal the rift between the transformed and the rest of the Xhaldian population—a rift for which he feels person-

ally responsible. Given the way the transformed have been
treated, I can only hope his conclusion is a realistic one.

Lt. Sovar stood alongside Dr. Crusher in the cavernous, marble-walled Verdeen Auditorium, and studied the
large, empty stage.

A moment later, Chancellor Amon walked out, his
footfalls echoing. The chancellor was anything but eager
to be there, as evidenced by his lack of haste in approaching the podium that had been set up for him. He
seemed humble, contrite, as he scanned the faces in
the audience.

The faces of the transformed.

Erid and Corba—who had recovered from her exhaustion, and who seemed to like Erid very much. Energy-
draining Nikti and toxin-making Cudarris, and three
dozen others whose names the lieutenant didn't know.
All of them were intent on the stage, wondering what
Amon might tell them that they could possibly want to
hear.

There were more of the transformed—nearly a hundred—in other cities around the planet, watching the
chancellor via a closed-circuit video system. Though
they had escaped the horror of what had happened at
Verdeen, they still had a stake in Amon's announcement.

Even Rahatan and his cohorts had been allowed access
to the event. Tessa Mollic, too, despite the man's in-
sanity.

As Sovar looked on, the chancellor took a deep breath.
"Before I say anything else, let me say this. I am sorry.
Very, very sorry."

"Do you expect us to forgive you?" asked a youth with
four arms, his voice vibrating with righteous indignation.

Amon looked at him. "No," he replied after a moment
or two. "I don't expect that at all, to tell you the truth. I
just thought you deserved an apology."

He put the flats of his hands together and averted his
eyes. "Please try to understand . . . I was concerned for

the people of this world. So concerned, in fact—so terrified—that I deluded myself into thinking it was all right to strip you of your freedom and your dignity. But, of course, it wasn't all right. It was a horrible thing to do, regardless of what was at stake."

"Those are just words," Erid responded, speaking so forcefully that his brother didn't know it was him at first. "We've heard plenty of them since we became transformed. We know how easy they are to say."

The chancellor shook his head. "No. *These* words don't come easily, I assure you. But as I said, I don't expect you to forgive me. I just wanted you to know how I feel."

"Isthatit?" asked Corba. "Isthatwhyyouaskedustocome here?"

It took Amon a moment to understand what she had said. "Not at all," he told her. "I asked you here for a very important reason." He gestured to indicate Dr. Crusher and the lieutenant. "As you may know, our friends from the *Enterprise* have been studying the genetic anomaly that triggered your transformations. And they believe they can reverse the process."

Instantly, a murmur wove its way through the ranks of the transformed. They looked to Crusher and Sovar for confirmation.

"Is this true?" asked a youth who dwarfed the others.

The doctor smiled. "It's true, all right." She turned to Chancellor Amon. "If I may . . . ?"

The chancellor held his hands out in welcome. "Please do."

The security officer watched as Crusher ascended the marble stairs at the side of the stage. Then he turned to see his brother's reaction.

Erid seemed stunned more than anything else. No doubt, he was having a difficult time absorbing this turn of events.

Amon stepped aside and let the doctor take the podium. "If you want," said Crusher, "I'll explain the science behind our discovery. But I suspect what you *really* want to know is what will happen if you're changed back."

She noted that the process would take a few days. She noted also that there might be some side effects—but that they would be minimal and temporary.

"On the other hand," the doctor continued, "the reversal itself would be absolutely permanent. Once your powers are gone, you'll never get them back again. *Never.*"

The transformed looked at one another. The vast majority of them were grinning. Some even embraced each other.

But Erid wasn't one of them. Neither was Corba. They looked as if they had already lost something precious.

Sovar was surprised. His brother had looked so miserable on the streets of Verdeen, so bitter about the way he looked and the discomfort he felt. How could he not jump at the chance to leave all that behind?

Dr. Crusher answered a few of the transformed's questions, then returned the podium to Chancellor Amon. The chancellor thanked the transformed for coming and wished them wisdom in making their decision.

As the audience rose and moved from their seats into the aisles, there was only one topic of discussion—whether to accept Crusher's offer. From what Sovar could see of Corba and Erid, they were discussing it as well. But they were also shaking their heads a lot.

The lieutenant's initial inclination was to go to his brother and try to talk some sense into him. Then he remembered what it was like when he told his family he was going to join Starfleet.

They weren't happy about it—Erid least of all. The boy had hated his older brother for the choice he made. He had tried to convince him not to go. And ever since, the security officer had felt badly about leaving. He had felt as if he let his brother down, as if he had abandoned him.

I won't do that to Erid, he told himself. *I won't try to influence him. Let him make his decision—whatever it may be—and I'll stand behind him a hundred percent.*

Suddenly, he realized his brother was looking at him. Seeking his counsel, perhaps. Smiling, Sovar began to make his way through the crowd.

Chapter Thirty-three

THE HOLODECK DOORS opened with a familiar hiss. Peering inside, Worf saw the same steamy, jungle clearing where his calisthenics program took place. Even the white-stone altar was in evidence.

The Klingon turned to Wolverine, who was standing beside him. "I thought you said you designed a holo-program."

"I did," the mutant told him.

"But this is the setting from *my* program."

Wolverine shrugged. "What difference does it make *where* you fight? The important thing is *who.*"

The Klingon frowned. "And whom are we to fight?"

The mutant chuckled. "Keep yer shirt on."

Worf was puzzled. "My shirt . . . ?"

"Be patient," Wolverine translated, as he led the way into the holodeck.

Worf followed him, his batt'leth at the ready. As before, birds shrilled at them from their perches in the golden foliage. Frightened-looking creatures peered out at them from between the trees. And the place stank as badly as ever.

"You could at least have changed the smell," he told Wolverine.

The mutant looked back at him. "What smell?"

The Klingon made a face. "You *must* smell it. It's—"

And then he stopped himself. Wolverine's sense of smell was even better than his own. The mutant had to be making a joke.

As if to confirm his suspicion, Wolverine grinned a mischievous grin. "You were sayin', bub?"

Worf scowled. "Never mind."

As they approached the altar, the lieutenant knew their adversaries weren't far off. After all, the birds were shrieking more loudly, the trees bowing deeper under the press of the hot, tropical wind.

Worf could feel his heartrate speeding up. He looked about, jaw clenched, bracing himself for the attack he knew would come.

"Where are they?" the mutant whispered.

The Klingon glanced at him. "You are asking *me?*"

Wolverine shook his head. "They should'a pounced on us by now."

Worf sighed. He had a feeling this was going to be a disappointing experience. But then, what did the mutant know about holodeck programs? Especially those in which—

Suddenly, he saw the branches part to the left of them. A powerful-looking figure in orange and brown garments moved like a cat out into the clearing. His pale blond hair was wild, the look in his eyes a feral one, and his clawlike nails were almost as long as Wolverine's.

"Logan," the man rasped hungrily, displaying his fangs.

"Sabretooth," the mutant replied. "It's about time."

"Wait a minute," came a slow, deep voice from an unseen source. "Don't shred him till I get a coupla shots in."

251

A moment later, there was a crack and a tree fell down across the altar. Behind it, a gelatinous mountain of a man in a black tank suit stepped out from concealment.

He wasn't alone, either. Another adversary followed. He was dressed entirely in black, dark hair slicked back across his head. To Worf's eye, the man didn't look particularly dangerous, but he was sure Wolverine had selected him for a reason.

"The Blob," said the mutant. "And Unus the Untouchable."

The living mountain cracked his knuckles and grinned. "I been itchin' ta get my mitts on you," he told Wolverine.

The one called Unus didn't smile, but his eyes seemed to twinkle. "That's right," he said. "We owe you and your friends. *Big* time."

He had barely finished speaking when there was a commotion to Worf's right. A flight of birds took off screaming into the blood-red sky, followed by a pounding that made the ground shake beneath the Klingon's feet.

A pounding that sounded oddly like . . . footsteps. And they were getting closer moment by moment.

Finally, another gigantic figure shouldered his way into the clearing. But this one wasn't grotesquely flabby like the Blob. He was a mass of corded muscle encased in brown and crimson body armor, his headgear more a dome than an actual helmet.

Wolverine grinned. "Hey, Juggernaut. Glad ya could make it."

The behemoth's eyes flashed like blue fire. "You won't be glad for long," he thundered.

Wolverine glanced at Worf. "Looks like they're all here, lieutenant. But don't let 'em fool ya. They're actually a lot tougher than they look."

Eyeing his adversaries, the Klingon shifted his batt'leth from hand to hand. "Tougher, you say?"

"Yup."

Worf smiled. "Good."

Perhaps this wouldn't be such a disappointment after all.

Picard looked around the table in his observation lounge, which had never been so crowded before. Not only were Worf, Riker, Troi, Crusher, Data, and La Forge present, but all the X-Men as well.

"Thank you for coming," he told them. "As I noted, we have a number of subjects to cover." He turned to his first officer. "Commander?"

Riker launched into his briefing. "When we first saw the Draa'kon in orbit around Xhaldia, we wondered what they were doing there. Now we know. They weren't just there to kidnap Xhaldia's budding superbeings. In point of fact, they had *created* them."

"Created them?" La Forge repeated.

"That's right," said the first officer. "You see, as many as thirty years ago, Draa'kon geneticists found a genome that would produce certain combat abilities in breeding stock."

"To support Draa'kon aggression against other species," Crusher noted.

"Exactly, Doctor—just as Khan and others engineered human genes in the twentieth century. But the Draa'kon ran into a stumbling block. Their DNA rejected the genome."

The captain saw where Riker was going with this. "So they sought out a gene pool without that particular problem—one that would bring forth a crop of super-powered warriors."

"Apparently," said the first officer. "Finally, they found such a gene pool on Xhaldia—though it was a tiny fraction of the population. After that, it was simply a matter of introducing an airborne virus that would sow the right genetic seeds—and produce a sprinkling of mutant Xhaldians some twenty-two years later."

La Forge grunted. "Incredible!"

"However," Riker said, "once the transformed learned to use their powers, they would become difficult

253

to capture. Therefore, the Draa'kon would only have a limited window of opportunity to harvest their crop."

"A window," Picard continued, "that we have managed to shut." He eyed his first officer. "But tell me, Number One . . . how did you learn all this?"

The first officer shifted in his seat. "Actually, sir, it was Wolverine who obtained the information."

"Wolverine?" the captain echoed, turning to the mutant.

The man in the mask just grinned at him.

"Yes, sir," Riker confirmed. "In an . . . er, interview with one of the captured Draa'kon."

Picard frowned. "An interview in which Wolverine no doubt employed his own, unique brand of persuasion."

This time, Riker smiled along with the mutant. "No doubt," he said.

The captain sighed. It wasn't always easy dealing with these X-Men—and Wolverine especially. Still, he could hardly argue with the results.

"Thank you," he told his first officer. He turned to La Forge. "You have the floor, Commander."

"Thank you, sir," said the chief engineer. He looked around the table at the X-Men. "You'll be interested to know I've figured out what went wrong with your time-space transport."

"Excellent," replied Shadowcat. "So what was it?"

La Forge turned to Nightcrawler. "It was Kurt, here."

"See that, elf?" Wolverine grunted. "Ain't I always said yer more trouble than yer worth?"

"Stick it in your two giant ears, mein freund," said the teleporter with a smile.

Storm ignored her teammates' good-natured banter. "In what way was Kurt the cause of our problem?" she asked.

"Good question," said La Forge. "You see, when Nightcrawler teleports, he picks up traces of something called verteron particles—which we've come to associate with subspace travel."

"Ye learned that in yer examination of 'im?" Banshee wondered.

"That's right," the engineer replied. "And once I knew that, I suspected it was a contributing factor to your inability to get home. But I didn't know how verterons alone could be responsible—and I couldn't find out the easy way, because I didn't have access to the timehook Nightcrawler had used."

"So what did you do?" asked Archangel, looking genuinely intrigued.

"Well," said La Forge, "I thought about the fact that you could have shown up at any point at all in timespace—but you showed up in my particular universe, not too long after we'd seen you last. I decided that couldn't be just a coincidence. There had to be something drawing you to those coordinates."

"And what was it?" Shadowcat prodded.

"That's what I wanted to know," the engineer told her. "Since you turned up originally at Starbase 88, I figured I'd make that my next research stop—figuratively speaking, of course. Contacting Admiral Kashiwada's people, I asked for their security logs for the month preceding your appearance. And that's where I found the lead I was looking for.

"Remember the other timehook—that one that brought us home? As Captain Picard told Storm, it was misplaced in the course of its return to us. But when I went over the starbase's cargo logs, I found a reference to something that sounded a lot like it."

"On Starbase 88?" asked Colossus.

"On Starbase 88. So I asked them to analyze it for me. And guess what? It was lousy with verteron particles."

"Ah hah," said Nightcrawler. "The plot thickens."

"Wait a second," Shadowcat declared. "I think I get it. There's some kind of connection between the timehooks—some method of communication Kang built in, that may not be obvious to us."

"That's what I was thinking," La Forge said. "Maybe

to keep the timehooks from trying to jump to the exact same coordinates."

"Okay," the girl replied, "that works. Anyway, at some point, the starbase is exposed to verteron particles, and so is the timehook in its cargo bay. And the one Kurt's using has already been contaminated with verterons. So when we try to use all our hooks at the same time, to get home . . ."

"The nature of the link changes," said the engineer, impressed by Shadowcat's grasp of the situation. "It becomes like an elastic band. And having been stretched, it snaps back again—until it drags you back to the other timehook, which happens to be in a cargo bay at Starbase 88."

Banshee whistled. "And 'twas brought to *this* point in time because, before then, th' other timehook had nae been exposed . . . and th' altered link had nae existed." He smiled. "Pretty heady stuff, 'tis."

"Now what?" asked Nightcrawler. "Am I to be drawn and quartered for my role in this?"

La Forge chuckled. "That part's out of my hands, I'm afraid. But you'll be glad to know the last timehook is on its way to us even as we speak. After we cleanse it of verteron particles, you should be able to use it to get home once and for all."

"Here, here," said Banshee.

Archangel nodded approvingly. "Nice work, Commander."

"I try," said the engineer.

Picard turned to Dr. Crusher. "Your turn, Beverly."

She leaned forward. "What I have to say isn't all that complicated."

"If I had a nickel for every time I heard *that*," Wolverine muttered.

Storm shot him a look.

"As you know," Crusher continued, "I programmed a replica of Professor Xavier in the holodeck. Working together, we were able to devise a process for reversing the work of the Draa'kon genome—in other words, turning the transformed back into normal Xhaldians."

"And?" said Colossus.

"Having studied your systems at a cellular level, I think I can adapt what the professor and I came up with to rid *you* of your mutant gene as well."

Crusher watched the X-Men's faces, as the significance of her announcement sank in.

"In other words . . . make us into normal humans?" Colossus asked.

Banshee's eyes narrowed. "The same as the rest of society?"

"That's right," the doctor told them. "You wouldn't be mutants anymore. You would be *homo sapiens.*"

Shadowcat stared at her. "But . . . we don't *want* to be *homo sapiens.* I mean, don't get me wrong, we don't love the idea of being persecuted because of what we are. But that doesn't mean we would trade it for anything else."

"We've risked our lives to remain mutants." Storm pointed out. "And to be accepted that way."

"In fact," Nightcrawler said slyly, "the only people who've offered to make us *homo sapiens* in the past are our *enemies.*"

Crusher smiled. "I had a feeling you'd say that. Still, I had to give you the choice."

Picard nodded. "So you did, Doctor." He looked around the table. "And that concludes our agenda. Thank you all for coming."

Everyone got up and left the observation lounge. However, the captain lingered. So, he noticed, did Storm. She gazed out the window at the stars, as she had that time in his ready room.

"Commander Riker told me of your exploits in Verdeen," he said. "They sounded rather colorful."

"No more so than your adventure in the shuttle," she replied.

Picard frowned. "May I ask you a question, Ororo?"

The mutant turned to him. "As you wish."

"When you first came aboard," he said, "we had a conversation. We were talking about the demands of leadership."

She nodded. "Of course. I said that leaders seldom enjoy stable relationships—which is no more than the truth as I have observed it."

"Yes," said the captain. "But you also seemed on the verge of mentioning an exception to that rule. I cannot help but wonder . . ."

Storm gazed into his eyes. "Are you certain you want me to answer that question? To answer it even as I am leaving, most likely never to see you again?"

Picard considered the wisdom in what she was saying. He took a breath, then let it out.

"Perhaps not," he said softly.

For a moment, silence reigned in the observation lounge. Then the mutant came over and took the captain's arm. "Suddenly, I have an urge for some herbal tea."

Picard smiled. "As you wish."

Chapter Thirty-four

PICARD STOOD ON the periphery of Cargo Bay One, flanked by his first officer and his ship's counselor. They watched as Geordi and Shadowcat conspired to set the coordinates on the last remaining timehook, surrounded by the other X-Men, Commander Worf, and a handful of *Enterprise* officers.

"And that's it," the chief engineer announced at last.

"It's ready?" asked Wolverine.

"As ready as it'll ever be," said Shadowcat.

The X-Men looked at one another. Clearly, they were gladdened by the prospect of returning to their rightful timeline. However, it also meant leaving their newfound comrades behind—if not for the first time, quite possibly for the last.

Wolverine clapped Worf on the shoulder. "Don't ever change, bub."

The Klingon's mouth pulled up at the corners. "Once again, it was an honor fighting beside you."

Shadowcat hugged Lt. Sovar. "Take care of yourself,"

she told him. "I mean, you'll have to, now. You won't have me to look after you anymore."

The Xhaldian grinned. "I'll do my best."

"You sure you don't want to stay?" Geordi asked Nightcrawler. "We can use a man who teleports on his own."

The X-Man shook his blue head. "Your universe is too exhausting, mein freund. I prefer a place that's nice and restful, where I just have to battle the odd villain from time to time."

Dr. Crusher exchanged good-byes with Archangel, Data with Colossus, and Banshee with Lt. Robinson and Lt. Rager. Storm, on the other hand, separated herself from the crowd and approached the captain's smaller group.

"I will miss you," she told them. "All of you."

"And we you," said Troi, smiling sadly.

"Next time," Riker commented, "I'll trust your instincts. I promise."

The mutant nodded. "I am grateful."

Picard glanced at his officers. "If I may, I would like to have a word with our guest."

Alone, was the implied ending of his request.

Riker and Troi looked at one another.

"Of course," said the counselor, taking her colleague's arm and walking away with him.

Storm regarded him. "Yes, Captain?"

"Good luck," he said. "Not that you will need it."

"Everyone needs it," Storm replied. She touched his face with her fingertips. "Goodbye, Captain of the *Enterprise.*"

Then, tearing her eyes away from him, she turned to go.

"Ororo," said Picard.

The mutant looked back. "Yes?"

"My name," the captain told her, "is Jean-Luc."

She smiled the smile of a delighted child—one who had found a friend to help her stave off the darkness.

Then she rejoined her teammates in the center of the cargo bay.

A moment later, Riker and Troi returned. Neither of them said a word to Picard. They just stood with him and watched the X-Men gather into a knot around Shadowcat.

There was no flash of light, nothing at all to warn the captain of the mutants' departure. One moment, they were there; the next, they weren't. It was that simple.

Still, Picard felt richer for having known them—and one of them in particular. One might even say he felt . . . transformed.

Epilogue

WARREN BLINKED AND realized he was somewhere else. Not in a cargo bay on the *Enterprise,* but in a meadow surrounded by fragrant pine trees, where birds sang and flitted from branch to branch.

He recognized the place. It was on the grounds of the Xavier Institute for Higher Learning—the exact same spot where he and his fellow X-Men had arrived after they left the *Enterprise* the last time.

At the time, they had believed themselves home. Then they had been bathed in a bright, blinding light—and the next thing they knew, they had turned up on Starbase 88, in another reality entirely.

Warren looked at Ororo, who was standing beside him. The two of them were afraid to say anything. They were waiting for the other shoe to drop.

But it didn't. There was no bright light. They stayed right where they were, apparently fixed in time and space.

Finally, it was Colossus who broke the silence. "Unless I am mistaken," he said, "it seems we are home."

"So it does," Banshee agreed.

"Back in Salem Center," Nightcrawler declared.

"Where we belong," Shadowcat added.

Home, thought Warren. *What a nice place to be.*

Filled with a sudden rush of exhilaration, he spread his great, white wings and soared straight up into the heavens. And he didn't stop for a long, long time.

Hidden behind a stand of closely grown pine trees, the omnipotent entity known as Q removed his sunglasses to watch Archangel ascend into the vibrant summer sky. Replacing his glasses, he folded one leg over the other, sat back in his lawn chair and sipped his pina colada.

"You see?" he said to the gigantic personage standing beside him. "I told you it would work just fine."

The Watcher, eons-old scion of an immortal race, shook his massive, hairless head and adjusted his majestic robes.

"I have seen one being after another tamper with the integrity of Time and Space," the Watcher replied in his expansive, echoing voice, "Kang being a prime example. Yet none of them ever seemed to obtain the results he desired."

Q grinned. "That's because none of them were *me,* Watcher old bean. A yank here, a tug there, and the *Enterprise*'s timehook—which was in storage on Starbase 88—wound up saturated with verteron particles. That, in turn, drew the X-Men to the *Enterprise*'s universe, where they were eminently available to help solve the mutant crisis on Xhaldia. What could be simpler?"

"The Xhaldians called them *transformed,*" the Watcher reminded him. "Not *mutants.*"

"They're all the same to me," said Q. "The point is the X-men were in the right place at the right time, and Xhaldia's all the better for it."

"And why do you care so much about Xhaldia?" the Watcher inquired.

Q cast a sidelong look at him. "I thought you people just *watched*. No one said you asked *questions.*"

"Nonetheless," the Watcher pressed, "you must have had a reason for sparing Xhaldia so much misery."

Q thought for a moment. "Let's just say I've got my eye on the Xhaldians and leave it at that, all right?"

The Watcher frowned. "I can hardly do otherwise. I, like all my kind, have sworn never to interfere in the affairs of others."

Q chuckled. "And a lovely policy it is, my friend—though, I must tell you, you don't know what you're missing."

Suddenly, he snapped the fingers of his free hand and made his pina colada vanish, glass and all. Then he stood up, snapped his fingers again, and the lawn chair disappeared as well—along with the sunglasses.

"Well," he told the Watcher, "got to go. You know how it is—places to grow and people to be. But don't worry—I'll be in touch."

The gargantuan figure nodded his head. "I'm certain you will be."

Q smiled mischievously. "Perhaps sooner than you think—though *sooner* is such a relative term."

Leaving the Watcher with that morsel to chew on, Q snapped his fingers a third time—and, at least for the moment, vanished from the X-Men's reality without a trace.

About the Author

Michael Jan Friedman is the author of nearly sixty books of fiction and nonfiction, more than half of which bear the name *Star Trek* or some variation thereof. Ten of his titles have appeared on the *New York Times* bestseller list. He has also written for network and cable television, radio, and comic books, with the *Star Trek: Voyager®* episode "Resistance" prominent among his credits. On those rare occasions when he visits the real world, Friedman lives on Long Island with his wife and two sons.

He continues to advise readers that no matter how many Friedmans they know, the vast probability is that none of them are related to him.

IN STORES NOW

X-MEN®

WATCHERS ON THE WALLS

The new novel by
CHRISTOPHER L. BENNETT

From Pocket Books

Available wherever books are sold

Also available as an eBook

www.SimonSays.com

Turn the page for a preview. . . .

Jean Grey flew on the edge of space, straddling the teeming mass of life that was Earth and the infinite death that was the void, and contemplated the balance.

Oh, all right, she confessed, deflating her own poetic moment, *the* Blackbird*'s doing the flying, and Charles is piloting. I'm just along for the ride.* Specifically, she sat in the co-pilot's seat of the X-Men's RS-150 jet aircraft—or, rather, their heavily modified descendant of that Lockheed Aircraft prototype, upgraded with technology the Skunk Works engineers could never have contemplated. Technology, courtesy of the Shi'ar Empire, that allowed the *Blackbird* to take the concept of a high-altitude reconnaissance craft quite literally to new heights and permit this little jaunt to the fringes of the mesosphere.

Still, the contemplation was real enough. The view up here was a striking reminder of the events that had given Jean her special perspective on life, death, and rebirth. Sacrificing herself to pilot a damaged shuttle through a deadly radiation belt, she had been joined with the all-powerful cosmic Phoenix Force. The entity had cocooned her away to heal, in exchange for borrowing her identity, a piece of her soul, and living as Jean Grey for some time—only to die as Jean Grey, sacrificing itself to atone for the evils it had unleashed when the temptations of human passion had driven it mad. Jean had later been revived with no knowledge of those events, but her borrowed essence and memory had finally returned to her by a roundabout route, making her whole again—so, in a sense, she had been reborn twice. Her powers now were far less than her doppelganger's had been, though greater than they had been before. Hence her ongoing lessons with Charles Xavier to test and refine her evolving powers.

How ironic, she thought. *I was Charles's first student, all those years ago. And yet despite everything I've been through, here I am still taking classes.*

Learning should *be a lifelong process,* came Xavier's mental "voice" into her mind. It was not his way to intrude on others' private thoughts, but Jean had made no particular effort to shield hers. After all these years of telepathic rapport, there was little between her and Charles that was truly private anymore. In many ways (and she did keep this thought more to herself), this man knew her more intimately than Scott Summers, her husband, ever would.

But even so, sometimes Xavier could still surprise her. "So what did you have to teach me that required flying us all the way up here?" she asked.

Xavier smiled, turning away from the controls. "Are you familiar with the avant-garde composer John Cage?"

Jean resisted the impulse to rummage around in his surface thoughts for the answer; that would be cheating. "I can't say I am."

"One of his most famous works is a solo piece, usually for piano, entitled *4'33"*. It has three movements, adding up to that total duration, and each one consists of the instruction 'Tacet'—be quiet. And so, for four minutes and thirty-three seconds, the artist performs silence."

Jean's fiery-hued brows angled upward. "Sounds like a very lazy composer."

"The point," Xavier went on patiently, "is to encourage the audience to listen to the silence. Rather, to discover that there is no such thing as silence. Even when the performer doesn't play, there's still an abundance of sounds to be heard. The sounds of your own breathing, the rustling of the audience's clothes, the creaking of the floorboards."

"The yawns of the audience. The trilling of cell phones they rudely forgot to turn off."

"Even those. The audience, the environment, it's all part of the performance. It's the source of the music. And it's a unique performance every time."

Jean was starting to see where he was leading. "So we're here . . . to contemplate silence?"

"Exactly. In a somewhat different way, of course, since we're not in the midst of an audience. The goal is to get away from the psychic background noise that humans generate all the time, the mental voices against which we have to close our perceptions to if we wish to have our thoughts to ourselves. With no one around, it should be possible for you to open up your senses and still be essentially alone in your mind—well, present company excluded, of course, though I can shield my thoughts from you. The goal is to contemplate that quiet and see what you can discover within it."

It was an intriguing prospect, and Jean let the professor sense that in her. "But I don't know if we're far enough. Even this high up, there's still going to be a background buzz from the Earth."

"I know. What I want is for you to focus your attention away from that. To extend your senses out into space, into the void." He paused as a thought struck him. "Essentially I'm asking you to try to read the mind of nothingness."

She took that in. "And what do you think I'll find there?"

He shrugged. "That's for you to discover."

"Okay, then." Jean leaned back in the seat, directing her eyes toward the black of space as a focus for her mind. She hesitated to open up to it, though. She'd been in space enough times to know that emptiness. She had memories of the Phoenix Force soaring through it unassisted. She could grasp, as few humans could, just how staggeringly huge and empty it was. She couldn't avoid a fear of becoming lost in it. *Couldn't I just read a politician's mind instead? Or one of those people who leave their phones on in the theater?*

Maybe, she had to admit, there was another basis for her unease. What if, when she opened her mind to the void, some other cosmic force were to sense her and try to join with her? It was an irrational thought; given the immensity of space, the odds against such a freak occurrence happening twice were literally astronomical. But it was hard for her to shake off. Maybe she hadn't come to terms with her past as fully as she'd believed. *Hm. I haven't even started listening to the silence, and already I'm learning about myself. Maybe Charles is really on to something.*

So Jean took a deep breath, calmed herself, and tentatively opened up her telepathic senses. It was the same method she used to reach out to someone's mind and know their thoughts, except this time she directed it outward, going against her reflexes and reaching toward the *absence* of a target, the ground instead of the figure. Her awareness strove forward, pushing on through the void, searching for something to connect with, a flaming arrow racing toward an unseen target. *No,* she told herself, instinctively sensing that this was not the way to proceed. *Not so directional. Outward, not forward.* The arrow dissipated, spreading out into a cloud of consciousness . . . and yet that was a poor metaphor, for the cloud was made of nothingness, nothing except pure perception. She let go of the image, let go of any concept of localization. There was no fire, no cloud, no Jean. There simply . . . *was.*

Yet still there were presences to be felt, vague impressions, shadows in the black. Charles's mind; even with his thought processes screened, the more elemental functioning of that supercharged mind still created a strong aura about him. But she could filter that out through long familiarity. Beyond it, there was more. Tiny voices, not even minds, little more than bundles of sensation and reflex. The millions of microscopic insects that inhabited the *Blackbird,* that resided on their own bodies. An audience of dust mites, ruffling their programs and stifling their coughs.

And still there was more. A pervasive sense of mind, of awareness—not so much of thought or will. Just   *something* at the cosmic level. The telepathic carrier waves of the universe's superbeings? Was she sensing the gaze of a Watcher or an Eternal sweeping across the cosmos? Or could it be something purer, more primal, endemic to the universe itself?

But those were questions for later. Now was not the time to analyze; now was the time to perceive, to absorb, and simply—

Suddenly a psychic noise blasted through her mind, a devastating burst of terror, aggression, and pain. She screamed.

"Jean! Jean, are you all right?" It was the professor, calling her back to awareness. She shook her head, pulling herself together.

"Something . . . out there, something powerful . . ." No. Not as powerful as it had seemed at first. She'd had her psychic gain turned up to maximum to listen to the silence, and suddenly someone had screamed into the mike. These were normal minds, but they were in terror. They were in battle. It was all too familiar a psychic stench.

Charles nodded, acknowledging her wordless observations as he brought the *Blackbird*'s sensors to bear. "Several thousand kilometers above us, but closing fast. Two ships in pitched battle. No . . . one attacking, the other trying to flee. It can barely defend itself." Jean knew he was getting this as much from his telepathic scans as from the sensors.

"I can't tell who the attackers are. I can't sense them. A robot ship?" Jean asked.

"I don't think so. I can feel . . . someone inside, but I can't make them out. Something about their technology, their shielding, must interfere. As for the others . . ."

Jean nodded. Multiple species, none she'd ever sensed before. They were displaced, deprived—refugees. Their minds were too full of battle, too fixated on raw survival, to let her read much of anything else yet.

"They're heading for Earth," Xavier said, somewhat unnecessarily; they wouldn't be this close to the planet by sheer chance. "Allowing for evasive maneuvers, their course seems to be taking them toward the northeast U.S. They shouldn't land too far from New York."

Give me your tired, your poor, your huddled masses yearning to breathe free, Jean thought. "If their attackers let them get that far," she said. "Charles, I think you should—"

"Yes, Jean. Try to hail the attackers on the radio. I'll see if I can project my thoughts through their shielding." It was a sensible division of labor, given how much stronger his mind was.

But what to say? "Attention, attacking ship. Please break off your attack. There are defenseless refugees aboard that vessel, parents and children." Something they probably knew and didn't care about, but worth pointing out anyway. "Um . . . on behalf of the X-Men, representing the people of Earth, we ask that you discontinue any acts of aggression within our airspace. Please acknowledge." Big talk, considering the fact that the X-Men had no formal authority to speak for anyone, and that, indeed, their existence was barely tolerated.

Now the ships were close enough that Jean could see them as points of light in the distance, tumbling Earthward with beams of energy flickering between them. One beam struck the smaller, fleeing point of light, causing it to flare up, and for a moment she feared the worst. But it remained intact, and she could still sense its minds. However, as it passed in front of the Earth's bright clouds, she could see it trailing vapors behind it. The instruments showed that it was no longer under power, falling on a ballistic course that would bring it down in eastern Pennsylvania. The larger ship continued its pursuit, but its bolts were being diffracted by the atmosphere, and friction was forcing it to slow, letting the refugee ship pull ahead. She could sense the refugees struggling to bring their vessel to a safe landing, and there was just enough hope in the pilots' minds to tell her there was still a chance. She was already putting the *Blackbird* on an intercept course. "Charles, it's close enough that we can get a team there soon after it lands."

"Right." She could sense his mind reaching out, checking the current status of the active and reserve team members, seeing who was available at the moment. Then the familiar call went out. *To me, my X-Men!*

Printed in the United States
By Bookmasters